I WAS TRYING TO DESCRIBE WHAT IT FEELS LIKE

I WAS TRYING TO DESCRIBE WHAT IT FEELS LIKE

NEW AND SELECTED STORIES BY

NOY HOLLAND

COUNTERPOINT
BERKELEY CALIFORNIA

"Rooster Pollard Cricket Goose," "Swim for the Little One First," "Fire Feather Mendicant Broom," and a portion of "What Begins with Bird" first appeared in *Conjunctions*; "Chupete" in *Web Conjunctions*; "Absolution" and "Boulevard" in *The Quarterly*; "At Last the Escalade" in *Antioch*; "Monocot" in *Kenyon Review*; "Jericho" in *Denver Quarterly*; "Time for the Flat-Headed Man" in *Open City*; "Milk River" and "Pachysandra" in *New York Tyrant*; "Blood Country" in *Western Humanities Review*; "Pemmican" in *Milan Review*; "Love's Thousand Bees" in *Unsaid*; "Luckies Like Us" in *Columbia*; "I Was Trying to Describe What It Feels Like" and "Perihelia" in *No Token*; "Instructions for Xu Yuan Flying," "So Says the Post Mistress," "Music of the Old," "Querido," "Courtship," "Matrimonial," "Put on Your Crowded Body," "Hunger Is the First Emotion," and "Cuernavaca" in *Notre Dame Review*; "Once I Wrote a Story" in *Big Big Wednesday*; "Tally" in *Epoch*; "Blue Angels," "Vegas," "Home Improvement," and "Sinew" in *Story Quarterly*; "Not So the Donkeys" in Cosmonaut; "Search and Rescue" in *Catapult*; "Duende" in *Agni*; "Ringneck," "Bitty Cessna," and "King for a Day" in *Fence*.

The Library of Congress has cataloged the hardcover as follows:
Names: Holland, Noy, 1960– author. | Holland, Noy, 1960– Orbit.
Title: I was trying to describe what it feels like : new and selected stories / Noy Holland.
Description: Berkeley, CA : Counterpoint Press, [2017]
Identifiers: LCCN 2016040258 | ISBN 9781619028463 (hardback)
Subjects: | BISAC: FICTION / Short Stories (single author). | FICTION / Literary.
Classification: LCC PS3558.O3486 A6 2017 | DDC 813/.54—dc23
LC record available at https://lccn.loc.gov/2016040258

Cover design by Kelly Winton
Interior design by Megan Jones

Paperback ISBN 978-1-61902-593-6

COUNTERPOINT
2560 Ninth Street, Suite 318
Berkeley, CA 94710
www.counterpointpress.com

Printed in the United States of America

for my children

CONTENTS

I WAS TRYING TO DESCRIBE WHAT IT FEELS LIKE

ORBIT

At NIGHT, WE KEPT WATCH FOR TURTLES. WE MADE OUR bed one bed to lie across together, our pillows pushed up in the window we had popped the screen from. There was a broken place in our yard, and in our yard, our garden. We could lean up onto our pillows at night and watch out over the garden.

This was in the yellow house; it was swallowed up by trees. Vines grew into the kitchen.

This was the summer our father left. Our mother lay at the back of the house.

There were trains at night, and whippoorwills, and the sounds our mother made at night went out across our yard. We moved Mother's bed to the window—so she could see the sun and moon, so she could see the garden.

We let the animals harvest the garden—the mule deer and the whistle pigs, the rabbits nosed through our broken place—the things you have to kill to catch.

It was easy, catching turtles. We leaned into the light from our window. My brother whistled a marching call to tease the turtles two by two: Sugar and Vernon, Oscar and Doll. That was what

Orbit had named them. Every turtle we caught, we caught again. We carved their names with a crooked nail in the soft shells of their bellies. Our names, we carved in the trees.

We named our bird dog Bingo then. Our father had named her Jane. We let her come sleep in our room with us, in our beds, underneath our bedsheets, her head on Orbit's pillow. We kept Bingo's tail in our pockets. Our turtles, we kept in a wooden box, or we let them loose in our mother's room before we carried them back out into our woods so we could catch them over again. We kept their box beneath our bed so we could hear them if they moved at night.

We heard Mother sing at night—Mother Goose and birdcalls. Whenever she was singing, when we could not help but hear her singing, Orbit flung the bedsheet back and went out through the window. I went to Mother with saltines, Popsicles, to feed her. She pulled the bedsheet up across her mouth, held it below her eyes, and danced, veiled—her arm dipping above the sheet, her hand fluttering out at the end of it. I heard her hips twist.

I heard the field mice, shredding her clothes, in the dresser.

When Orbit came back with his bike from the lake, I sneaked to our bed and pretended to sleep—so he could wake me, so we could hunt for turtles. Some nights he did not wake me. He curled under his sheet at the foot of our bed, and I would feel our beds rock; I would hear the box springs shudder and creak and our bird dog—curled up at the edge of our bed—moaning, her head underneath Orbit's pillow. I pulled the sheet over my head to listen—to his hand pumping his tiny prick, to him breathing.

Orbit brought jars of tadpoles from the lake, scooped from the weedy shallows, and frogs, gigged and bleeding, he tried in the coming days to heal. He sewed up the frogs with needle and thread, patched their lesser wounds with gauze, practiced amputations.

Without Mother, we broke rules.

We ate with our fingers, if we ate at all. We said, *Fingers were made before forks.*

We put tadpoles underneath our beds with the World Books, the box of turtles.

We popped the screen from our window—so we could lean out over our windowsill so we could watch for turtles. When our wonder beans swung, there were turtles. Orbit was feet-first, shouting *Geronimo!* dropping past the windowsill before his bedsheets settled. He kicked away from the side of the house, lunging backward, gaining yard to the garden.

THIS IS WHAT was; this is what can have been.

WE WERE QUEEN Mother and Orbit, we said, the summer she lay at the back of the house, the autumn, the spring. Our father was other places. Our father had sat with his hat at his feet, useless in the kitchen. When he stood up, he stood up walking, moving to the door.

We did not try to stop him.

We do not try to stop him.

We are Queen Mother and Orbit of the night birds and the terrapin, of the tubers and of the leaving trees.

We are a ruckus of arms in the head-high weeds, bent-kneed, dropping to stalk on our fingertips between the rows of corn. In the squash, we drop to our hands and knees, to our bellies—elbowing, dragging our legs, too loud in our moving sounds to hear past ourselves for prey. We watch down the rows for the beans to swing; we keep an eye on Bingo, who is standing on the windowsill, watching over us from our room. We have her broken-off tail in our pockets, and rabbit's foot in our pockets, and the crooked nail we name them with—our Sugar, our Vernon, our Doll.

Oh, we are so lucky! So grown, how blessed, such seers!

We stop in the dirt to listen.

We know Mother watches for us. We are sure she is listening for us. There are strays, after all, wilding fields, and fire—and we have seen houses splintered by wind lift like leaves from their yards.

We listen for the closing up, the hinged, hydraulic sound of the keeping shells of the turtles. Orbit howls and I, Mother and I, watch him—cat-backed, my brother, a boneless pounce of boy into a sprawling thicket. He thrashes through the vines and leaves; we see a flash of scrawny arm, a ratty patch of hair. A sorrowful moan leaves Bingo, her havocked, swallowed trill. We see my brother's legs jerk straight, Mother and Bingo and I—then nothing. He lies with his feet poked out of the beans as though he has been grown over.

"It's Sugar," he explains to me, and hands off the turtle.

A GREEN MOON is the best moon, Orbit claims, for turtles.

Our mother claims in a green moon, as rare by far as a blue moon, our father comes home and carries her out and, hand over hand, runs her up the flagpole in our yard.

We hear her pleading with the Pope at night, blind-gigging geese at night.

We have our Gander in our yard, our trough for frogs and tadpoles.

Sugar, we have, and Oscar—soon—to knock at our legs in our pockets.

Orbit claims that if they would let you, held open against your ear, you could hear the sea in Sugar, in Oscar, and so on—in turtles we have not yet caught to let us listen to them there.

Sugar is cool underneath, where the shell smooths and smells to me of potatoes. Our potatoes, left to freeze, will grow hard as bone in winter, food for vole and shrew. Turnips we grow for their slick skins swelling in the press of earth; beets for their rough and knuckly peel we peel back in bed with our kitchen knife in our room I was first to be born in, our yellow house stooped and winded as far from town as from the sea.

pitchfork,
MoonPie,
tarpaulin,
Lipton's,
hangers to mend the fence,
morphine—

Not the sea I hear in Sugar, but my brother saying *penknife*, Orbit saying *saltines* to put on the list for supper. But town is a long and, even in the cool, blistering walk through the hollow.

We keep near her, Mother on a good day taking toast and tea, a day when the sound she makes at night is not Mother Goose but Mother, the words we know of her, her calling over the windowsill my brother and me by name.

NIGHT TO NIGHT, *day to dark, very night of very night,* Orbit recites to the undershells as white as the buffed soles of our feet come bootless to the turtles. We learn in the dark with our fingers what, with a crooked nail and a kitchen knife, by candlelight we have named them.

We take our time to name them. We lie with our chins hanging past the foot of our twin beds. Turtles are shy when they open, the swung-down half of a moon of shell a ramp the kept inside of them might lift up and walk out over.

In me, also, is a flap of shell—hinged, according to Orbit, open when I squat to pee, and when I am finished peeing, drawn shut accordingly ahead of the hooked and wrinkled neck the size of Orbit's thumb and mine. The skin of a turtle's neck—as the skin of our mother's neck—is fit to be shed at the side of a road, our mother not a mother to sing before this jack-in-a-box of cheeks rouged with the skin of beets we peel to pop out when we want her.

And we want so much of Mother.

In bed, the dark between our sheets keeps the smell of lumped dirt, of crops we have left, of Mother—if we touch her before we leave, or when we come back to her from the garden. We smell ourselves of the garden. We smell of Bingo—who smells of her kill she has left in the woods and who sleeps her dog's sleep with her head underneath Orbit's pillow.

Orbit's pillow, since our father left, has become our dog's pillow; Bingo's name we changed from the name we never liked all along. The nights since then, since our father left, Orbit curls at the foot of his bed, thinking I am sleeping.

But I am not sleeping.

His boy's breath I am of him and of the fallen dark with him. I am the keeping sheath of him, slipping on his penis.

I see him reach his hand out. I see him turn his hand to let our Bingo lick it clean.

WE TRY TO lure the turtles out with shiny slugs and straight-pinned flies, with the luck of rabbit's foot saved frozen from the garden.

We are lucky when they open.

They are so shy.

We try to pry them out with kitchen knives and pliers, to burn them out with candles, mute things, toothless. Do they know it when we sleep? Do they rise up in their old homes and walk out in our room at night?

But we are not sleeping.

Maybe they dream.

Might it be not the sea we hear, but some lurching yellow dream we wake to keep from dreaming?

I am no weak sister gone to kneeling through the house at night to harvest lint from carpets, to polish and to clean. I am not afraid to sit darkly among our things and in the room where Mother sleeps, or is not sleeping, to sing, or am not singing.

But I do not sleep with Mother, shall not when she lifts the sheets and pats our father's place to lie against her in their bed.

Our beds are one bed, my brother's bed and my bed. We lie across together.

But I would go, should Mother call—between this room and that, between sister and daughter. Or if she does not call, I will go to sit and watch her dreaming.

····· ····

YOU WILL KNOW the place, should you ever come, as soon as you have seen it. You will see it from the dirt road—the house leaning, and leaning, slumped—from the narrowing road from the hollow.

Should the stone in the road you are walking past lift up on its legs and move, pick it up. It may be Vernon.

The spotted dog is Bingo, her paws webbed for swimming.

The goosenecked goose is Gander, hitched with a rope to the trailer hitch.

And the swaybacked mare—what of her? She lay in the grass behind the barn that stands beyond the slumping house and squeezed out her dead filly.

And of the mother?

And of the father—what shall we say of him?

IT WILL BE done as soon as the father comes or not—until he comes. The father will come by truck or train as fathers betimes are wont to come. Or by some flight of fancy.

Or he will not come.

Or he did not go, and shall not go, but stayed in Tuscaloosa.

Tuscaloosa is a good town. There are fathers in Tuscaloosa. There are no cars in Tuscaloosa, no guns, no books, no telephones, no telephone book to finger through waiting for dark to come.

Or do you not wait for it?

Or do you live in Little Crab? Mightn't you live in Oneida? Might you not wait for a father to come, driving himself in a vented rig, with a feather alight on the bill of his cap in the dash-light light of the cab of his truck, driving chickens by night to Oneida?

I was born in Ohio. My mother was someone, chances are, I never might have known.

Do you know Oneida? Would you take my word for what I would tell you about Oneida?

Ask anyone.

Ask my mother.

Is it pretty somewhere near Oneida? Is there a boy you know named Orbit living on the outskirts there?

Ask yourself any old thing you might think of to want to ask yourself, or not to want to ask yourself. Will it be done, for instance, when it is done? In a heartbeat, will it? In a whimper?

Old Mother Hubbard lived in a cupboard covered with pudding and pie.

Who saw her die?
Who saw her die?
It was I, said the fly, *with my little teensy eye.*
Who caught her blood?
Who caught her blood?
It was I, said the fish, *it was I, in my pretty silver dish.*

•••• ••••

WHEN DADDY COMES, Orbit claims, I will show him.

I will show how—in the tree, turning above the dogs—we keep the filly safely there to show him when he comes. The lean-to, I will show him. I will show him the broken place where the animals crawl into the yard.

Do you know where Turkey is?

How does a turnstile work?

Turtles have been toothless for one-five-zero, zero-zero-zero years.

This one is Oscar. Oscar, meet Doll. Daddy and Doll, meet Oscar.

After a single mating, Doll can lay fertile eggs for years.

Will they all at a time break open?

She will not show them. Our Doll will not show me even her belly still.

And if she is not with them?

If our Doll is old and sick and nodding by the road one night, who will there be to show them? And which way goes to the paved road and on to the yonder sea?

I have not seen it. I have not seen the sea.

I see crows.

I know there are buzzards banking turns up there.

I KEEP THE flies from Momma. It is my job to keep them from her. The sky is yellow. The fields and the fields and the fields are green. The lean-to is blue. My name is Orbit.

"Oh, you're that little Gibson boy with buckeyes in his britches."

"Momma," I say, "it's Orbit."

But who am I to tell her? Who am I to Momma? What am I to say?

For luck, I shook a buckeye down to clatter from our buckeye tree. She put it in her mouth.

Our dog is Bingo. We gave Bingo *Bingo*. *Bingo* is a dog's name. We took *Jane* away.

So is it Jane's or Bingo's tail we worry in our pockets?—broken, ropy, gyplet tail Daddy cut away. So maybe it is Daddy's. But it is in our pockets.

Our goosenecked goose is Gander. If Gander is our Christmas goose, will we take his name away? And will it still be Christmas? Will Daddy come to carve the goose when she is dead who took his name and, with it, died away?

Sometimes I cannot hold my breath for Momma's long not-breathing. I keep her sheet snugged under her. *One Mississippi*, I count. *Two, three Mississippi. Four.*

Outside is the garden.

My bike is in the garden.

I hold my breath between our breaths so she will not stop breathing. But sometimes I breathe. I cannot keep from breathing.

There is the lean-to. There are birds to clean. There is the light to think of. Already the day is so long past the coins sun-dropped through the leaves of the trees of the locusts calling *Phaaaraoh*, past jarflies and dragonflies that stitch the air above our lake, our house shadow flung as far and wide as both our yard and garden.

Still there is no sign of my sister.

But surely she will come.

Cissie will want to be the one when Momma wakes up screaming, and Momma wakes up screaming—*What time is it? Oh, let me up! I have got to get into that kitchen.*

But there is only sun time here, and the fickle moon in the trees at night, and months that pass from things that bloom and rot in our dark garden.

There are wonder beans now. There are turtles.

UPON A TIME the times we did not sleep, Daddy shunt the hall at night to lock us in our room at night when we were not sleeping. There is no lock to lock now. Now is the door and the hall and the door any boy can follow.

You can see our house at night. We leave the porch light on at night. You can see it burning.

Once Daddy came to our room at night when I was afraid of the dark at night, of the night sounds and the dogs at night and in the woods the cows at night, though days I saw them feeding. Then

I did not sleep with Oscar then. Then Cissie's bed was one bed and my bed another. I did not sleep with Bingo. Then Bingo slept on the floor of our room, before she slept at the head of my bed, before the two-dollar truck would run, before she got my pillow. Now it is Bingo's pillow. Now it is Bingo's tail for me to finger in my pocket.

I am not a scaredy.

Only but to shoo the flies a boy would need to look at her. I am small to bathe her or try to keep her eating.

But I am not a scaredy.

I am like my daddy.

My bike is in the garden. My lamp is in the breadbox. My straw, my shreddy shoes.

And I am in the garden now, my feet are in my shoes. Whooey.

Cornstalks left and splinted peas, the scrabbly path that splits our yard, oh fast, our moon, the window left, our porch light left on burning late for Daddy not to come, or to come when I am hiding, sly as sly Geronimo, a scrap of a boy in the tree limbs hung with copperheads and gawking cranes that ghost across our lake at night.

Nights!

Oh, the tree frogs!

What boy was I to be afraid ever of the tree frogs? Ever of the blat and twang, the rasp and scraw and cruck of things—the warbling, the mournful, the leaves of the trees fallen all sunken to a churchly calm to keep me up with Daddy?

I kept up with Daddy. Daddy creaked like trees.

Daddy smelled like creosote slathered on our wooden shed, our leaning fence, our barn my bike thrums and rattles past—a swift bank, a cock-kneed swoop he showed me. House and barn and creek bed gone, turtles gone, a moon, a stunt to make my momma gasp to get down to Daddy, to hold her breath for Daddy—no hangdog on the fence we built to fence the bending hill we built the barn to squat on.

No spotty clerk, my daddy, not a man to cobble shoes.

Did he not know the names of things to call the nightly sounds by? By cricket, by screech owl, by croaker?

My way is quick: the barn, the slough, the hidden field. My way loops through the hidden field, between the vaulting stalks of weeds so near I have to hold my breath—to stoop, unmooned, no smoothened pass, but the sting and smeary green of greening knees to steer by.

My name is Orbit.

Joe Pye, milkweed, mullein.

The lake is low. My bike is old. You can hear it coming.

In the leaves are cans to kick where I tip my bike down. My lamplight is on. My Dixie straw, my gigging prong, my knack I have among the trees for soggy calculation, my skinny pole, my skiff I have to stand up in to skinny past the trees by night by night-blind navigation.

I hear such frogs.

They fall to feeding when I pass them.

But I do not pole past them. I shine my light across them—long of toe and yellow-eyed and wide mouths to pry open.

Slow now, and soft to go.

You have to go so soft as me to catch them in the laps of trees, gawky in your narrow skiff in the lapping shallows. The weak place is the white place that bloats out when they call. They flap and bleed when you gig them.

I let Bingo taste them. I let Bingo lick my hands when I have slicked my hands at night.

But I do not croon. I do not pitch and moan to see our Cissie curl her toes underneath our sheets at night when Momma is still singing. And Momma is still singing. Momma is always singing.

I pry their mouths open.

I scrape my straw down into them—and breathe.

THE GREEN-HEADED AND the long-legged and the black flies hatched from the spit-gobbed weeds tick by day at our windows. Inside the flies are flies inside and in the frogs flies inside and in our house also and also in Bingo worms inside—hook and whip and ringworm worms and worms left to feed in Bingo's heart—pale, mute, sluggish, plumping in the bloody rush in the blinding heart dividing.

Until at last Bingo's heart tears open. Can.

Surely it will not tear open.

Momma will not tear open. The filly did not tear open. I cut the filly with a carving knife to turn above the dogs at night safe from the limb of our tree.

When Daddy comes home, I will show him. I will show him the broken place where Bingo comes into the yard.

Bingo is Bingo.

When Daddy comes, Bingo is Jane.

Tonight is the light of a greening moon a boy can see to ride by, and else to ride to sea by. Daddy will not come tonight—when Momma is still singing, when Bingo is not Jane.

My sister's name is Cissie.

Our momma's name is Cissie.

You can hear us calling. You can see our house at night. We leave the porch light on at night.

You can see us calling.

·•• •••·

THERE IS THE dirt road, the paved road, the airport.

Should we walk to the dirt road, we could not hear her screaming. Should we walk to the paved road, we could not see the porch light. But should we walk to the airport?

If we cannot hear her screaming, if we cannot see the porch light, no porch, we can see no house at night, no dogs to see who run their dreams beside our father's bed at night now that we are leaving, and we are leaving. The dirt road that starts at the graveyard, or ends, if you wish, at the graveyard, and begins, if you wish, at the paved road, to take us to Oneida, to take us to Tuscaloosa, takes us out in the snow some night to walk the rising tide some night until our hats start floating.

But that is not our want, we claim.

After all that we have claimed of it, this seems not the road at all.

THERE IS A yellow house I know set back from a road I know.

There is a well there. From the well comes the sweetest water.

We have no bucket.

Shall we assume, then, the well is dry? Shall we say there is no well at all, no yellow house, no mother?

And if a mother, what shall we say of her?

That she is pretty?

That she is quick to dance a Charleston in her rhinestone shoes?

Very well, then. She was pretty. She was quick to dance a Charleston in her rhinestone shoes.

Shall we make a claim from on airship high how the road comes to look not a road at all but a rope to knot a loop into to kick a chair out under from, or from yellow porch to pin oak tree to pin a mother's trappings from—her gold lamé, her taffeta, her brocades flown across the sea or boated in a ribboned box from some shop we have not thought to think of yet in Hong Kong—her girdles, Mother's hard brassieres, her gowns back-slit with a kitchen knife—greenish, blooded, nylon—children, usurers, thieves—her nylons to pull past our chins at night to steal from our mother's room at night that we might well be on our way, well down the road I would not claim as clothesline or hangman's noose, no ribbon to bewitch in a young girl's hair to flutter by chance in your slowing rush down the old road, or the new road, the dirt road, the paved road, headlong to get to Ohio?

IT WOULD PLEASE me to think you might think of me as a girl you picked up driving once, or thought to pick up driving once, who says, as we ride, nearly nothing.

That we have met in a dream, you might think.

That we have eaten pork chops—this would please me. We have left the last bright diamond field, the shrinking glare of hamburger joints, of car lots and Circle Ks, dog tracks and Sears.

YOU ARE SO pretty.

Is there nothing I can say to you?

Is there not a vein you love lashed beneath your mother's skin she lets you fiddle with your fingers?

Must you follow with your fingers the broken and the boldened road, the turnpikes, the highways, the lists made of names of towns to go, sitting beside your mother's bed for the last breath breathed out at the back of the house and gone?

You may go now.

But will you come back?

Will you not come to hear her calling you late from the wide field, from your hay forts and strewn caves—the thin rain, the cities?

The cities flee from my windows.

I do not rest much. A run of music, a plain door, in the hard streets the sound of horses sends me on.

I push on. Sometimes a door opens.

Sometimes with some man spent in me, Mother comes to me tugging her catheter, the limp, blooded tip of it, out from where I have forced the tube into Mother's—I want to say—womb.

Is it possible to be gentle?

Her skin is a yellow bruise. Mother dents where you touch her.

I am like her. Each day I am more like her.

I have her hands, my mother's mouth, her long, straight body.
Go fuck yourself, Ohio.

WE TIED OUR mother by our wrists with scarves and to the bed
stalks by our ankles. We had a great stash of morphine, a run of
hot nights of a sweetened cast that clotted in our throats. We had
gizzards. We grew scales. We had feet.

We were bottom feeders.

We were flat out over our lake by night with each a stone to
ride by. Our stones grew smooth. They sunned all day. We found
it warm to hold them. We eased the stones over the rim of our skiff
and the water rose on the flank of our skiff and rose again for my
brother. Our skiff nosed up and flattened. Our skiff nosed down
and flattened.

We had chosen each one stone. We held them. It was all we
could do to hold them. We tipped, tucked over, dropped ourselves
into the water.

All the moon long, we fell.

The stones rode against our bodies. We fell past breathing,
shapeless things.

It was pleasing. Our lives grew strangely pleasing.

We were told the lake had no bottom. It was said the lake had
no bottom.

Our lives grew strangely pleasing.

Such creatures—whiskered, feeding things, shelled things—we
bumped past. We came upon the lake's dark bottom.

Did you think we would die of it, Mother?

EVERYWHERE WAS A bruise on her, and the flecked wounds of our needles. Her bones scraped underneath her skin—we could hear them, when she moved at all, when we helped her turn in bed. We turned her to salve the whitening sores that mouthed out from the weight of her bones, from the weeks, the months, she lay there.

We brought pretties. We brought her things to smell. We brought our mother bits of things she used to think to speak of. There were smoothed things—leviathan, terrapin, Pawnee. We moved along the silted bottom. Our hearts thrilled in our ears.

She waked up screaming.

Orbit waked up screaming.

The sky stayed the same pale haze.

Her cookware and cameos, a deck of cards, her cigarette box, needles, nylons, we buried out in the garden. We dragged our beds to the garden. Sometimes we sang.

We brought slingshots. We had Bingo and kitchen knives, a certain native know-how. The days grew dusty. The fields were tipped with ocher.

We bound our mother with her bright scarves by her wrists to her bed, by her ankles.

Our turtles scuffed in the garden. We had shards of pot and bone, rabbit and whistle pig; dogs dug under our broken fence to nose over us in our garden.

Mother called out.

Bingo chewed up her slippers. Bingo chewed up a rhinestone shoe Mother used to dance the Charleston in—years back, days back, should you ask her. Ask her would she show us, and Mother would be our scissoring knees, our wild arms on the screen porch, a thumbnail, some harvest, any old green or fish-belly moon it would be our want to ask her.

We planted the rhinestones two by two with a foot between in the garden. We grew. We were still growing.

We carved our names in our arms.

No rain came, no father.

Orbit stayed out in the garden. I would leave Orbit out in the garden. A house is so dark inside when you have been out in the garden.

I wore bracelets of leaves, Mother's gold lamé.

"Mother," I said, "it's me."

"If you say so," she said.

I said, "We were out in the garden."

"I see. And what did you sow?" she said. "I've seen no moon to plant by."

"No moon, Mother. No motherlight. By twos we planted bright stones to lead us out from the garden."

"Stones, child?"

"Stones, Mother."

"And what of your mother, child?"

"We will dig her a hole in the garden."

"And how will you face her, child?"

"As I do, Mother. With a difference."

"Then face her south, then. But will you bind her?"

"No, Mother."

"But you will face her? Will you build for her a simple box that the dirt not burst her eyes?"

"If you wish, Mother."

"Are you certain, child? What wonders the dead accomplish. But the living? Oh, uncalmable, a palsied, mewling sack. To breathe, I am cinched and watered. This is a child's love, child? Child, you call this love, child? Love?"

We could see her from the garden. We tied rabbits by loops of string to cornstalks in the garden. We kept Gander. We filled a trough for frogs.

I held her. It was all I could do to hold her.

"You are trying to kill your mother," she said. "Are you trying to kill your mother?"

UNDERFOOT IS A millet of bone. The road opens out in a graveyard.

Will you drive on? Have you seen me?

Do you see that they cut us bone to bone to sort through what might grow in her as we had grown in Mother?

The wound gapes, leaks bile. Mother cannot swallow. Mother's veins collapse. For months, the doctors come and go back out into Tuscaloosa.

For months I will not lie with her and then one day I lay with her and in the nights thereafter and after a time to lie there, curved into the wound in her, I think to grow in under her, bone by bone, my toothy spine her long wound's tongue and groove to seal her.

I think, if ever he comes to her, my father will come to feel me there, if ever my father should touch her—and to feel me I think would please my father as I pleased my father once, my chipped spine my mother's skin will come to overgrow in her.

I can make her please him.

I rouge her cheeks, tease her hair, her slack sex sponge clean.

He will feel me. Our father cannot but feel me—a bone-hard nub of bone in the soft, in the bowly hot suck and leech and long swim of Mother.

Get me out of here. Unmother me.

OH, THE AIRPORTS of Ohio. There are salt bluffs in Ohio, roads to take run slick by rain to drive into my Ohio—these wasted acres walked off, strewn caves, my caverns scraped, stripped mines, ravines.

I cannot get free of her. She is tongued, gashed; she towers. A door will open. She finds me eating. She finds me lacking. I am in some mall or lobby, some truck stop or Sears, six stone set in some riverbed, she finds me. She finds me on the road some night as like as not in your rig some night where we have maybe swung wide in the gone seas of Ohio.

Listen, you. You, Einstein. Hum up, boy.

•••• ••••

BUT THERE IS more. There is always more.

There is yet light enough, and always some motel out here with walls as thin as ice, enough breath: night: talk enough to kick a stone to town.

Let the sun so top the trees, it sits on a boy's head like a cap he has long since lost the thought of, thinking *pitchfork, MoonPie, tarpaulin, Lipton's*—a boy to count and count again the worn heads of the silver coins singing in his pockets.

It may be that you know him, knowing enough at all events to conjure a name to call him by when the road from out of the hollow climbs to widen in the shut-down, dead heart of Oneida.

Or maybe it is not Oneida. Maybe you know some farther town his daddy drove through in a two-dollar truck—to find what, who could guess at?—what would only ever anyway be but a name Orbit guessed at, spelled out—the names with his mother's knitting needle scrawled across his sister's skin, Cissie's back bared and arms, her legs, her girl's skin given to rash and welt, so that riding back in the back of the truck Orbit could dig down far enough for the names of the towns to welt enough to read the letters plainly.

It takes so little to please me.

I think of Orbit in the back of the truck thinking, *Slow,* I think, to his daddy, but saying only to his sister, *Cissie, faster,* saying, *Make it go faster*—as though she might so surely will the body as to will the letters of the towns gone through to sink from the unsunned white of her skin too long, to Orbit's mind, lasting— with town coming on, and dusk coming on, and with the saltiness of his sister's skin, the first faint taste of blood.

I think of them in the bed of the truck with the spare wheels and empty cans, the crap their daddy took with him that leaves a left boy thinking how small, how truly stowable, a boy like him might prove to be to be among the whatall a man with an eye to head for town might have picked and taken.

In time, his daddy will come. They will mend, in time, the broken place by now so long by lost dogs, mule deer, and so on, so long by now worked through that the greased hairs even of the whistle pigs fly from the fence curled back to a wire-toothed snarl.

All day, the porch light burns, all night, and of late by now, room by room, in the windowed rooms the lights of the house come up also, so there is light throughout also—a tall house, storied—light enough that, driving by, you are apt to let your window down to listen out for dancing, a glimmer of voices, some bit coming across the field of familiar song.

But, quick now. Drive on. They have already seen you passing.

···· ····

As soon as Momma goes to sleep, I go back to Momma's room to light the light back burning. Momma dreams. The wind creaks the pin oak tree grown up in our yard at night and you can hear the dogs at night and sometimes someone's car goes by unlighted, with its engine off, if I am in the garden.

My bike is in the garden. Nights when the wind and moon come up, its spoked wheels turn.

I am growing tadpoles.

There are three-hundred and sixty-five different kinds of tadpoles. I keep a trough filled up for them to grow up in in the garden.

Cissie sits out in the garden. Soup pots, she sits with, and wooden spoons, lipsticks, purses, the lipped ends of cigarettes snubbed out in the corner drawer—she takes even the drawer to the garden—the scarves in it and soft-skinned gloves that Bingo will find and, by and by, dig a hole to bury. Cissie drags our beds to the garden, her bed and my bed, so at night I sleep under Momma's bed and sit by day at the foot of her bed to see myself what the day will bring for Cissie to take to the garden.

She wears one hat one day and leaves it out the next day to come inside for another.

Some are feathered. On some of them, the brims are wide the wind bends up.

The snubbed ends of cigarettes Momma keeps in her corner drawer, Cissie takes in her corner drawer to smoke on in our garden. But they are still our momma's.

I say to Momma, "Nome."

I know Momma sees out but I say, "Nome."

I say it is not the pearly crown our momma bought to marry in when Cissie crowns the fence with it, windy in the garden where the hung veil blows.

Plus also dresses—jewely, gowny things hanging in the pin oak tree Cissie picks from in the morning, picking for days the black cape hung with black flapping threads that Momma used to dance in—to dance in. But she does not dance like Momma. When Cissie starts some loopy jig for a boy with half a head for it to chance a leg to look at, even our birding Bingo stops to watch like me instead.

But also there is Momma. Cissie puts the music on and Momma lifts the bedsheets up for foot room and room enough for her knees to twitch, her rocking hips left gownless in the drifty light the lifted sheet lets in.

I do not say, *Did not*. I do not say, *Nome*.

I pull her sheets away from her, from her feet turned out at the foot of her bed—but she does not say, *Orbit*. Cissie does not say, *Orbit*.

The filly hangs from the pin oak tree with still the show of Momma's gowns until there is just the one gown to pick from in the morning.

I go out in the morning. Some strange bird sings. I go out with goldenrod poked into my buttonholes to walk beneath the trees with her, the bright sun high by then, with only still the filly hung to ornament the pin oak tree Cissie picked clean.

It is a yellow morning. The hems of the curtains in Momma's room blow where we can see outside the house across our yard.

Cissie says, "Say it is when you want to sleep and I'm your bad dream, see."

Cissie's hands are hard and dry and running down my neck I dream.

She says, "Hold still, Orbit."

She says, "Say I am the shadow that you walk on down the road at night, but it is yet so dark at night you do not think of me. You do not remember me. But there will be some dream. Say I am in the garden. Say I am some old yellow sleep come climbing up the stairs at night to walk you to the garden. Come. I walk you to the garden."

I can smell the rain clouds building out above our lake, the long, chuffing thunder come swift to drive us home. I think how we rode home. Sometimes Cissie's skirt rose up and sometimes Cissie's hair rose up and caught between my teeth and in my mouth where I had breathed it. Still no rain fell. Cissie had said when the rain would fall, then there would be no nests of bone the kingbirds make, then there would be no sister, calling from a rocking skiff to swim across the lake to her. I swam to her to: *Orbit.*

We do not turn back.

We go on walking until we cannot see the garden, until I cannot see the lean-to showing blue between the creaking trees I have not shown to Cissie.

The bird we saw in the garden comes scrawing out its strange song it sings for us to follow, so we follow, seeing the bird wait in the trees for us when we stop to lift the heavy gown to leave the weight of fallen leaves and needled dust we walk through, that Momma's gown gathers up, dragging, as we walk. We walk to a ledge where a brook runs through, where the sun drops sudden through the leaves of the trees like something we have asked for, something we would shy away to make a noise to ask for.

Cissie lies down. When Cissie lies down, through the pearly crown's fishnet veil, I can see the bird shadow sweep across her face.

"I want to fall asleep so long the kingfishers steal my hair," she says.

"My hair is so long," she says.

Cissie spreads her hair beside her for a pillow for my head. She makes a bed of Momma's gown beside her I can lie on. Now is no bird nor shadow now, no mark where we have named the trees to see to find our way by—no tailing dog, no broken fence, no way for us to know now if Momma howls nor sings.

"Do you think I'm pretty, Orbit?"

"Yes and no. Sure," I say.

"I think we better go," I say.

"Oh, shut up, Orbit. You could hang yourself at the foot of her bed and Mother wouldn't think twice of it."

Cissie has a beaded purse and in the purse a plastic bottle. She unscrews the top from the bottle and puts the bottle in my hand.

"Try some of this," she says. "It's good for scrapes and bruises."

Inside is as blue as the lean-to's blue, bluer than a blue sea I have not swum in.

"What's it for, Cissie?"

"To make you want nothing. More of it—you want that. But otherwise nothing."

"But why should I want nothing?"

"Oh, never mind, Orbit."

So I take a big sip from it, another sip like Cissie says.

She says to lie here. We have to lie here. The kingfishers, if we are still, will steal our hair to knit the bones to nest upon the water.

Today is not a wind at all even on the water. I know today our lake is bright, so you can see your shadow gone to pieces in the water. Still if ever you swim, your shadow swims with you.

Once a bright leaf falls. Once I saw a silver fish trail me in the water. Even if I swam hard, even if I did not quit, when I quit, I saw the fish beneath me silvering my shadow gone to pieces in the water.

The fish was as quick as my tongue. It was small enough to swallow—small enough to swim inside my mouth if I had let it.

I wish I had let it.

Momma says that, in her mouth, spiders have spun a web and webbed her toes and fingers.

Maybe you also feel it. If it is bright you see a shadow, even if your eyes are closed, fall across your face. But I think you can feel it. I feel Cissie's shadow, I think, fall across my face. Then I feel Cissie's heart start to pound against my face.

"Open your mouth, Orbit."

•••• ••••

IN MOON LAKE, catfish grow as big as boys and dogs.

The lake was once a bend in the river.

There is a lake nearby where our father grew up that goes by the name of Reelfoot. Beneath it is a fault called New Madrid, the stress falling on the first syllable, the open *a*, the plea: New *Ma*drid. At the time of the earthquake that formed the lake, the waters of the Mississippi ran backward.

•••• ••••

LET ME SAY I stood in our stand of corn, seeing the wind move the drapes out past Mother's window. I heard them—they have those little weights in them that beat a slow, tapping sort of sound against the clapboard. When the wind stopped, the drapes hung flat against our house.

IT GOT TO be needles.

She was begging me for it. The morphine we had, the bottle the doctors had given us, was enough to kill off the whole house of us and the swaybacked mare, too. Mother ranted to get up out of her bed to get up into the closet to it where she had seen me keep it.

I gave her enough to sleep through it, is all, so that she would quit begging me for it.

That was all.

It got to be she quit begging me for it, quit begging or sleeping or eating at all or wanting at all like she used to want to have something cleaned or moved in the room like she used to want, or to be touched. Mother lies there, her sheets to her chin, drawn flat the way Mother lies now.

I SAID, "HOLD still. You lie here, Orbit."

I held him.

I could see the way we took, the curved mounds the gown had left when we lifted the flounce from the dust and leaves.

I said, "Now we have a secret. Now you know what I am glad of most: Mother doesn't speak my name."

···• •···

WHEN I HAVE raked the glass and nails across our yellow road at night, when I have washed our momma's feet and filled the trough where the tadpoles swim and, with the cast-off hangers Cissie strew beneath the pin oak tree, mended the place in the wire fence the wiry coats of the dogs snag on, I ask her.

"Can't we go now?" I ask her. "Haven't I stayed?"

Cissie is with the rabbits down squatting in the yellow dirt. She has dirty knees.

"You know we can't," she says. "What about your mother? We can't just pick up and waltz off to the fair."

But I say, "Cissie."

I had not meant *Cissie*—not thought of her, that she would go.

I say, "I thought me and Bingo might would go down to the fair."

TONIGHT IS JUST the slough to cross, the stubbled stretch of dusty field I bent my spokes and, days ago, punctured both my tires on. Now is no thrum nor rattle, no swoop I keep my breathing from.

I go by foot, by flattened path. I leave my bike in the garden.

I take my pail, my hollow pole, my chicken necks and fishy eggs the whiskered fish are wise to. The list Cissie makes of things to buy, I take—but I leave Bingo.

There is no sign of Bingo.

At the lake is a new moon, shining. It is best on a night when the moon is thin to lie alone in your metal skiff to listen for your skiff to tick and slur with the swim of the snakes' thick bodies. They are in the deep part you dive into with stones to ride, or sometimes, by some skinny chance, you find them in the shallows. I pole out from the shallows—past pale frogs squat in the laps of trees I since have grown and done with. Such frogs—some harmless, yippy, simple-sighted house gyp's easy prey.

It is a hard row open-handed out to reach the deeper water, a clever eye that catches sight, by thin moon, of their mouths. It is the best a boy can hope to see is see inside their mouths. Else there is a place to look where you can see the water welt, which you have got to watch for.

Then you have got to lie down.

Then you have got to listen.

Listen: I know it is cold down there at night against the water.

Because also, it is August. Also I was dressing, thinking only of the haze of heat that lies on us in August. Still I wait here; you have to wait here. Maybe there is fog here, the thin moon down.

I don't think they hear me.

I have got my chicken neck poked onto my hook I strung from my pole our daddy gave me. Maybe they can smell it. They smell with their tongues.

DO YOU KNOW there is a good chance that tadpoles see a simpler world than we humans do?

We can see their legs inside them, their pinpricks behind their toes of their tiny ears. Their ears are not like our ears.

A boy can hear the frogs. But frogs hear only frogs, I hear.

The frogs cannot hear Momma. The frogs cannot hear Cissie out singing in the wind at night to lost dogs if they come.

But maybe they won't come. Maybe since I fixed the fence, then it will be just snakes tonight to come into the garden, and garden snakes are garden snakes. They are not like water snakes, which rob the nests the kingbirds make if ever there are calm days and no wind on the water.

Now is not a wind at all to move you on the water.

Do you know where the Pacific is? Because there is a frog I heard of there which lives on some island there, which I would like to look at. It is not like our frogs here. It is very rare, I hear. But I would like to look at it.

I can see the water welt starboard past my metal skiff I kneel up in to paddle. So I cast out, I think to cast out. I have my stone to stone them with if I miss my pail. I have my pail, my good stout lid on it, which Daddy says you have to have if you are ever going to make a nickel at the fair.

But first you have to cast out.

Come on, Orbit.

I bet some egg-sucking snake lives there, where the frogs live out on that island there, and this is why they do it—the little ones.

They are not like our frogs.

They are not like turtles. Their eggs are not thin eggs like Doll's that she leaves out by the road some night for snakes maybe to find some night while we are in the garden.

And they are not like tadpoles. They do not swim. Their legs grow up outside them, growing in their mother's back—her back as smooth as Doll's smooth back they squat on so the weight of them pocks themselves a place in her that she will have to carry.

I HAVE GOT to cast out.

They are so near.

But Bingo is not with me. If Bingo does not look for me and Cissie does not look for me, since I have said to Cissie we are going to the fair?

I have got to paddle. But to paddle since I saw them near?

So I have got to lie here.

Maybe they are under here. I am not a scaredy.

I am going to lie here. It is safe to lie here. I am sure to lie here that it is safe to lie here, that it is safe to listen at the skiff for the tick, for the slur they make, the barbed fast boil of the cotton-mouths' thick bodies.

IN THE MORNING, I see raincrows cawing in the trees.

I have seven quarters, fourteen dimes, so many nickels yet to count and dog's tail in my pocket, pool to play in my pockets, since it is just a rough road nobody ever comes on much to climb out on from the hollow.

Sometimes if a car goes by, I think, *Is that a car gone by, unlighted with its engine off, if I am in the garden?*

Is Bingo in the garden?

I watch for her in trucks gone by until one truck is a pick-'em-up truck that the fellows in it turn around and turn back around again to drive it out ahead of me to wait for me to follow.

The one fellow says, *All be,* and the other one goes, *Shew.*

"All be," the one says, "will you look at them shoes?"

"Damned if it ain't that scoundrel's boy," the other goes. "Shew."

"Will you look at them goddamn shoes?"

I have put my squeaky shoes to ride clean atop my pail until I near to town.

"How far is it to town?" I ask.

"Fur. Fur enough. Oh, fur."

"What ye got shut in that bucket, boy?"

It is an old pick-'em-up truck with dents and rust and muddy clumps and cans thrown back in the back of it, rattling tools and antlers, shot shells, I see, and leafy wads and the misspat spray of tobacco juice but: true. It is a far piece, true, by road or wood for a body to get to town.

"Cottonmouths," I tell them.

"Cottonmouths? Shew."

"Ain't but two kind of snakes he's afraid of. Live ones and dead ones."

"You git back in the back then, boy. Shew."

I put in my lidded pail, my stone for luck I have kicked from home, and before my legs are swung to clear the beaten-up sides of the bed of the truck, we are hell-bent howling down the road run to rut and ruin by the last good trough of rain.

I keep my pail from tipping. I catch my cap. I dust my shoes.

I am so lucky! By hoof bent and ailing truck, by day and dark, I'll reach there.

What boy is this?

Buhl Parson's boy!

Pray, boy. A peek, boy. What have you got in that bucket?

A hole, ma'am. A dancing toad. A six-legged armadillo.

Come riding, else walking, they come, poor of shoe and pocket it is my good luck to fill—prayerful old disheartened hearts, one and all for music come, for dancing and the girly sweet of candy in the air. For Clem, come, always Clem, and for the carnies barking: *A whale! A whale! The great white Clem!* Harpooned in a covered truck they haul him fifty counties in.

Forty-nine foot long of him!

Nigh on seven tons of him!

None but a shoaty eye to show and nary a tooth nor tongue in him!

A marvel! A wonder! An amazement to behold!

Come on, boy! Move on, miss. Come back, boy, he is smooth back here—I will let you touch him.

Yes, but, mister, can you tell me this? Tell me how old Clem is. I want to know how old he is. Is he as old as that turtle is, come flippered from the selfsame sea which he has got a glass trough of which we can see him swim in? Is he that old, your Clem? Is he?

Oh, move on. Will ye git on, boy. Go win yerself some gew-gaws for your sister at the fair.

HERE IS WHAT I figure—a quarter and two nickels which I will have to part with once to see Clem at the fair. Before, a peek inside my pail would set you back a nickel, but then was when I went the last with Daddy to the fair.

I have seven quarters. Now if I charge a penny, five times is a nickel, so for five times two times, I can see Clem seven times for every ten lids seven times I lift up at the fair.

I put my hand against my throat so I can feel me say it—*Clem, Clem.*

Buhl Parson's boy. Old Buhl Parson's boy. Clem.

But by and by, we are bumping past where the road forks for the fair.

I knock my knuckles against the window. The one fellow rides with his head hung back to show the whiskey slugs he takes that his long throat moves to swallow.

"Righto," he says. "Okey doke. Hold yer horses, Slim."

The truck shoots out underneath me. Broken jacks and rusty cans, headless screws and sockets sail, skipping the ribby bed of the truck. I am flopped back, paddling for a hold to grab. I find my feet to stand up, and duck the limbs of roadside trees.

We are going faster.

And we are getting farther.

So I have got to figure: tarsals and metatarsals, greensticks, spirals. Tibia, fibula, femur. There are two hundred and some-odd bones in the human body. Of these, I have broken eleven legs, thirteen arms, twenty-two toes and fingers.

I spy string to make a splint with and slip it in my pocket. But then I see my pail. I see the fellow driving us, still driving us with his elbow bent to stick out his side window. So I figure. I turn my boy's back on them so they can't see me tip my pail, so they cannot see Oscar, so it is just my pail they see I swing outside the window of the one who goes *shew*.

"Shew," he goes. "Shew, boy."

I let my pail swing in at him, closer every time it takes for him to guess ahead and back again, back to the lucky fib it has come to me I told him. *Cottonmouths*, I told him. We are proof of it—slung wheel-locked in a dusty skid I tip my cap at the finish of.

"I thank you, sir. And you, sir."

I hop down in my shiny shoes, with my turtle worked to the seat of my pants, to march—oh, slippery whelp!—the short piece to the overshot tin trumpet's call to the fair.

···· ····

OH, BUHL'S BOY. Buhl Parson's boy.

So now I have my bucket. I have my yellow house I know, set back from a road I know, and if I walk to the back of the house, I see the rope, the pulley, the open mouth of thick pipe set in the drilled ground.

At the bottom of the pipe is a bucket.

I cannot see it. But I can say that it is filled.

The bucket Orbit leaves in the back of the truck, since I have said so, is empty. It is lidded. But—that drunken night or another, on some parched curve or another, on some hardscrabble county road—suppose that the bucket tips over. Suppose it is found tipped over.

THERE IS A story I have often heard told in Tuscaloosa.

There was a boy in a fishing boat on the lake near Tuscaloosa.

I am not so sure it was August. It may be later, toward winter, the breeding season, when the nests are seen to rise in the lake and the eggs, it is said, of the cottonmouths are moving deep in their bodies. Onlookers on the banks of the lake claim the boy fell from the fishing boat. The boat was narrow, they say, not a deep boat, not a boat you would find to be hard to rock and, rocking, to get tipped over.

They dragged the lake there.

It occurs to me to wonder why it is they dragged the lake there. Maybe it is something that must be done, that there is some sort of decree about, nothing you are left any choice about, but I am guessing that someone, some family one, thought it was something that should be done, that someone ought to take it upon himself to have the lake be dragged. And when he had, when the lake was dragged, when the body of the boy was on the bank you see the snakes sun on there, when it was seen there, when people gathered there to see it—the body, the boy it is said to have looked by then to have rolled down a hill as boys do, but that this boy, punctured, spun out of a breeding nest, it is said that the way this boy looked, it was a long hill he had rolled down wound in barbed wire—then was the father, I wonder, was the sister, was whoever it was who had decided for the boy that he ought to be brought out of the lake and seen on the smooth bank there—were they, even then, that father, that sister, were they thinking ahead even then to how it might be told again, and knowing that it would be told again, how the story, the spectacle, the outrageous trick by common blood forevermore recast them?

Or before then, I wonder, before that, before the body had been seen at all, before the nets, the slow boat, before it was decided to drag the lake—then—even before then—before it occurred to any-one that someone was going to have to decide to have the lake be dragged, or not—I am not saying yes, or no, only that I wonder—no, that I suspect—hope, I hope I am not alone in this, in thinking that in the decision made there was likely to be, apt to have been, some notion—that in the spectacle of the body, in the freak show of the body, was the promise for them, the endurance for them, of some fresh exile, some uneasy glory.

···· ····

"CLEM?" CISSIE SAYS. "You saw Clem? And how is Clem, Orbit?"

I have not got prize one I brought Cissie from the fair. I have not got Oscar, and not my pail I took him in, so now I have to use a pan, which it is just a shallow pan I sneaked out from the kitchen. And the trough is almost empty. In the trough is just a puddle left

where the few tadpoles left over swim since Cissie dumped the
rest of them, which I will pick up by their tails to count them in
the garden. Each by each, I will line them up, snoot to tail in the
yellow vein, to fold them into the smooth leaves to bury them out
in the garden.

"How come Bingo isn't out digging up the garden?"

"How should I know?" Cissie says. "It isn't me who took her
off and left her at the fair."

But I did not leave Bingo. I say, "She did not come."

I am at the kitchen sink to fill the pan I thought to try to sneak
into the garden.

"And what if Daddy comes?" Cissie says. "Maybe you think I
could borrow your pail to fix him up a chicken."

But there will be no pan she needs and there will be no chicken.

Momma rests her hand on her wrinkled hair like there is a hat
to keep there, like there is a wind inside the house only she feels
come. But this is not the garden. The night wind does not come.
The filly does not hang inside to turn above the snapping reach of
stray dogs should they come.

I know why they come.

I say it is not for her, but I know why they come.

We light the lights back burning. I fix back the broken place to be
again a broken place so when our Bingo comes home, she can scoot
into our yard. I leave the windows open so we hear her in our yard.

But how will we hear Oscar? Cissie brings our beds from the
garden. Our beans are stripped in the garden. So how can we see
Oscar coming slowly should he come?

And Sugar should she come?

You can see the lights all burning. But still the dogs will come. It is still so hot at night that even with our windows closed we can hear them come.

So sometimes they are open.

Sometimes, with our windows closed, you cannot hold your breath enough long enough in Momma's room to stand the smell to sit there thinking why they come. So sometimes they are open.

Sometimes Momma watches me lift the windows open.

Sure—I know there are dogs out there.

I know with the windows up that Momma hears the dogs out there fighting for the filly in the yard when dark is come. I lift the windows open. I know dark is come.

I know should our daddy come, then there will be no talking then of sleeping in the one bed Cissie makes of two beds we sleep in in the pantry near to Momma's room.

But there will be the lean-to.

There will be our broken place our Bingo by and by will find, and there will be our Gander still, honking in our yard.

Still, Bingo does not come. I thought with the other dogs surely she would come. "Come. Come."

They said, *Come on, boy. You cain't see from there. Why, it's Parson's boy—old Buhl's boy. It's Orbit.*

They put me on the bandbox by the stage, where I could see.

I know the girl was watching me. I saw she could see me in the tent light there. I could hear the carnies singing *Clem* out there.

•••• ••••

MAYBE I AM mistaken. It is not unlikely that I am. But I do believe
it was August. I am almost sure it was August. It is the order of
things I am never quite so sure of myself of. I would say that Orbit
went to the fair before we missed Bingo, though, before we went
to the lean-to, though—because I remember thinking then, when
Orbit had gone to the fair, I remember having to remind myself
that it was just so quiet then because my brother had taken our
dog with him. Because it was so quiet, you see, and I would have to
remind myself that they were going to have to walk, Bingo and my
brother—they would have to walk a ways just to get themselves to
a place in the road where I know you can hear the fair.

So it would be a while, I knew. It would take those two some
walking, I knew, just to get to the goddamn fair. I knew I ought
to get myself to where I didn't need to remind myself that it was
bound to be quiet—that there were just the two of us, that it was
going to be quiet a while because it was just going to be me for a
while who moved in the house with Mother.

There was not yet rain then. There was not a sound, I know, of
rain coming down on the roof of our house—because it calmed me,
that sound, the sound of rain on the tin of our roof, so that now,
surely I would be certain now to remember that I had heard it.

The car for nights we had heard coast by—I didn't hear it at all.
It was only, I think, myself I heard, mostly, I think, my feet I heard
on the old boards, walking through the rooms of our house I heard
when it was just the two of us, when Bingo and Orbit were gone.

It is best to keep secrets with the dying, I think.

It would be our secret.

I drew the sheet back. I fixed the needle. For weeks, she had begged me for it—to be done with it. And then she stopped begging at all.

I did not rest much. I was waiting for her. I was waiting for some sort of signal from her. The names Mother had I knew of for things I knew fell away. Still I thought there would be some signal, you see; I thought there would be some way for me that Mother would find of asking me, something I could do or say, so that there would be some way to know, so that there would have been some way to think it wasn't me who wanted it, that it wasn't my want at all.

It was quiet; it would be quiet.

It was just me with Mother then—no fathers then, no doctors, no dogs in Tuscaloosa.

I CANNOT SAY how many days it was that the other two were gone. I know that the rain came later. The sound of the geese was later, the lake, the lean-to—I think of these as later. I think sometimes that the quiet then, that whatever it was that happened to us happened without our speaking then—that this is why, now—this is what it is now that makes it so hard for me now to remember what happened, to believe that anything happened.

But this is silly.

Orbit was gone, and Bingo was gone, and I was at home with Mother. I stayed by the bed with Mother. I kept the filled syringe in her drawer.

Before we took them away from her, Mother kept her cigarettes on the nightstand that stood beside her bed for all the nights of all the days I myself could speak of. It was the one thing she seemed to remember, the one thing Mother insisted on—on having one of her hands free to reach across her bedsheets with to pick up one of her cigarettes that we had long since decided she had had enough chances by then to get burned up in bed with, and us in bed with.

But she would reach for them. She would feel around on her nightstand for them and bring her hand up close to her mouth, with her mouth a rounded shape she made as though she were really smoking, as though she were somebody my age then practicing for smoking. For all the times I sat there and saw Mother reach for a cigarette, still when it was quiet like that, when we were alone in the house like that, I would catch myself thinking that Mother had reached for me.

There was a restlessness in me. It is hard for me to explain it. The weeks passed, the days. Years pass.

Years pass.

There are houses. Favorite dogs have died.

I cannot explain it.

A redbird flies at the windowpane. A river turns tail on the sea.

The shadows made by the pin oak tree pooled on Mother's bedsheets. She tried to kick them off, to sweep them off with the backs of her hands, to go out. She was always wanting to go out. When the last of the shadows left the room, the sun had dropped over the sea.

This was when she had gone out before our father left home. I had heard the bones of her hips crimped against the kitchen counter. She was peeling something, washing. Whatever it was, she put down. She went out.

She used to let us go with her.

There were geese those years I know Mother loved, and the pelicans that follow the river. I know Mother loved the river.

We were walking with her on the levee one day. We were behind her. She reached her hand behind her to stop us. We were to go back. There was something she had left in the oven for us that we were to eat for dinner.

We listened for her. We left the porch light on. Orbit dropped marbles in an empty can he set inside the door of our room and, from the can, walked a string from our room down the hall to wind around the knob of the door so that when she came back, we heard her.

There were times we did not hear her. We popped the screen from our window. The tree frogs had started to call. The call grew louder, quickened toward dark. Whippoorwills walked the road until dark, calling themselves out slowly.

Did you think we would follow, Mother?

WE LAY ON our beds by the window, our pillows doubled beneath us, to see across the field. Our field was silted. Our potatoes were fists in the ground we tilled—held out, rooting.

We grew restless.

We sang.

A horse and a flea and three blind mice, sitting on a tombstone shooting dice. Horse jumped off, fell on the flea. "Oops!" said the flea. "There's a horse on me!"

Boom boom. Boom boom.

WE NEVER FOLLOWED her to the river. Our father was in his room. We kept on having to remind ourselves that our father was in his room—that we should be quiet, that it would be dark before Mother came back, because it was a ways to the river and back. We would fill a plate for her and leave it to warm in the oven for her so that she would eat some dinner.

And then this stopped also.

The fields were burning. It was the time of year our father went out among the other fathers to burn the grass in the fields.

Our field was burning. We spelled one another at the window-sill. We could smell the grass still burning. The flames were brief, guttering birds.

We saw her.

She was growing old.

We saw the light of her cigarette drop at her feet from our window. Then we did not see her. We did not think we could see her.

We called out. We thought to call out. Ash rose to our mouths in the field.

•••• ••••

I DID NOT dawdle. Cissie says I dawdled there, but I did not dawdle. It is just a long way there. I came quick.

I did not have shoes. I did not have Bingo with me going there or coming back, and coming back I came by foot and I did not have shoes. I did not have Oscar, not my pail to bring him in and not my pail to rest on, turned up, tired by the road. And it is such a rough road.

But I came quick. I came in my sock feet. I had swapped my shoes.

I swapped them at the tent. Also all my coins I had which I had not yet parted with—I swapped them at the tent.

My shoes,

my coins,

my lidded pail,

my fishy eggs,

my chicken necks,

my stone I kicked for luck from home,

my store list Cissie gave me—

lost, and worst of all is Oscar lost, and worse by far is Bingo lost, and also figure tadpoles lost, folded in the yellow leaves since I left through the field.

There is always Clem there. The Ferris wheel was broken. But there is always Clem there, and the turtle that swims in the tank.

The tent was flapping. I had on my shoes.

"First off," the boy said, "you got to remove them shoes."

I took out my coins I had. I took off my shoes.

They smelled like Daddy. The ticket booth smelled like Daddy. Where I touched my shoes and the ticket booth, I smelled him on my hands.

I had smelled the roe, too, and the chicken necks when morning came, the morning I went to the fair. My pail was empty. I knelt in my skiff to paddle. I had to paddle with my hands. My hands were rotty. First I had the necks to lob and the bright eggs of the fish to lob where the lake is deep where the catfish swim, so that when I got to the shallows, when I got to the bank of the lake, I could haul my skiff up away from the lake and rinse it out with my empty pail and tip it up so if rain should fall, snakes would not swim in it.

The catfish had to swim up from the bottom.

I threw the eggs and the chicken necks as far away from my metal skiff as I could make them go. But I could still see the fish swimming.

Even the eggs they swam for. The eggs were so small. The snakes came and went for the eggs, but the snakes were small also.

The fish were as big as dogs.

I saw them swimming. I threw the fish eggs one by one, but once I threw a bunch at once so the fish would fight for them.

But I did not want to see the fish. I did not want them bumping me.

I did not want to feel their whiskers pulling past my arms.

THE BOY WAS putting on my shoes. The boy was just a tall boy stepped up taller in the ticket booth. He was not an older boy much by far than me. When he walked, my shoes made squeaking sounds like the sounds they made on me. My coins played songs in his pockets.

I stepped up with the boy in the ticket booth. There was a mark on the wall of the booth which even tipped up on my toes I could not reach with my head.

"Uh-oh," the boy said.

I was too small, he said.

I had seen my daddy—he had walked into the tent.

Inside the tent the men were clapping. There was music when the clapping stopped. But I was still not tall enough. Even tipped up on my toes, I was not yet tall as that for the boy to let me in.

My hands were in my pockets. I could not make a run for the tent because my hands were in my pockets. I had to keep them in my pockets.

I listened for him. If I listened hard enough and if I stayed still long enough, I heard Oscar's neck come out and sometimes, too, his feet came out and I would feel him walking on my legs between my pockets.

I HAD HEARD him, on the bank of the lake, in the weeds as soon as the sun came up. I had pulled my skiff up. I had my lidded pail. Oscar's feet made slow scraping sounds when I put him in my pail.

The boy had a scar on his forehead.

I thought the boy had sisters. I thought the boy had a stone to kick, or to keep with his hands in his pockets.

But he did not have sisters. I gave him my store list Cissie wrote, since he did not have sisters.

But he did not have pockets. I thought all boys had pockets.

I thought all boys had sisters, girls to carve their names in trees and in the shells of turtles boys can carry by their pockets.

"How old did you say your sister was?"

How old do you think Oscar is? How old are you, Cissie?

I swapped my shoes, my lidded pail, my Oscar who I held up in my pants between my pockets. I swapped until the boy in the ticket booth promised to let me in.

It was dark almost inside the tent when I first went in. The stage was empty. The men inside stopped talking. I could not see them yet, coming into the dark from the bright outside, but they saw me.

They said, "It's Buhl's boy. Why, Parson's boy. Hey, Orbit."

They smelled like piss and horses. They lifted me up on the bandbox so I could almost see. But I did not see Daddy. I was on the bandbox, sitting, seeing over the hats of the men, but I could not see Daddy.

"Somebody tell Parson that his boy has found him here."

But I could not hear Daddy.

On my hands, I could smell my shoes. I heard the thick flaps of the tent beat in the wind outside the tent and the boy walking out in the wind outside. I could hear my shoes. It was just the trees I heard and the wind which beat the flaps of the tent and the squeaking steps my shoes made and then the music started. The girl had feathers in her hair which flew out when she danced. The light

shined down along her. She had a jerky way of dancing, a tooth
which as she danced I saw her loosen with her tongue.

"Quit that," Cissie says. "What is it now, Orbit?"

I pull the porch light on.

I say, "Oscar will not come tonight. Will he, Cissie? And Daddy
not the next night?"

Not even if we hear the cars go quiet past out there. You cannot
see the trees out there. Tonight the trees are quiet.

Even if that boy left him there to find his own way home from
the fair, still there would be the road to cross, the slough, the stubbled field to cross—so even if Oscar came on, even if Oscar did not
stop, it would be high time by then, by the time we maybe saw him,
to polish our swapped shoes again to be on our way from home by
then to see Clem at the fair.

There is not a leaf that turns. There is not a drop that falls.
There are not the trees to see until the bright heat lights them.

"Is that all, then?" Cissie says. "That's what you wanted to
ask me?"

We leave the porch light burning.

Momma is in her room.

We try to go how Momma went when Momma could leave her
room. We walk along the dirt road which quits against the paved
road the river runs on beside of and takes the boats to sea. Ours is
just a small boat. It is just a lake boat. It is not a boat to ride the
river out to sea in.

The river moves fast.

It sweeps beneath the limbs of the trees which bend along the broken bank. The rain clouds stay at the river, at the crooked lake the river left.

Go on.

The pelicans go on.

We do not turn back. We go on walking down, catching onto the limbs of the trees to reach the high wall of the barge, the low rail of the sloping deck we use the chains to climb to. The chains come up from the river. We swing our feet up over them to monkey up the slope to the barge, the mud of our shoes dropping past into the passing river.

I say, "Be careful, Cissie."

The river goes to sea. The sea ourselves we have not seen nor had the taste nor smell of.

We lie on our backs on the deck of the barge. We lie so our heads hang away from the barge, listening to the river. Sometimes a river turns back.

"I saw a girl at the fair," I say. "Her hair was kinked and yellow. It was not like your hair. I did not want to touch her hair."

MY HANDS WERE dirty. My hands smelled like Oscar smelled and my hands smelled like Daddy—like the shoes I wore to the ticket booth, the eggs I threw to the whiskered fish, the necks I threw so I could flip the skiff so snakes would not swim in it.

She danced. The men were hooting. They were calling for the next girl, calling for something else. She took her top off, her thin brassiere. She took her time with her panties, tugging so they fell down, so they were on the floor. Then she quit dancing. She got down into the webby chair folded out in the swinging light. She let her legs drop open.

She pushed the eggs up into her—three, I counted. Four. Maybe I lost count of them.

Maybe they were Doll's thin eggs.

Maybe they were the kingbird's eggs, crowning in the gash she dropped her legs apart to show us. She popped them out again. I saw her watching. I saw she could see me in the tent light there. She lobbed the eggs over the hats of the men.

I did not want to catch the eggs. I did not want to touch her skin, and not the small eggs that broke and left in her no shell I saw, no shut place she could open.

Say the river turns back.

Say the river turns back, sucking at the sea to turn, will the pelicans turn back also, Cissie? Will the salted fish turn back when the sea has turned back to run back into the sea itself in the turning river?

Go on.

Our lake is our lake. Our barge is chained here.

Go on.

The fair stays here for twelve days. Then is yet the next town I can think of that it goes to. Then the fair stays eight days. Then figure for the next small town as small by far as our small town, it stays for maybe ten days. I cannot figure.

Maybe I lost count of them. I counted nine and seven—nine eggs going into her, seven coming out.

Plus there is this also—also to think how many times to figure in a fair night they can fill the tent to do it. It is not a big tent. And where they find the eggs she keeps, plenty more would come. Twelve, say, eight days, ten days spent in Little Crab, plus maybe days in towns to go I have not even thought of. So say another two towns. Say she does it twice a night, since maybe they won't wait for her to let the tent get filled. She is seventeen, say, or maybe she is twenty. Maybe it is nothing you can start before you're twenty. So maybe she is twenty. Couldn't she be twenty?

MAYBE IT IS not a redbird. It could be a kingfisher bird.

Couldn't it, Cissie?

Because don't the kingfisher birds steal bones to knit them on the water?

The bones could be our Bingo's bones, the small bones of birds she kills, the bones of Momma's fingers.

Couldn't they, Cissie?

Because maybe it is not a redbird. Maybe it is a kingfisher bird.

Maybe it flies at the windowpane because kingfisher birds need bones and hair and there are the bones of Momma's hands and the hair which falls from Momma's head and the hair which falls from your own head and from my head also.

And we have bones also.

HER SHOES WERE dirty. Momma's skirt of her dress was dirty. I felt the cool where the skirt of her dress, where the cloth of her skirt, doubled back, was wet from the river still.

Our mouths were burning. The fireflies were burning.

"There, now," Cissie says.

"Let's go now," Cissie says. "Hum up, Orbit."

The boats are moving. The lamplights are on.

But we are not moving. We are not moving. Our beds are one bed. Our lake is our lake. Our barge is chained here.

Go on.

She is here with us now. She will die with us.

Go on.

•••• ••••

THE BIRD CAME back when Orbit came back. I heard it hitting at the windowpane again.

It kept on at it. For a time I could not see it. I thought at first it was mud Orbit threw, but there was no mud to throw, no rain yet to pock the dust to clop against the windowpane so that I would lean across her bed and say through the window, *Orbit? What is it now, Orbit?*

But he did not throw it.

He was working at his tree.

His ax made hammering sounds working at his tree. The blade was shiny. The light that fell from Mother's room, Orbit chopped

the tree by. There were pieces chipped of the bark of the tree and of
the pale wood of the tree scattered in Orbit's shadow as if it were
not his shadow but a still pond by some accident he had stepped
in there.

He swung the ax back. He had choked up on the handle. I saw
it slipping in his hands. The window sweated. I let it close then.

I saw the bird swoop down then from where it sat in the pin
oak tree, where the filly shook in the pin oak tree when the iron
head of the ax homed, and so I pushed it up again, the window,
the shadow of the window sash lifting on my brother's back—and
the bird banked.

It was a redbird.

I saw that it was a redbird. It was common.

I pushed the window open enough to lean out past the windowsill to be heard above the chuck of the ax. I saw he had
not eaten. I saw the plate I had brought to him gathering wood
chips still. Orbit's shirt hung down from the waist of his jeans
for a rag to keep to wipe his hands and the shadow had lifted
away from his back and gone off into the leaves of the tree and
I leaned out.

"Hold your hands out for me," I said. "Let me see your
hands."

I saw his shirt was stained and wadded. He kept his back to me.
He went on with the ax.

I said, "Stop it. You've got to stop it."

I said, "You ought to come inside."

But I could not stop him.

Even when the tree was down, even with the filly down, dragged away from the pin oak tree, I tried to tell my brother that Bingo would not come.

But I could not stop him.

I could not stop any of it. I knew she would not come.

···• •···

OH, TO BE a junkyard dog and run the woods with Daddy!

Gander knocks his beak on our door at night. I keep my vole in my pocket.

I say, "Lookit, Cissie."

I take my hammer.

It is Daddy's hammer.

It is my vole I found. It is in my pocket.

"Lookit, Cissie."

I put my vole on the porch step.

She says, "Stop it, Orbit."

But I do not stop it. I do not stop it. I go on hitting. I hit it on his head.

···• •···

I WAS PEELING potatoes.

In the sink, the mounding strips of skin gave off the smell of turned earth. Everything had stopped growing. The fireflies lay in the field.

I saw Orbit walking between them with his shoes off in the field.

He was walking to reach the place in the fence he had mended before he left for the fair—he had forgotten. I could see that he had forgotten. His hands were ragged. I saw that his cap was frayed.

I peeled all we had of potatoes.

Orbit I suppose had not eaten much in however many days it had been, and it had been a ways, I knew. It had taken my brother some walking, I knew, to get back home from the fair.

I boiled the potatoes and poured off the water and added what we had of milk. We had a good dollop of butter. I let it melt some. I used two colors of pepper. I salted the potatoes in a metal pot and mashed them together with the tines of a fork and spooned them into a casserole.

Orbit was burying tadpoles. I was sorry about the tadpoles.

I listened outside the door of the room when he went in to talk to Mother. He told her about the tadpoles, about Clem he had seen and the girl at the fair, about how he thought he had seen Daddy.

He didn't say a thing about Bingo.

He fixed the fence back. I mean that he pulled it apart again so that Bingo could get back through.

He got the ax out.

It was almost dark when he started. He kept at it, working into the next day and on into the next dark. I carried a big plateful of potatoes to him and set the plate down in the path in the yard beneath the crooked limb of the tree Mother used to read in.

She read limericks. She wore knee-highs.

I closed her mouth some. A tooth had abscessed. The side of her face had swelled.

•••• ••••

THE ROPE I used was rotty and thick and there was the hanging weight of it, I said the waiting hang of it. When I went out on the limb of our tree I could see our momma's bedroom from, I saw that the knife blade bent and caught with never so much as a nick in the rope I had lobbed across the limb of the tree I had climbed the tree to saw through.

So Momma said to me, "Orbit, so why don't you cut it down?"

So I cut the damn thing down.

I found the ax our daddy used, which I had seen him do it.

After the tree was well and down, it was easy with even a flimsy knife to cut down past the hide of her into the long neck of her, the blade going quick along and smooth behind the soft muzzle even Bingo had fought to get at, that I had seen her jumping with the other dogs to get at. The muzzle was torn from them and hard-blooded and soft-haired still to want to kiss, but I did not stop to kiss it. It was near to yard-dark and soon to watch the darkened woods, I would see the dogs.

So I went quick.

I had not thought to think it yet that Momma said my name: *Orbit*.

So, Orbit, so why don't you go ahead and cut the damn thing down?

But I had not thought *Orbit.*

I was thinking of the filly still and the knife blade pulling deep in her and the dark shapes of the dogs I saw bunch up in the field. The light from Momma's window fell bright before the field. It was all the light I worked by. I worked to get the hide free the way once Daddy showed me.

First you put her head back. I had put her head back. At first the knife went smooth.

It was how he showed me. At first the knife went smooth the way he showed me down the front of her, smooth all down the neck of her. It was just a knife I had I sneaked out from the kitchen with and then the light to work by, down by night from Momma's room.

I heard her name me in her room.

It was just the one time. I only heard her one time.

At first the knife went smooth.

····• •···

WE PASSED THE barn. The slough was dry. The lake was left by a river.

The lake was dropping. Where the skiff had scraped on the bank of the lake, the paint was flecked and silver.

I did not know why we had come there. I remember the snakes were blind. My brother brought the bent skin he had found in the woods that the snakes by then had begun to shed, and a turtle—Vernon, I remember—and chicken necks, and the rhinestone shoe he had found of Mother's that had not been chewed or buried; he brought tadpoles, I remember, a poke of frogs—a damp stash he had gigged in the trees—a flat stone, a kitchen knife, a lamplight, though the sun was high, though the moon would rise behind us.

Our house lay bright behind us. We paddled out with our hands. He threw a frog, a chicken neck. He threw an old bone from the garden.

We waited.

I did not know what we were waiting for.

We were quiet.

I did not know why we were quiet.

The lake slapped at our skiff underneath us. I sang. Of the cranes in the trees I sang of, and of the pelicans I sang of, no cry came.

I sang, *Oh, what a bird is the pelican! His beak can hold more than his belly can!*

But Orbit didn't want me to sing. We were waiting for the moon, I thought, for the sun to fluke in the sea, I thought. I thought he would tip us over. He threw great wads of tadpoles out and the rhinestone shoe of our mother's out and our Vernon gone scudding out in a slapping rain of frogs.

There was something he was trying to show me. He kept stepping up onto the thwarts of the skiff to look for it to show me. But whatever it was was not out there, or he could not see it out there, and Orbit started to scream at me that I wasn't really trying, I wasn't really looking, but he never did say what to look for, see. I never really knew what it was he had brought me out in the skiff that day he had wanted so much to show me.

That was August. It must have been August.

Because I remember Orbit saying to me that the snakes were blind. I know that it is dog days, that dog days are August, that these are the days the skins lift away and the snakes themselves go blind.

···· ····

SOME DAYS THE crows are blue if the sun is yellow. The lean-to is blue all days. The weeds are going yellow. Tomorrow if the leaves are green, the next day the leaves are red if they are not yellow.

The girl's hair was blue, then yellow. I did not want to touch her hair.

The redbird was a redbird before I touched the redbird. After, its neck was broken.

I chopped the pin oak down.

I should not have done it.

A tadpole's legs are dark inside, as small inside the skin to cut as when a fly is yellow. I did not want to see the flies. First a fly is yellow. Then are yet the legs to grow, the thin wings and eyes to grow, though first by night by Momma's room I chopped the pin oak down. I know our momma saw me chop the pin oak down.

Here is what I figure:

But I cannot figure.

Figure there are flies inside.

I pulled the flap back. I had to light a light inside.

Inside the filly are flies inside and in our house also. Also in Bingo worms inside and in our house also. Inside the snakes are fishy eggs and maybe frogs also, and in the fish also. Inside the frogs are flies inside and in the filly also, in maybe Bingo also. Maybe fishhooks also. In the whiskered fish are fishhooks and maybe ducks also. Maybe Vernon also.

There could be a dog.

Then if me and Cissie dove and held our stones and sank with them until we sank to the bottom of the lake and we lay on our backs on the bottom of the lake with our stones on top to hold us, we would hear our dog.

Because I bet she is digging. We would hear our Bingo digging.

Because she is just our dog.

OUR OSCAR PUT his flap down and walked between my pockets. True.

But I cannot figure *true*.

The pin oak tree is down. The filly, I dragged to the lean-to. It is my lean-to, true. It is my vole I found. It is in my pocket.

If the vole is my vole, is its head mine also?

Is it my head also?

Once it was the vole's sharp head. But if the vole is not now, if it was and is not now, its head is only mine now, its feet, its tail mine also.

My broken head,

my feathered neck,

my ropy tail my daddy cut—

mine—

my muzzle also,

my long toes, mine,

my yellow eyes,

my bones of Momma's fingers, mine.

She will be mine also.

ONE MISSISSIPPI, I count, *two*, to know the seconds by. I think she is not breathing. I try to keep from breathing. But sometimes we breathe.

Her mouth is open. I thought Momma sings. But Momma does not sing, I know. There is no such song she sings that only she can hear, I know.

I take my time some. I wash my finger. I put it in her mouth.

One-five-zero, zero-zero-zero-zero—I cannot remember the zeros it should be—the toothless years the turtles pass. But a tongue, I know, our turtles have, a toothless frog a tongue, too, else it would not sing. Else you would not hear it sing.

It is getting looser. I work it with my finger some—a sharp tooth, Momma's dog tooth.

A goose's tooth, you cannot pull, though Gander knocks at the door come night, though maybe you could pull his tongue to quiet down the yard at night—if you broke his neck first. If you had a pliers.

They are Daddy's pliers.

I work the gum up. I shut the curtains. I pull the window closed.

Listen: between day and dark, you hear them. With my breath I breathed in Momma's room between her breaths, you hear them.

But the frogs are not calling me.

"Open your mouth, Momma. Open your mouth, Momma."

I thought they were calling me.

But they are not calling me.

They are calling Momma.

•••• ••••

COME.

The trees are green still. The cows can be heard feeding. I will keep quite near.

Only come, if you will, from the dirt road that ends, if you wish, at the paved road. Where there is dirt, the path will have been worn smooth. Where saw grass, the blades are broken.

Cross the slough, the levee. I will not be far from you. The way is perfectly clear.

From the levee, you will see a high, red bank gouged by the flow of a river. True: perhaps there is no river.

Perhaps the almanac is right: there will be no river this year.

But the road—there will be the road, yes. The arroyo, yes. Some truck stop, some Sears. Some fair-grounded border town of tooled belts and Kewpie dolls, dirty-shirt dog shows, souvenir spoons.

Remember he kept a rabbit's foot saved frozen from the garden. Remember a vole in his pocket.

I left the doors both open—Mother's door and our door. There was something Orbit wanted to show me. He kept bumping around in the hall for me, to wait for me, to show me.

I put my shoes on. The sun was dropping. Mud swallows sang in the eaves. We crossed the yard, the garden, stepping over the boughs of the pin oak tree.

"What is it, Orbit?"

We were marching. We crossed the hidden field. The geese flew so high above the field, I could hardly hear them. I could not see them. I looked away over the trees as we went, thinking that I would see them.

We walked on. The path we walked, I could not see myself to follow. Still I followed. The shade was spotty when we reached the trees. I saw a swatch of something blue showing between the trees.

"This is where I come to think," Orbit said.

I saw he had made a lean-to with a tarpaulin in the trees.

"You brought me out here to tell me that? This is what you had to show me?"

NO RAIN FALLS. No birds swift past. On the bank of the lake is a shallow skiff the river bend has come to. The river is quite near. The wide boats going slow to sea, you can see from Tuscaloosa.

Tuscaloosa is a good town. There are doctors in Tuscaloosa. No guns, no books, no telephones. But a river—yes. A yellow house, a lake near Tuscaloosa.

The lake is deep, the river. The door to the house is open. Inside the door is a woman's purse. Inside the purse is a pair of gloves. The purse is open. The door is open.

In my mind is an empty room Mother walks into when I speak.

But this is silly.

I sat on my hands in the parlor. I closed the window. I drew the curtains.

Listen to me, Orbit. It was not the sea we heard. It was not Ohio.

It is just a sound I like to hear, the name *Ohio*.

He said, "Come on, Cissie."

I saw the bird first—it was a redbird. It hung from its feet from a string from a limb the tarpaulin was lashed to.

Orbit folded the flap of the tarpaulin back. There were rows. At the mouth were rabbits he had brought from the garden whose necks you can break with your thumb. We stepped over the rabbits to step inside—we had to light a light to see by. I was too tall to stand inside.

He said, "Close your eyes, Cissie. Open your eyes, Cissie."

A blue wall hung with a gaggle of frogs—pinned, quartered. A yellow cat. A turtle—the beaked neck of a turtle, the dark shards of shell. Orbit had teeth in his pocket. He had a pitchfork, looped with snakes skinned from behind their angled heads, and mice—pink, puny, hairless things Orbit had driven the pitchfork through, that you could see the prongs of the pitchfork through.

"This is where you come to think?" I said. "You brought me out here to tell me that?"

There was a pin oak tree in our yard. In the tree was a crooked limb—

What of it?

She read limericks; she wore knee-highs.

The yellow cat is a yellow cat.

The blacktop runs beside the river, to sand against the sea.

What of it?

Orbit pulled away the filly's hide, the slab of her rib with the toe of his shoe. He nudged her open.

THE WAY IS easy to see—to see her, to word her, to be shut of her. I cannot get shut of her.

Come. There will be a road, an airport. There are lights so bright at airports, you can hear them burning.

Come. Forget about Ohio. The salt bluffs, the sea.

The door is open.

We may go now.

You may leave us.

I drew the sheet back. Needles, implements, morphine, salve. It would have to be needles—the body seen, the witnessed skin. The light grayed, blanched her. Mother's skin grew weak, and pulled away.

Mother, please.

I love you, Mother.

A signal, a word. If she spoke, I did not hear her. Maybe she asked for water. Maybe a light was on.

I drew the sheet back. Her gown was twisted.

No rain came, no father.

When the rain came, it stayed, the wind, the no-time of waiting through—the dry, disordered days, dog days, days of heat and of the wild cry of geese faintly above the fields and in the dusking garden.

She is years dead. She is dying. I am in some airport.

Everywhere, even where there are no paved roads, still there will be an airport—a strip to portage to, pebbled or clayed, what have you, beaten grass swept of light.

The light is leaving our windows. The Naugahyde booths are dreams.

I draw her gown back. Our mouths are open.

No birdsong, Mother? No silver fish?

Very well, then. Very well, then.

I fixed the needle.

No fathers then, no doctors, no dogs in Tuscaloosa.

There was nothing I could do for her, nothing I could not do to her. I rouged her cheeks, teased her hair. I harvested beets from the garden.

Go on. Go on. There is not a place in you I will not work into. I work apart bone.

The bland root of me swam between her bones.

The fields are planted. The door is open. The trees are green still. *Go on.*

I cannot remember you.

I unremember you.

For years I do not dream of you.

Go on. I give back nothing.

THE WEEKS, THE months, they gave me something to do with myself. I had a sense I liked of myself—that I was needed, that there was a great givingness in me, a patient, damaged, holy sort of hardheaded love in me.

Love. Say love.

That I waited, say, since I waited—not to say or have it be said of me that what I did I did because there was not patience enough in me, enough faith, love, talk in me, that what I did I did because there was such a rush in me—there was a great hurry in me.

Come. Quickly. Come.

The lights are burning. You can hear the lights still burning. I can conjure up a dream for us, the Dopplered wheeze of an engine, a tire song on a paved road—

But this is easy. To conjure a dream is easy.

To upstage the dead is easy.

I take—I give back nothing. I have had my children scraped from me—accidents of fucking. No wide swim, no brackish suck. But the reamed cunt, the scoured earth.

The Buick in flames on the highway. The breakfasts, the tea.

Love. Say love.

Say something, anything more—that you are sick, or lonely, some wild boy gone to seed one night, some buckaroo I loved one night farmed apart on scag one night, one night when I was twenty. That you are oceans to cross from home, let us say.

Or nothing. Let us say almost nothing.

In my hands are the hands of your mother.

Let us go now. She may leave us.

Look, you. You, newborn.

Has there been no dream we met in? No Naugahyde booth we met in in some tawdry airport bar?

Here's to you, love. And to you, my sweet.

The fields are burning.

So, go. Go on, go on. Run tell the doctor, the children, the schools. A signal, a word. Only whisper.

Light out.

Winter wheat, corn counties. Cave Hill, Carthage. Caspian, Ocoee, Reelfoot, Sargasso.

There is always the next place to go to get to to light out of.

The road lapses. Snow falls—schools close, dog tracks, airports. There will be some airport.

From the soft palm, the girth of tumor in her—let me say, let it be said of us, of myself and of my mother said—in a Naugahyde booth, in a makeshift bar, in the shaking heat of an airport said— some lesser god from the greening rift—beaded, slicked, a pale sheen—a long cock broke to probe me.

Newborn, adieu. *Asante.*

To you, lad. And to you, my sweet. May we have a good long romp of it.

For who will love what we love?

What bright house?

What reading tree?

Who will love our dead for us, the wormy dog at our feet at night, the harpooned corpse of a baleen whale we walk a day to see?

I COULD NOT hear her. I saw her talking. Mother for hours made sounds with her mouth in a voice not as loud as breathing. I leaned my head near. I felt her breathing.

She was saying thank you. Mother was saying thank you.

After all the months of it, the careful doses of morphine, the dressings, the scarves? The Popsicles and floating pears, swabbed teeth, open sores, bludgeoning heat, neighbors, neighbors—for this, she thanks me?

The long box we build for her we break her bones to lie in.

Mother kept a cot at the foot of her bed certain nights I slept in. I was sleeping. When I waked up, I found her dead.

I pulled the drapes shut. I closed her mouth some. I knew to close her eyes.

I left them open.

I untied the scarf I had tied Mother's foot for weeks to the post of her bed with. I had taped a needle to a vein in her foot. I took it out. I got the sheet off. I took the catheter out. She had bled from her mouth. I wet a washrag. I took her gown off. Her gown was bloodied. I took her pillow. The blood was dry. I wiped her mouth off. I rinsed the washrag. I wiped her neck some. I wiped her shoulder.

We had a big barrel we burned in.

I burned the gown, the pillow sack. I burned the washrag.

I got her arms straight. I turned her feet in. I got her rings off.

We put on lipstick. We put her rings on.

Day came. Men came. Rain.

We sat for the men with our hands in our laps with all that was ours in the parlor.

BLOOD COUNTRY

The wind came down from the mountains and drove the fire across the plains. The fire burned fast and bright now and everything living moved with it, the jackrabbit and the antelope, the coyotes flushed from their dens. The badgers dug in. He tried to think of it. He thought of his wife but he had lost her name.

He rode with his back to the mountains going blue in the dark coming on. A light was burning. He needed to reach it. He rode holding to the horn of his saddle. He did not ride so much as hang there as in some shoddy western. He felt the heat of his face. His face was on wrong. The wind pressed against his back and made him cold.

Her name was Prairie. Prairie was his girl, his wife was what? The wind parted his horse's mane and blew it eastward. The pronghorn would outrun the fire but cattle would heap against fences until the fire burned them alive. The prairie was shortgrass prairie. Land of his youth. Blood country.

His horse walked calmly and the flames moved off from them and ash made the going quiet. He slept he did not know how long before his horse spooked and started. A rabbit bounded through the burnt grasses, wind lifting and twisting its hair. Somewhere a bird dipped past. A clump of roots flared.

HE DID NOT wake again until the ranch house. He had been in the mountains, he explained, pushing cattle. It was a young horse. He did not know anymore. He had a wife he knew, could he call her? He didn't know how to call her. He had forgotten the number. Town was hours. He had parked his rig somewhere. Somebody else had been with him. He could not bring up her name, he meant his wife's name. His head was breaking. He was vomiting between words.

He said, I think my name is John. He tried a number. It was somebody else. He had lost his sons' names, his mother's. He tried a number. I think I am John, he repeated.

AT LAST HE reached her. Elaine was her name. She came to him, a good woman, and nursed him the years in bed. He had been thrown, he supposed. Maybe his horse had reared up and hit him.

He lay in bed for years and tried to think of it. He flew into rages. He had seizures. The doctors worked on him. His jaw had been thrust into his brain. His mind wasn't right, it would not be right again. He could hear his eyes rolling in their sockets.

He was dangerous, the doctors told his wife. His wife was thin and weak and her hair fell out. You need to do something, the doctors told her. She came at them with a rake.

He heard mice half an acre away. The sound of opening a bag of potato chips knocked him to the floor. His boy dropped a horseshoe behind him; his face swelled as if struck.

He went nowhere. Bed to kitchen to bathroom. He meant to take his life but something stopped him.

He was forty when the horse wreck happened. He was fifty when they brought him out again into the wind of that dry country. What was expected of him, who would recognize him, how was he to behave?

The grass had come back. Sun had whitened the bones against the fences.

He could not run right but he could stand. He could ride a horse, he discovered. That's what saved him. He kept to the plains, to the coulees. He rode anything. He broke colts with his boys. He roped calves at the local rodeo.

In the fall of that year he was thrown by a colt and dragged by his boot from the stirrup. His boy found him. He was living still. The wind tumbled his hat into a coulee. The boy studied his father—the mess of his face, the years ahead. He saw his life spent. He saw his mother with her robe hanging open.

His name was Trinity. His father twitched in the grass. Jackrabbit, coyote—on anything else a man took mercy.

Trinity, he repeated. Goddamn it, pop. I'm your boy, pop. I am your boy and you are John.

MONOCOT

HE SERVED A FEW YEARS IN THE MERCHANT MARINE AND so named his sons Anchor, Hawser, and Rudder. The names amused him. The boys didn't come to much. The eldest killed a girl he was in love with, a crime of passion, you likely recognize the arc of the story.

The father grew water oaks strewn with epiphytes that looked like creatures of the sea. Bromeliads of many colors. The plants were bizarre and harmless. If you wanted to hurt the man, you hurt these.

After long months at sea without women, the father fell in love with a delicate, flinty girl who went by the name of Penelope. To watch her mouth as she spoke—he would give anything. She loved him briefly and they married. Her feet were always cold and her teeth ached and she ate nothing but tiramisu.

They watched a film one spring night about a speed skater stricken by a crippling disease. Exquisite, such ease, like something winged—the way she moved across the frozen expanse. It was as if you were watching music. Then the wreckage, the counted hours.

A beetle, caught in the lens of the projector, kept walking across the screen. It was a thousand times too big.

The marriage was over.

They were driving home, after. He wanted to know why.

A rabbit loped along the shoulder, keeping pace with their car. She couldn't begin to say, but it was over. She had her bags out the door by morning, monumental in the sun.

He moved south for the heat with his third wife, mother of his three boys. For years the boys played Who Would Win? A tsetse fly or an elephant? An anchor or a hawser? Diabetes or a Colt .45?

The boy rowed her out in a dory on flat water at dusk and strangled her. The eyes were the proof, the marks on her neck, even after the lake had done its work. She had looked like her mother once, people remarked, as consolation.

The father grew calla lilies also, and drank water from the throat of the bloom. The blooms were extravagant, cousins to the lethal datura, succulent in the moon. Best by far were, to him, the bromeliads, slow to grow and scrappy, needing nothing but mist and sun.

SEARCH AND RESCUE

A CLIMBER FELL TO HER DEATH TODAY FROM A CHALKY face in the Rockies. Rush hour, happy hour, dusk among the cities of the plains.

SHE LAY WITH her face to the sky. As though an offering. Patch of bright. A broken parakeet.

WHITE FLECK OF a jet descending. The picker-uppers—quick with the news—clairvoyant or just plain lucky.

THESE FREE CLIMBERS, the woman, that boy on El Cap—they must move with the mind of another. Free climb, free to fall. Don't think of it.

DID SHE THINK, as she fell, with a buffalo's mind—tumbling, no more, once a pishkun, driven into the sun?

NO MORE. HERE'S to you. It's your birthday. We search and search and rescue. Feeble-sighted. Slow.

So how, so fast, do they find her—nature's homely helpers? By the eye, is it, by the nose?

By the look of the balding white man, the Lakota supposed: scavengers. By the smell. Feeding on the rotting meat of their sweet-faced cows.

No thumbs—what the African once thought of the white man. Imagine that this is so. Had been so. What changes? Colt .45, etcetera.

By the time the kind boys from search and rescue arrive, the woman is eaten clean. Sounds a little grim, but really? Why not let them carry you, flesh of your flesh, brainy heads, into the indigo heavens?

Tongue of bright foam is the stream. Lift of the wind, a slow ascent. To you, my life. Splendid.

PACHYSANDRA

ROSE CALLED.

I said, "Hello, Rose."

"You sound funny."

I was lying on my back with my legs in the air trying to make a baby with my mister. I had his seed in there. My poor egg had slipped out to meet it.

"Can't you come out here and help me?" Rose pleaded.

She had bunions. She had busted her elbow stirring oatmeal.

I was busy. My mucous was of a quality. I had just the least clutch of eggs left out of the millions I got when I started.

"Get off," my man said, "and I'll do it again."

"Is that Tonto I hear?"

Tonto snorted. "She'll talk all day if you let her."

"Just send me the obituaries," Rose said. "I want to see if I'm in them."

COME MARCH, ROSE called again. I wasn't doing anything. I was solo again.

"I broke my back," she said, "reaching for butter."

"For butter?" I said. "That's ridiculous."

"I bought you a ticket. I'll send Rudy."

Rudy was the help. He was wicked. His eyebrows made a lovely shade for his eyes. He was Hopi and his hair shone like butter.

I said I'd come. I flew across. Landed in the land of enchantment. I'd been a girl here. Been in quicksand in the big muddy river. I scrambled out.

No Rudy.

But who after all can blame Rudy after all we've done?

I caught a taxi and went straight to the hospital where I had come out into this world.

"WHO WAS THERE," I asked, "anyone?"

"Gotcha. Big Ed and Snicker Bar were somewhere in the back."

Gotcha looked up weepily whenever Rose said his name. He worked to sit up and tipped over. Rose fed him off her fork at the table.

"I like butter," Rose told me. "Is it so much to ask?"

Her back was cracked in three places. She broke like pencils. She had a hump you could set your mug on.

The doctor said, "Doll, if you can get her to walk. Get her at least to sit and eat."

"Eat?" I asked him. "She will vomit in her plate."

I hated to so much as touch her.

Rose broke a finger dialing the telephone. She snapped the neck of her femur off stepping up the step from the driveway.

March, and the jonquils were blooming. I had brought a few stalks to the hospital in a peanut butter jar. A bee buzzed in the cup. It made me sleepy.

"Are you sleeping?" I asked her.

"I will be."

I WENT HOME while Rose slept to scrub up the house. I'd find a nurse and sort through the cupboards—the blackened fruit and applesauce, the chewed-open boxes of Jello. Rose had cans from the 1940s. Sacks of sugar hard as adobe. She had a hip-high stack of aluminum pans the city delivered her meals to her in.

I'd move the bed. She needed a hospital bed, cranks and pulleys. The handsome doctor said so.

Under her bed I found droppings and newspaper, stuffing tugged from the mattress, insulation, sponge. I found the ossified stools of her dachshunds, still ruddy from Kibbles 'n Bits. The cretins snapped at me while I worked: Big Ed, Gotcha, Snicker. They pissed on my lumpy pillow. They ate every bristle of my toothbrush and threw it up in my shoes.

"You could take them to the vet," Rudy suggested, "and ask if they are in any pain."

"And if they are?" I asked.

I COULDN'T DO it.

Rose had saved those dogs from the gas box. They had no manners. You couldn't blame them.

Gotcha had a tumor in his bowels. He puffed up and walked his belly raw on the carpet. Snicker was missing an eyeball. Something ate Big Ed's hair.

They chased mice and never caught them. Cockroaches feasted at their food bowls.

Candles went limp in their holders, helpless in the heat of the desert. Every doorknob was choked with elastics Rose had saved from the paper for years.

I ROLLED MY sleeves to my elbows, afraid to have something run up them.

I slept blasted on the beach with Tonto one lovely week in Panama City. A ghost crab scooted up my pants leg. A fiddler crab sat in my eye socket.

"You made it up," Rose said, "but I like it."

The handsome doctor thought Rose was my mother.

"My mother is already dead," I told him. But then I wished I hadn't.

I WISHED I hadn't come. I wished I had Tonto to work with still, slow in a sunny bed. My time was passing.

Rose said, "Whose isn't?"

I held her sweet hand and looked out. A jogger streaked past the hospital window. He weaved between cars in the parking lot, sweating and showing off. He looked like Rudy.

He was Rudy. Rudy was supposed to be high on the Spanish tiles patching leaks with cut-in-half coffee cans. Half Rose's roof was cans. Rudy sprayed them a desert amber, glopped them in with a fat seam of caulk.

"Let me out," Rose pleaded, "before he knocks the house down."

She reached for the handsome doctor, her eyes sparkling in her head. She was jacked up. They call that comfortable.

That house was coming down around her ears. For forty years the roof had leaked. The walls shed stucco like continents the English ivy had dug its fingers down in.

Everything Rose knew needed helping—Rudy and the gas-box dachshunds, her defaced and stricken elm. She knew a one-legged boy she took cookies. She married a man who was dying and spent her honeymoon in the hospital. A year later they were picking out coffins. The Big Pink. The Satin Amplitude.

"If you find me with my throat slit," Rose told me, "look for Rudy."

I LOOKED FOR Rudy. Rudy was turning cartwheels in the street.

I was still inside cleaning. I cleaned up the oatmeal, the butter. Everything felt buttered. The soap grew mold, a green velour. The chairs wicked piss from the carpet.

I thought of hanta, death by mouse, amazing what can kill you. Rudy stayed away.

I bathed the dogs and they bit me. I set the organ to play "Moon River" and scrubbed my knuckles bloody.

THE HANDSOME DOCTOR let Rose go. I got her squared away in her rented bed with the hand crank and the pulleys. Her house was clean but she didn't like it.

She liked yard sales. Topiary and porcelain, other people's pictures. She liked chubbies in bikinis and butterflies climbing the garden fence. Reminders, little helpful hints, tea tags and winged cookies: *Next time order the shrimp.*

She liked bacon fat and Jimmy Dean sausage.

She liked her bed I took apart.

"Rudy helped me," I lied.

Rose said, "Stonewall Jackson slept in that bed," she swung her feet until her slippers dropped off, "before he burned Atlanta."

WATCH IT, GIRL, *those luscious*
    mounds of ice cream topped with cherry
    Can be the source of extra
    pounds that people note . . . just barely.

"I LIKE YOUR mouth," Rudy said. "I like your buttocks."

He brought his women to the pachysandra that grew beneath Rose's window. I watched them in the streetlight doing what people do.

I tried missing old Tonto but couldn't.

"There's something about you," I told Rudy.

"Maybe this?" he said, and showed me his package.

"SOW YOUR WILD oats on Saturday night, hope the crop fails on Sunday," Rose liked to say.

When there was moaning in the pachysandra, Rose said, "Open the blind and let's see."

Rudy waved at us. He was kneeling in leaves.

He was killing her with it, how it sounded.

Big Ed ran laps around the bed legs. His stool hung from the hole by a hair.

Something was leaking from Gotcha.

A pair of roaches chased Snicker from her food bowl until she was too spooked to eat. Rose fed her in bed, the TV blaring, her eyecup buzzing with flies.

Rose kept TVs on in every room of the house—half the day, all night. I woke to car chases, shootouts, Rose thrashing in her bed. We kept her jacked up. We lost track of the bones she was breaking.

We lost Gotcha, who had leaked for too long. There was a big rusting freezer in the basement stuffed with meatloaf and frozen lettuce. Citymeals for a dollar. Individual portions.

Rose had us put Gotcha in with them. He would keep.

"Throw the lot in there and bury me with them."

RUDY CARRIED GOTCHA down.

"Psst," Rose said. I can think of no other way to spell it. "Hopi eat dogs," she whispered. "They dance with chickens. They dress up like ravens and snakes."

Rudy carried Rose to her Naugahyde chair. He smelled like Gotcha. She fell out of it.

Rudy said, "You meant to."

Rose spat at him. "I'm starved. Give me a leg to gnaw on."

SHE QUIT EATING. She didn't care if she lived. They gave her something for it.

We gave Rose a siren flashlight for her to call us to her bed, to her chair. *Wao wao wao*, it went.

She motioned for me to bend near.

"Check on Gotcha," she said.

"Gotcha's dead," I said.

"Exactly."

He was there but an ear was missing. I turned him over to hide the deed.

I TOOK TO Rudy.

My next little egg went out. I picked life, was my way of thinking, despite the blah blah blah.

Rose said, "If at first you don't succeed, keep on sucking 'til you do suck seed."

Wao wao wao, the siren went, but we kept to the pachysandra, doing what people do.

Rudy had me knocked up come April.

Come April, Snicker died of poison. We found her in back in the sunshine, blown up and leaking foam.

"Get out," Rose said.

I had nowhere to go.

She said, "I'll tell you a cute little story."

She made Rudy sweep the flagstone where deer mice pissed and lived.

"There once was a little Indian," Rose began.

Drool crept from her mouth to her ear. She had hairs in her ears. I offered to pluck them. I plucked her whiskers. We drank Pabst from cans and watched the window where Rudy lay the pachysandra down.

No Rudy.

No Rudy in that house long enough it seemed he must be gone.

I took a photo of the last place I saw him—his buttered hair, his silken tongue. He took Gotcha, bundled up like a baby, already starting to thaw.

Rose said, "I never did have any babies. I never had brothers or sisters. My neighbors have been awful good to me. We make our choices," she said, and drifted to sleep, and waked and said, "and then we lie in them."

I lay in bed and felt the baby kick me, mine and Rudy's. Rudy was wicked. That didn't matter to me.

I couldn't say if the baby mattered to me or if it was just something that happened, like breaking the neck of your femur off on your way to driver's safety.

I caught myself in the mirror, pulled my face toward my ears. That was better. I didn't look hard.

I touched myself and kept going. I went until the bees bunched up in my lungs, thinking, *Rudy, Rudy*—slow until they lit out through me, how lovely like they used to do.

IN THE MORNING I went to the hospital and had them scrape what Rudy gave me out.

I would not have been much of a mother. I went for shitbags. I liked to sleep late. I liked people who could work their own spoon.

I stopped in for caustic green chili. It made my head sweat. It made me cry until I couldn't stop crying. I flirted with the waiter and stiffed him, getting back at Rudy.

ROSE WAS SINGING when I walked in.

> *Won't you go on, Mule,*
> *don't you roll those eyes,*
> *you can change a fool*
> *but a doggone mule*
> *is a mule until he dies.*

I pried the window open. Something had shit in the grass. Maybe elephant.

The pachysandra was still matted down. I felt it for heat like a campfire the cowboys have ridden out from.

THE TELEPHONE RANG. It hadn't done that before.

"Is Spanky there? Hey, Spanky."

"Spanky?" I said. "Rudy?"

"Git back here, little bunny."

It wasn't Rudy. It was those characters down the street.

That night I tied a rag around Big Ed's jaw to stop him yapping when I went out. Even outside, I heard Rose sleeping.

It was just me and Rose and Big Ed now.

I walked to Spanky's. It was right down the street.

There were hookers outside in Barbie clothes. Strippers inside in sequins. They danced in cages. They lunged at the bars.

I ate French fries. I drank a nice cold Coke.

"YOU KNOW I love you forever. But if you pour me a Coca-Cola I'll love you forevermore."

Pot roast, frozen lettuce, prunes.

Chicken leg, frozen lettuce, peaches.

Meatloaf, frozen lettuce, pudding.

Pot roast, frozen lettuce, prunes.

NO RUDY.

"I could take you out."

"Only way I'm going out is in a coffin."

Rose quit singing. She ate a grape here and there if I skinned it.

She quit letting me pluck her chin hairs out or work at her ingrown toes. Her siren weakened. Her organ quit.

She quit sitting in the back with Big Ed. Come May, Big Ed was finished, dead of having lived.

I STARTED IN the far room pulling plugs on TV sets, the murders and the heartbreak, the vim and vigor of the news. The sound

closed around Rose. She never noticed. I pulled the last prong and
her room went *oooo*.

Now it was me and Rose and long desert days and three square
meals she wouldn't touch anymore.

The siren gave out altogether and Rose had to call me by name.
She forgot my name. She forgot I was there.

When she saw me she said, "Who is it?"

I went to her attic and tried on dresses—much too short, far
too wide.

"What do you want to do today, Rose?"

"Swing on the bars?" she said, her hands hooks beside her chin.

Her room filled up with butterflies. She was suffocating in them.

RUDY SENT A photograph.

His chest was heaving from the dance he had danced. His face
was shining, and the brave lovely wings of his back.

"We need air," I told Rose, "a little sunshine."

Every day was sunshine.

I suggested, "A little Tang party and tea."

I brought Lorna Doones to the front stoop where the rest of
a world went by. The dying elm was spray-painted "DISCO." A
punk pinched a loaf in the grass. I thought I had never seen it but
I'd seen it a hundred times.

Rose struggled along behind her walker to the lip of the front
stoop. I tossed her walker in the pachysandra. I hooked my arms
behind her neck and knees and swung her softly up.

My bride, I thought, my balding doll. But everything in her was breaking.

"Oh," Rose moaned. And then, "Move it."

We lay on our backs breathing. The grass was pokey and dry beneath us. The leaves did their thing in the sun.

Rose held out her hand for a Lorna Doone. They were perfect. They were from the 1960s.

She would be dead before she got it to her mouth.

"Tell me something," I told Rose. "Tell me a cute little story."

"Fuck off," Rose said.

I was choked up. I ate slowly, my love, my last Lorna Doone, my old bloody country.

AT LAST THE ESCALADE

WELL WORTH IT, WELL WORTH IT, THE LAST OF THE legendary glaciers and cell phone service besides. They have seen a wolf and bighorn sheep and a hundred cheeping pikas in the rocks and a pair of boxing marmots.

But the littlest is a little let down. They have to get back to Ohio, back to the hover-mother and school. He has to pee. *So bad.* He can't stand it. So the father pulls off at Sunrise Gorge. There's a waterfall and people around. Soon the water is falling in the sunlit gorge and the little boy is peeing on a little rock and the big brother pees on a bigger rock and the father has his out, too.

Here a bear appears from between the trees and stands a while to watch them. It's just watching.

They can't pee anymore. They have waited so long to see a bear they can scarcely even believe it's a bear.

"It's a bear," says the bigger boy.

The father says, lowly, "Boys."

It will eat me first, thinks the littler boy, and the bear thinks, *Indeed.*

The father makes a gutsy father sound and stands his ground bravely between the bear and his boys and the bear leaves the path to trot around him. The bear wants that little boy. That boy is doing exactly what his father says and walking backward toward the Escalade but the bear is trotting frontward at him. The boy turns and runs, which you are *not* supposed to do, but, lucky boy, because the bear turns and opens his mouth at the other brother.

Don't run, say the pamphlets, don't shout.

"Don't run!" shouts the father and now the other brother is running too and you can bet if they hadn't peed three seconds ago, they would all be peeing now. The bear is closing in on the bigger boy, the bigger boy is the father's favorite boy, it's true. The father runs shouting down the path at the bear with his car keys scratching in his pants.

At last the Escalade.

But the doors are all locked, the littlest boy tried, so the boys try diving under the car. The bigger boy is giggling now, it makes no sense but so what.

A crowd has begun to gather, *oh, a bear*, they have waited so long to see.

The bear takes a swipe at the boys beneath the car. The boys roll across the gravel to the other side, so the bear trots over to the other side and takes a swipe and they roll off again.

The crowd loves it, how like a circus, stupid but you have to admit.

The father shouts and waves his arms and the hover-mother sips iced tea with a sprig of mint with the shades cinched tight while her boys roll fast and away from the face and the terrible yellow claws of the bear and the dreadful meaty breath of the bear and the little one bleeds, nicked in the ribs, and socks his brother for laughing.

The father makes a claw with his car keys thrust between his chubby fingers—to do what, he doesn't know, go for the eyes, but instead he whips his keys at the bear's awful face—you guessed it, the car is still locked.

A button springs out from the little boy's shirt and turns like a top and lies down.

But let's keep to the bigger picture, to the sipping and swiping and the stone the father heaves and at last to the father on the hood of his car, his beautiful car, at last to the father on the roof of his car, Bluetooth and drop-down screens and, my God, the chrome, the leather, but what passes now through the vast mind of the bear we will never know.

Pity, disgust, despair?

A bush of ripened berries? A juicy beetle? Bees?

We can't know—what a shame, we would like to.

Happily our story stops here. The bear takes a last swipe across the hood of the car and leaves a mark in the luminous pearl they will decode the miles home to Ohio. The mark is a bigger version of the mark on the littler boy's ribs.

The father takes it to mean: *buckle down.* He quits carousing. He finds a job he can stand not to hate every day and loves his boys like a crazy man he never was before.

NOW, the day shouts. *BE SOMETHING.*

Be free, one boy thinks, *in a flap tent. Be a bird in an eaten tree.*

He plans to fell his first goat with a bow he carved and pack the meat out in a rucksack in bloody, cooling slabs. Forage for parsnips and mushrooms. For luck, he will carry that button. For love, he relies on a chickadee who lights on his steady hand.

For now, he's still under that Escalade his father is pounding on.

His poor father has yanked his shirt off and he is flapping it like a rodeo clown, oblivious at last to his beautiful car and his ugly patchy blubbery gut—it's alarming, but that's the idea. He has bloodied his nose with a button. He is shrieking like a peacock and sobbing and clutching himself in the chin.

The bear rears up and walks into the shade like a man he never hopes to be, and a woman claps, uncertain—applause—no lonelier sound in the world.

My heart, my heart, the father sobs, and the sobbing sounds like choking, which it sort of is.

In a minute every tonto watching will hurry off not to miss the nightly feature, happy hour, buffalo tongue, lucky us, we can eat them again, snatched from the brink of extinction. *Yippee.*

PEMMICAN

V ERONA WAS A WOMAN WHOSE TOMBSTONE WOULD read: *I asked little.*

SHE HAD A boy named Little Five Points and Little Five Points wanted a mouse.

The rig cost her sixty-three dollars. Sawdust. Wheel. Glass house. Food. Little Five Points wanted all of it.

His first mouse, he named Verona. All night of both long nights she lived, Verona sprinted without the least complaint on her squeaking wheel. She was a plain mouse, and seemed to know it. Little Five Points made a brown house for her with a curtain of pleasing beads. They passed the hours happily, small boy, plain mouse, until the third night, when death took her. Nobody up to now knows why.

NEXT CAME BASKET and Macaroni, nothing but trouble with these two. These were fancy pants and iconoclasts, spotted from tip to toe. The clerk handed them off in a paper sack. He had a mirror glued to the top of his shoe to look up ladies' skirts with.

"Hurry home," he suggested, and they did.

THIS GOES BADLY. Fast.

They are driving. Little Five Points holds his paper sack duti-
fully between his knees. The stinkers eat through the sack. They
make off with his stiffened French fries and his pemmican and his
goo. They live a life of furry princes in the tunnels and vents of
Verona's car and trot up her skirts while she drives.

SHE DRIVES INTO a moose, *numero uno.*

NUMERO DOS: SHE drives into a drunken bear.

VERONA BUYS THREE more mice for her boy. She thinks maybe
the problem is numbers. She carries them home in their glass house.
Surprise! Little Five Points picks out the prettiest to pet. The mouse
nips him and Little Five Points whacks it against the wall. It dies
instantly, what a relief.

HE NEVER DOES name the others: they fall to eating each other
before he names them and Verona walks what is left of them into
the snow by their wrinkling tails.

It could be worse, Verona reminds herself. They could
be thriving in her car with Basket and that patchy Macaroni,
eating the stiffened French fries Little Five Points forgets from
his box.

SHE SETS TRAPS for them. Sympathetic traps with a dollop of peanut butter inside. The car smells of pee and poopy dots. The trap doors swing shut but she finds nothing, not even a smidgen of peanut butter, not even a slick where the dollop sat.

POOR VERONA. LITTLE Five Points wants more mice. Verona has lied to him about all of them, about Verona and the nameless cannibals and almost catching Basket. "They got out," Verona tells him. "They went to live with the hair and the corn cobs and their little wild sisters in the walls."

LITTLE FIVE POINTS wants an ant farm. He wants to watch the red ants steal the black ants' babies and make the black babies slaves.

Little Five Points wants a boa constrictor.

He wants a baby reindeer.

Little Five Points wants a Gila monster.

Verona says, "Whoa."

Boa constrictor, Verona thinks. Maybe she can rent one?

SCENARIO NUMERO TRES.

Verona rents a cat from the shelter and turns it loose in her car. The cat howls all night and shreds the seats and snags its teeth in her forehead before bounding off through the snow. She comes into the kitchen bloodied. Little Five Points is spelling his name out with ketchup in his scrambled eggs.

He says, "F-I-V-E. Something red is on you."

VERONA PACKS THEM off to work, to school. She tries to reason with the mice while driving: the bitterness of winter nights, Little Five Point's happiness, the yellow wheel, etcetera. The mice sit on the cushy headrest, enlivened by heat and conversation, nibbling at their fries.

SHE CAN'T BRING herself to drive, *scenario numero cuatro*. She's afraid to even step near her car. She gets fired from her job for not doing it. The bank repos their house. They have to live in her car. The mice gnaw them to the bone, etcetera, and plump their nests with Little Five Point's lovely spun-gold hair.

NUMERO CINCO. SHE quits driving: the mice need heat from the engine to live. Ha. The stinkers freeze solid as wood frogs. Verona burns up seven tanks of gas, elated, spring at last, blasting heat through the defrost vent until the mice are crunchy as peanuts.

SEIS. THE FUCKERS prosper. Multiply. The babies spit out babies in the space of a week, mother of God, think of that, translucent pink collapsible sacks that clog the tubes, the tailpipe, an exponential increase, victors of the universe, Verona's car a mouse farm, should have made it Lucite, it's hopeless to resist them, savvy and hard at it like on the ant farms Little Five Points admires so in school.

LITTLE FIVE POINT'S papa comes back to them and kisses Verona on her seeping wound and loves her slow until sunup and brings her scrambled eggs in bed. He doesn't know what he was thinking to think he could live without her. He doesn't exist without her. *Tell me what you want, my life.*

Scenario numero siete.

"MATA! MATA!" VERONA shrieks, swinging her arms and dreaming.

They'll haul her off if she's not careful. She finds poopy dots in her toothbrush, poopy dots in her hair. Mice are all over her dreams.

"*Mata! Mata!*"

VERONA IS NO natural mother. The mice are one way she knows.

She tries a neck-snapping trap Little Five Points finds. He finds his mouse in her trap. She is never ever forgiven. He runs away at the age of six and passes his days in hiding in some ghastly European country: *scenario numero ocho.*

THIS HAS GONE on much too long.

Verona resorts to poison. They'll blow up slow with their tongues hung out. *Ha*, she thinks. But she can't do it. Verona thinks of the handsome Indian man who gave a talk in the town park once who said the white man ought to ask of the animal, "What do you know?"

He told a story of a mouse who saved a small boy from a buffalo stampede. Of dogs who sniff out your heart attack and whimper when your insulin spikes.

VERONA SHUTS THE door. The mice are convened on the dash-board in the numinous green of the speedometer light.

"What do you know?" Verona asks them.

"You have seven lives," Macaroni tells her, "and you already used up six."

"Your ex will never come back to you," Basket says. "Little Five Points will join the army and marry a dowdy Kraut."

"To get away from you, the little shit."

"She will plump him up and his hair will fall out and he will never remember your birthday, not one stinking time."

"Not one?" Verona wonders.

"She'll ruin everything."

"She'll vote for the wrong president. She'll sigh and roll her eyes."

Verona picks at a scab.

"A real hatchet," Basket says. "She'll hate children."

"She already hates them now."

"She knocks them on their heads off the monkey bars."

"She yanks downs their skirts in the lunch room when their trays are heaped with food."

Verona jerks her scab free and winces.

"Can we have that?" Basket says.

"Tell me one thing more."

"Deal," say the mice, excited.

Their whiskers quiver. Their mouths are wet.

"Soon, you'll write a story about us. You will hit a deer on a bicycle, thinking of how to be funny. Skip it, is our advice. You will be a teensy bit funny, but only when you think to say 'poopy dot.'"

"Poopy dot," Verona says.

"Very funny," say the mice, and squeeze two neat seeds onto the dashboard.

VERONA WRITES A story about a race of mice who grow themselves from seed, a tiny whole mouse in every stool they put out. The white mice steal the black mouse babies and train them to clean up carefully the wreck the white mice make of the world. They are friendly and obedient. They eat plutonium and plastic. That raft of garbage bigger than Texas that is floating around in the ocean? The mice nibble through that in days.

It is a children's book and grownups love it. The book sells wildly. Verona is stinking rich. She gives every nickel away.

She runs an ad for a Handsome Indian who replies pronto and falls in love with her. He makes a terrific daddy. Little Five Points learns to catch after all. He wrestles and grunts in the green grass and ties his shoes before school.

This can't last.

VERONA IS ON her last life: Basket and Macaroni were right. She picks a good day to die and dies happy, a saint almost, radiant and deranged, recalling the masses she raised up from nothing to make this a better world.

COURTSHIP

H E WAS OLD ENOUGH TO OWN THINGS. A PORSCHE. A boat. A biplane. The other men she knew were boys. She was weeding her father's radishes and singing with the radio when he flew overhead, close enough she felt the plane passing. Climbed up. Stalled and spun and plunged and climbed and flew upside down in the air. Marvelous. What it must feel like. Courtship of the birds. The serial monogamists, the polyandrous and loosely colonial. The lowly piteous squawking grebe sprinting over the water.

SO SAYS THE POSTMISTRESS

"EVERYTHING IS FOREVER NOW—" SO SAYS THE postmistress, and I won't argue. I walk home to find a hummingbird flown into the shed, thrashing in the dark of the rafters. Our raccoon stumbles into the shadows, fattened on cat food again. Honey-smelling succulent, a nightjar hunkered in the dew. Another day shut down. Blue curtain. Another letter dropped into the clamorous box. Dear Marcus.

ROOSTER POLLARD
CRICKET GOOSE

W E COULD DO WITH HIM WHAT WE WANTED. THE old people left and left Goose here and what they left was ours.

They'd have taken him if they could. They took the glass from in the windows, they took the crib from the bend in the road. Our pa would have to drag a new crib out to keep the corncobs in. They took the cow in the wet field lowing. They took the blind pig beating the barn.

Down from the house where our ma stuck tight it went barn and barn and barn and crib and next the pond-bridge over the pond next the brocade couch in the pond where they had gone and dragged it. They left us the couch and the road paint sure from wherever cheap they had got it. They left the washer machine with its top torn loose down on its side beside the barn.

They took the knobs from the doors and the rods for towels and what bulbs that burned they could reach up to and loose them from their sockets. Anything much they could loose they took and everything they left behind we got to keep between us. I got the doll from the johnnie I saved that simpered when I hit it. I got the trees and the wind in the trees and the pond with the couch and the muskrat traps and the green gone garish on it. Pa got the horse and the hills.

The horse we found between the barns where it had gone up and over. It had knocked its thick head on the road, Pa said. We were sitting in the truck.

We had checked the coop for chickens. We had seen that the crib was gone.

It went Pa then me then Ma in the truck with the baby asleep on her bosom.

They had hit it with a pipe, Pa said. Else it had gone up and over.

Ma got out like he told her to and went up the hill with the baby. I heard her high shoes on the road when she went and I heard when she stopped and rested.

The horse I heard and would hear again the queer high bird-ish sound he made, it hung between the barns. He was laid out between the barns.

I got the barn and the hay in the barn and the dust coming slatted through the rafters. I got the beat pail for corn I beat to spook the rats from the crib when I fed when I came from the bus from school. It was my job to feed the animals, to fatten cow Maggie to eat. I got the hay and the smell of the hay and the light snapping on on the barn.

The horse was Pa's and the hills he rode and the bees he dug that clouded him when he dragged the hooked plow with the tractor. The rabbits he dug he gave to me I kept in the bowl in the washer machine thrown out where the creek ran through.

I stretched the come-along out like he told me. Because the others never did have a come-along to crank the horse over the gravel with to take him off on whatever it was they had brought to move away on. So they left him laid out on the hump of our road between the high walls of our barns.

The horse was dead, Pa said, or good as dead but what was the thin long sound he made what were the lifting moons of his eyes when Pa came close with his gun? So he was good yet good for something.

A horse is worth something, easy, Pa said, you could sell him off handsome on the hoof in a blink they would buy him from Pa by the pound. We could haul him up on the bed of Pa's truck sell him off quick down the hill from us to pay for what they loosed from us the hooks and bulbs and sockets. And yet I thought to ride him. Yes. I thought to him: *Hup ho.*

I looped the steel loop around his pastern first as quick in the dark as I could. I walked the slack out. I worked the handle some.

I saw the light go on in the house up the hill and then Ma in the window passing. So they left a light with the chairs all gone so Ma could see to sit the floor and hitch up her shirt for the baby. The baby always goes to the one so I ask who is the other one for. She laughs. You are as bad as your pa. Get on.

There are chickens to feed and cow Maggie. Two cobs twice for Maggie. There are board fences sure to creosote and thistle to dig from the fields when it bolts before the purple crowns. I muck the stalls and soap the tack and vet Pa's dogs they run the fields flushing birds all day. I am his girl Cricket. I climb the big oak on the hill Pa's hill even after when it is hit and burns and the burn blacks my skin my clothes.

I work the handle some and the slack is out and I can feel the horse start to pull over the hump of gravel. He lets his long high sound. Pa says it is like a goose so Goose but I never heard a goose as that so long as that it warbled, not a sound like that and never since from bird nor horse nor man. Not even when Pa hit him.

He hit him in his head. Then was a sound a girl-girl lets, queerly sung and pretty. But that was some time after. That was when we shod.

First Pa thinks to work with him when he is up and well enough and we walk him down in the sun in the heat on the road between the barns. First Pa thinks to gentle Goose to ride him days we do not plow afternoons we do not need to hoe nor pick nor harrow. Pa went to him first going easy talking sweetly in his ear. *Hope hope.*

He never did hit Goose at the first the night when Ma went off up the road. She went up the hill with the baby quick her hair a knot on her brightened head he reached for when she rested. First it was me Ma reached for. Then after me she rested. I took the strength she had, Pa said, so after me she rested.

Pa gets the hills and the oaks on the hills the old people called the farm by. Ma gets the house she climbs to, her shoes tapping bright on the road. Our ma gets the boy not yet a boy for Pa to need to work the fields while he is weak and small. She gets the way he smells the way he gums her how he coos.

Goose lets his long high sound. I feel him shudder across the gravel the ratchet clicking slow. I see him rest if I rest and flutter his nose but Ma will have something fixed for us and sits her chair to watch for us and sheets on the floor she has spread for us and the light is gone from the barn. They have loosed it from its socket hung from the spavined wall of the barn. Get up.

I taut the line some. I bring him easy.

I haul up the traps in the muck by and by from the bank where the old people left them. The dogs come to drink from the pond. They beat out a flattened path in the weeds in the burrs that catch and mat my hair flown loose when first I found one. First how we knew to look at all was once I heard Pa's dog. She had her paw snapped up in the mouth of the trap in the gone-by weeds that mark the pond in the rattling pods come winter. Summer coming to its close. The fescue stiffly yellowed. And in the night Pa's dog cries out from the drawn-back lip of the pond.

Be slow. Our Goose.

See the road slopes up. *Take your time to calm you.*

His breath comes weak and shallows. I let the line slack. He throws himself to kneeling and his bones knock against the road. He shoves his muzzle down on the road to rest so his thick head saws above. Pa touches his flank with the gun. I ease up I think I am easing up, the line gone slack to tap the road but I can never see it quite I can scarcely see him stand but to see the yellow of his eye swing up and the white of his face against the road.

So he is up. I hear Pa humming to him slow and the coins in his pants when he moves to him going, *Ho*, going, *Hope hope ho*.

Pa ought to have a sugar cube, a cigarette to give him.

He throws his head up. The stripe in his head when he throws it streaks and see the dark will bleed it free, will from him in the darkness wick the whiteness clean away. It is like our pa has thrown it—how his bird dogs quake and trill.

You goose. First she called Pa so to tease him. But then she called the baby Goose and by and by each name for Pa I used to hear her call him by she picked to name the baby with and mine I had forgotten. Now we are only Pa to her and Pa and his girl Cricket. Moving slowly in the road.

He throws his head up. It is like our pa has thrown it, gone from the trees from the creek where he likes to work his dogs to the field. Good dogs.

We can do with him what we want to. Sell him off quick on the hoof if we like to grind his bones to give the dogs the inly tubes and organs keep them fed and fit and strong. They are field dogs, bird dogs all. Pa throws them the wing of the cutaway goose in the falling dark and the dogs at his feet and they stay they stay the wing dipping down until he moves his hand to school them.

And then his long high sound. And so Pa named him Goose for the goose for the wing he throws his dogs.

Goose lunges at Pa so much as he can but I have got him looped up still, Pa tripping back with his gun at his chest so I ratchet the line to hold him. I cannot hold Pa. Only watch him slowly falling. He takes a long time falling.

Pa's dogs bed down and whinge. *You quit.* But they are thinking what will happen what is next to come.

Time comes Pa thinks to ride him. Out between the barns. He rides to the oaks the lightning hits along the fence cow Maggie rubs to leaning while she fattens. Past the coop the chickens pecking slowly at their corn. Past Pa's prize yellow rooster learned to blind his favored hens.

Pa's dogs they are bird dogs all—but are they bird enough to guess at him? At Pa's prize yellow rooster? Who appeared in a fluff in the barn—the day Goose rode Pa past and every day thereafter. And sat his back thereafter. Who flew his coop to bide his days sitting Goose's withers—could they guess at such as him?

And at the day we shod him?

And of the bees Pa plowed?

I am not one to picture it not nearly even half of it not Ma in her chair past autumn not the wrangled plow. Nor Goose. The rooster shyly by him. Pa's. And then the rooster Goose's. Only walking back to rooster pecking gently at his hens.

Nor that. I had not pictured that. And not the picked-over eyes of the hens bright as the yolks of the eggs we take left seeping in their feathers.

Not the blood the baby lets not the milk the baby lets, Ma's shirt run pinkly through. Nor that. Him plumping at her bosom.

Time was I was Ma's. Nor that. Nor time was Pa was also.

Not Pa when I come upon him. He has dragged across the pond.

I am not cut to picture. To stand at the bank and puzzle out I am cut to cut and run.

The gun fires when Pa wallops the road. Then Goose is up and hanging.

The old people have come. I thought Goose had seen the old people come rolling home to claim him.

And so he hung there. What to do?

I touched the line once. They couldn't loose him. They could go on back from wherever they'd come and forget they ever saw him stood and pawing where they left him in a heap upon the road.

They could find another. There are others after Goose. There are Mouse and Pepper, Blue, Prim Sue, and Candysara. Cribbing at the barn.

I tie Pa's boot strings every morning. Did his boot strings loose I tied for him, did his pant legs make him fall?

Ma takes one pair and me another. We hem the legs on Pa's short side from the time when Pa was a boy my size and crumpled in his bed. Get up. And Pa could not get up and not. And not for a long time after. So is it mine or Ma's dread cross? Who take one pair and one another. We are not much with our needles. And Pa is fallen across the road.

He seems to quit there. He seems to quit and stiffen ready for the blow.

Goose would throw himself off from us. He would fly himself over the barn he thought come soft on his hooves in the field where he grazed with we two dumbly watching.

Then he was over. Goose flung himself on over. I heard his bones the clatter and snap his head a rind against the road broken wetly open. He lay there—his legs sprung stiff, his corded neck—his body hauled in chinked from stone to mark the field the fallen dead the bloody day forgotten.

Pa softly now, "Let up."

I held the line taut. I saw I held the line taut still from the coil where I let it.

The night sky stooped and held its breath, the trees bent too to listen—for the sputter and tick the quieting tide of Goose's reedy pipes and valves the rocking iridescent humps and hollows of his organs.

And Pa again, "Let up." Still I heard "Get."

Pa struggled up from where he fell and knocked the grit from his pants I stitched the sloppy hem and he nodded. Pa came at me with his hand high up. He had never hit me yet but still I stood to let him.

The line had cut some through. I had looped it over the curl of fur above the hoof you sell them on and it had dug some through. His eye had spun wide up in the dark to regard the stars above. The moon on its slow crossing.

His burblings—mine—my cross to bear, my thin bitten birdish shrill he let, my name though Pa had thought it—Goose. Goose and also Cricket. We were named for the sounds thrown from us, yes, for a dream's long-soured tongue.

And so I loosed it. I shook the line some. Nothing, not a twitch not a nostril flared no breath no lifting brisket. So I could do it easy ease the loop of cable from his pastern where I cut him. I felt the heat rise from him. I felt the give in my knees when I kneeled by him and the heat of the softened road. So we could winch him up now. He had made it easy. We would wait for the light for the morning.

Morning. *Hello, little farm.*

STILL WE WAKE to him up come sunup. We are sleeping all on the sheet Ma spread and Goose is scrolloping over the road.

I snip Pa's toenails for him, turn his hem and tie his boots who cannot reach to do it.

I can smell the barn. I smell in my hair the baby too he gummed it as we rode.

Pa clips the lead shank on him. He feels along his bones.

Pa leads him off between the trees, me and Ma standing out in our gowns she wears to walk in time the fallen dew the hill we climb to reach her. I sit the chair her chair to watch her, watch the nightshade fill behind her see the bats loop briefly through. Her small boy nearby sleeping.

At length when once the snow has come to keep us snugly home, Ma goes sunup to nightfall gowned else sits the bath from meal to meal the latch thrown once the baby walks to keep him always with her to keep him safely in.

She has heard us at our chores by then. We have backed Goose onto the slab by then. The rooster crowing on.

Pa's dogs spooked about for the moons Pa clipped for the tailings curled from his hooves filed flat to take the shoe and he cussed them. Cussed his horse his dogs. His runt with the mangled paw stumping in who sat with me at his knees should he sit should he think to nudge her head. Let her bump her ribs against him.

After her I found the others easy. You go by your nose through the weeds for the traps going low to the ground like a dog. Red fox I found and muskrat, coon and the paw of what I do not know in the muck cow Maggie made of the banks of the pond I would wade in the dry out into.

The old people could have found them caught in the dry time when they moved. Then I would not have had to. Would not have had to smell them then nor burr my hair to get to them nor haul them onto the bridge for Pa so Pa could see to flay or gut or what any else he did to them or sort the parts to bury.

We buried them back by the chicken coop in sight of the pond where they swam if they swam or only came and drank from. Soon the rooster flapped over the pond—his Goose had gone from the field. The rooster come to sit Goose's back to drub his back to calm him flapped in his grief to the couch when Goose passed come rain come sleet come snow. Crowing on.

His hens in the coop to hear him. I lay in my bed and heard him the moon sweeping past the stars.

Cricket you Cricket you.

See the white of his face swung up?

His bright eye webbed and curdled?

And then when we had blinded him and set him out in the field to browse I saw the skin seal and crumple how in the cold it was blent and gathered.

They will do it to a baby too, a rooster will give him half a chance he does it to his own. And his hens' eyes are small.

I lay in my bed and pictured it.

Pictured Pa when I came upon him.

I came upon him in the wet months yet the flying leaves the sinking grass the geese dropped from their wedges yet and scudding across the pond.

I had come on the bus from school. I skipped. I swung my feet through the fallen leaves to smell the sweet wet smell of them to smell the wind the needling rain that in the night had felled them. The leaves flew up and clung to me to the ratty flounce of the skirt I wore the bitten ridge of my shinbones. I stopped at the pond to peel them off me.

I could hear the tractor then. You turn the fields to fallow them. I liked to listen for Pa to know where he might leave the plow the harrow bed the baler.

I heard him. But I did not think Pa at first I did not think listen. I sang my song the coming home song against his note I had not heard and hope again to never. Still I looked about and saw him. He was wallowed up on the couch in the green with the yellow bead the pond was deep on the couch back scarcely showing.

He could not be Pa. He was something in the wet the old people left that had loosed itself from the muck as it went and yet it spit my name. With still our barns to pass between, the hill to the house to run. I ran. I ran the day the bees got Pa and ran the day I held his Goose in the washroom where we shod. But I did not run far. I heard him bellow. You try it try to run. Drop to your hands if the grass is high and dream he cannot find you there with your heart knotted small as the rabbits new-born he brings to you in the crown of his hat the days he plows to calm.

But I have never saved one. I have never saved one yet of all the ones he brings to me I have lost them all.

I LAY ON the bank and watched him. The longer I kept away from Pa the harder it was to go to him.

And yet I went to him. I knocked the bees from his neck for him Pa gone in his hurt not hearing me not a place on him to hold him by I held him by his hair. Through the green I swam him. I could have walked the pond but it took my shoes from my feet the silken bottom. Me and Pa dragged a stripe in the green where I swam where it folded against Pa's head. *Pa Pa.*

Once we grew a pig so fat even its eyelids fattened, ear and jowl and bursting cheek and by and by its eyeballs—squeezed—stood away loose from its head.

Then Pa. Bellowing out of the wallow. The cow to her teats to cool. The tractor run up on a stump and stopped and still at its ticking idle. I made my hands a stirrup—Pa's legs were too swelled to bend. *Swing up.* And from the time of riding shotgun years I knew which stick to muscle, which to back to raise the plow when once we had it scraping up loud against the road.

Ma in her chair past autumn. Us come up come dew come snow. The baby let to his knees at the screen to scream the day the bees swarmed Pa and Ma came out to swat at us going, "Gracious lord above."

Think back to when time was in her—my soft head broken through. Before that. When time was she was Pa's. Before my hair I grew in her that made her retch and swoon.

A girl. And her boy sick and small. I took the strength she had in her. I kept them up nights in her: their Cricket. Chirruping in the swill.

Boy, her boy, her funny runt. He could not be Pa's. Who came before they thought his name and stayed they had not thought he might for such a long time after. *Boy*, she called him. *Goose, you goose*, and *mister*—Ma thinking not to choose a name to have to have to call him by should he be taken from her.

We never took him from her. Even when he crawled. Nor say I ever came to her to cut my name most fine in her not before nor after Ma swelling as he grew.

I was all Pa's girl. The barns were mine and the hay in the barns and Pa and the trees and the cows. Cow Maggie leaned against me. The birds flew south by the stars. Barn and barn and barn and pond the road climbing out through the fields. Mine and Pa's, my pa's. The high quiet wobbledy stars. And Ma where she sat in the window was ours and sat in the shut-away buttery gold, the dogs at our heels the stars. Should you wish.

Ma's shirt bled pinkly through.

The seed-blown fields the wickerings. The slickened births and murders, ours, the fierce wide blowing day.

I TENDED TO him gently. Pa wallowing in the tub. He would swell to fit it. And swell till he could not budge from it and I would spoon a mash to him and keep the water cooled for him and nest his head in my pillow. His eye unloosed like a doll's. Fetch a sledge. Break him duly from it.

Pa's arms puffed out to float from him and seep in milky puddles, his skin so hot to touch it scalds. I did not touch it. I worked the coughing spigot, churned the cold to sap the heat slowly not to hurt him. And made as not to hear him, his voice not his no voice at all—a green sea grief a great whale culled and keening in its traces.

I daubed a paste where he was stung a curdly dull against his skin I first swiped bright with butter. Pa. Who plowed the bees it comes to me to see if Ma would see to him to see if she would tend to him but Ma would not have come.

Why seem at last to hear him? Ma would not have come.

And who was it came upon him?

And so I took it slow. I made Ma's clucks and muddlings and swabbed and slowly doctored him. I had no Goose to think of no price to fetch no mouths to fill no deed to hide the doing of.

No day yet when we shod.

"It's me, Pa. Pa, it's Cricket."

"Get."

I was not her. Not Ma and never Cricket quite but proof she had not come.

I TOOK TO sleeping in the barn else the sinking grass in the leaves unhinged in the wind. Pa's rooster nightly crowing.

Pa when he was up again and shrunk into himself again rode Goose unshod through our honeyed woods our creeks our windfall autumn. Among the lowly creatures named and ours to daily tend.

We are sloppy in our tending. Our swallows catch in the raftered dark our rabbits are turned from the fields. Fox we trap and whistle pig and the spotty domes of our turtles crush in the wet upon our road. And in our hay we gather. And too the narrow fellows sunning lazy in the stubble catch—snakes pressed between the flakes of hay as though we mean to keep them, and faith by them in the shut-away days the snowbound weeks we wait to breathe that the fields are strewn and rooted through with bees with bodies sleeping.

Pa wore Goose away his hooves split and curled and then a day I came from school Pa brought him to me saddled and swung me up to ride. Pa gave me a whip to run him with. Goose could not walk it looked to me he seemed to wince to stand there.

Up the hill I ran him.

We ran until Pa could not see and we let him gimp up the hill to us to snap the lunge line on. Pa swung me up again. So he could run us. So we might see she watched him run us. He stood at the hub of the circle we ran in whatever dusk was left to us and Ma appeared in the windowlight in her sorry robe. *Hup ho.*

The night closed in the early cold. Goose beneath me frothed and steamed and still my hands my skinny arms grew thick to me and shook. My bare legs burned beneath my skirt against the sweating saddle flaps and so I tried to hold them off so that when Goose tripped he threw me, he would throw me, I would fly through the trees like a doll.

QUICK THE SNOW the brittling cold. As quick the thaw comes on.

I trick Goose into the trailer then his blinkers on to calm him and grain in the bin to steady him after we have beat at him and cussed and poked and whooped at him till Pa has gone off for his gun.

After the day we shod this was. After the thaw had come.

No bird for us no Christmas.

The snow slumping against the barn. "You load the cur before I'm back else I am going to have to—"

To have to. Pa could do with him what he wanted—he was toddling off for his gun. I did not try to stop him but to think to walk Goose in.

Ma gone from her chair the tent jerked down we had hung at the hearth to snug in. Yet we were not what kept her. It was not in us to keep her.

And so I walked him in.

THE FIRST I saw I ran from him. I did not think Pa at first but is it dead or living.

This was before we blinded Goose before the time we trailered him our Ma going off with her wheelbarrow her boy in a bunch in the wheelbarrow how small against the road.

Before any of that. Before we shod this was. Before the rooster flapped onto the pond.

And yet I ran from Pa. Crept back. Before the bees died off I did. Before the fescue yellowed. I lay on the bank to look at him. The pods of the milkweed swelled and split and the seed by its silken feathery plumes as it was meant to do broke away.

AND THEN WE shod him.

The day was dull the day we shod him and cold before the snow had come and Pa sent me out to fetch Goose out of the withering grass where he browsed. I walked through the gate with my pail at my knees and called to him over the field.

He came to me.

He let me come to him, whinnying, that day as any other.

The days were dry then. The corn a stubble. The apples blew into the fields, a glut that year—I could find him. It was easy enough to find Goose—he was feasting beneath the trees. He quit to look at me. Pa's rooster pecking lazily a drubbing on his withers.

Pa had fired the forge in the barn the barn dark to me but for the embers there the shadows rayed and flinching the cottony raftered dark. Goose was shy of it, I brought him gently in, he was skittish.

I backed him into the washroom into the crossties where we shod. I leaned my chest, a boy's, against him. I felt my heart knock at the bone in his head his breath the wet of the grass he ate and sweet against my belly. *Hush.*

I kept it to me.

At the first even Pa was kind. He clipped away where the hoof began at the end to hook and tear. He kicked the shards the cutaway moons to his dogs to take to nibble at at the end of the barn and hide. He rasped the hoof flat, he picked a small stone from the frog.

The shoe nested in the forge on the fire. Outside, winter's early winded dark advancing slowly on.

The rooster stood to crow for it. That day as any other. But Pa when the rooster crowed jerked up and let his hollowed sound he made the day I came upon him swarmed. He jabbed Goose in his brisket. Goose already lunging. Pa gone to his knees on the slab.

The rooster flapped to the rafters. The sparrows swept from the barn.

He filed the hoof flat. You have to rasp it flat to take the shoe to ride the wash and hillside slopes to pass the house and Ma in the house to pass the coop the chickens.

Pa pinched the shoe from the forge—it was flaring, a shaking liquid yellow. He hooked the shoe over the anvil then over the battered nose—you have to turn it. Pound it to make a fit of it bore the slim squared holes.

I knew Pa's knees were swelling—I had heard them knock against the slab. His long face pinched and fallowed, I saw, who saw ahead as I knew he must the bruisy syrupy blue of skin the selvage pressed of the pants I hemmed sloppily upon it. I would have to cut Pa's pants from him—from the burl the knotted sickened joint and ice or lance or sit to bend or what any else Pa thought to show he could bully through the doing of and so we two kept on with it so we two said nothing.

He punched the nail through—once, three times again, on the one shank and then on the other. To keep the shoe fast. To drive the nails through—square and blunted. Eight in all. I knew the sound and counted.

Pa held the shoe against his hoof. The shoe was hot still it was hissing and the stink of hide of hair or hoof the twangy burning smell rose up and Goose threw himself against me. Pa held him. He did what he could to hold him Pa he kept him wedged against the wall we hang the tack the lead shanks on the picks and forks and shovels.

Tell her that.

He tapped the nail in.

Tell your ma I tried to calm him. That at the last we twitched him. To make it easy. I meant to calm him. I put myself between you tried to keep you safe from harm. No harm meant. You could not trust him. He was game but you could not trust him. He would throw you into the trees he would he would drag you across the fields.

I let Pa twitch him. So I could hold him. So the day might come I thought so of the weeks I sulked to school.

Pa drew out Goose's lip where the stripe blazed through the velvet soft that veered across and snatched down the twitch the silver bars upon it hard and twisted. It was easier then to hold Goose shaking quiet on the slab. I drew his head down slowly and pressed my face to the white of his face how soft where the stripe swept through.

Pa tapped a nail in. He went hoof to hoof in the graying light. *How quick the dark came on. Tell her that.*

But I could not yet think of Ma of what we would need or not to tell but thought of the day I would ride our Goose in my boots to school. I would tie Goose off on the chalky racks the city kids lash their bicycles to, would come to him between the bells to curry him to feed him.

Hey, horsey girl.

Of course they teased me. Would. Who wished to be me.

How I pressed my heart to his brisket.

Pa wedged each hoof between his knees his shoulder thrown against Goose hard to keep him tipped against the wall we hang the leads and halters on the shoe for luck to hold him. I felt his breath against my chest a wind drawn rough across my throat and felt the cool the whips of spit the snot swept down from his nostrils yes and of his mouth the velvet there where the stripe blazed through.

You get. And the rooster too. *Get get.*

I kept the loop of his mouth pinched fast the twist in the loop that made him wheeze that made him drip and gurgle. And still I could not hold him. I was sick in myself to hold him so so Pa could shove and cuss at him so Pa could treat him roughly.

He swung the rasp back.

It would not be long.

We would leave our tools and the cooling forge and make our way up from the barn. Soon enough.

Then I could cut Pa's pants from him. Who cannot reach to do it. Who have not kept him from it. The selvage dug well in.

Pa kept on as I knew he must who knew by him the way of things who knew to watch him swing his rasp he swung at Goose's head his knees enough to think he's mine. He is mine he is mine he is mine.

Will be.

I will cook and clean for him and sew and scrub his feet for him and shine his boots and buckles.

Keep him safe from harm.

Say that.

Say that is easy—to lose an eye on the washroom wall on the hooks and nails we hang tack from he could do it to himself tell her he could do it easy.

That he is fractious. He is meant to be worked and strong tell her. How quick the dark came on.

It came on.

Pa beat at Goose about the knees the rasp struck in behind and hard where you can hear the bones in him where you can make him buckle.

I would not have pictured it—that you could make him buckle. That Pa could fell him in the crossties hanging ready for the blow.

Goose dropped to his knees his rump yet high as if to let me throw my foot my leg across and ride him. My hat flying up to school. *Wheeo.*

He quit there—to let before Pa came at him his last breath ratchet through. And then Pa came at him.

I thought how the white swept up. Pa fallen across the road. *Wheeo.*

Because Pa could not have rolled from him. Pa could not have moved.

He swung the rasp back. He brought it hard across his head his rolling curdled eye I saw.

Cricket you Cricket you.

Quick a girl's sweet warbled note. Quick as that the wettish thuck the jellied seep of his eyeball burst the flies the puss like honey.

We set him out then. When it was done then. I walked Goose out on his blinded side and set him loose like Pa had said back in the back and hidden field the deer came to to lie in. We walked up the hill and washed our hands and sat and ate our supper.

She had fried three eggs for supper for us as Ma had come those weeks to do no matter what Pa said of it and three again come morning. And Pa said nothing of it and not again when light had come and Ma went out with her boy in the snow that as we slept flew down. Her tracks went out to the fence I sat the days Goose ran the sloping field and turned toward the barn and quit there well shy of the bend in the road.

She came back then. I put my mind to it—to the tracks I had to go by. There were two of them going she left in the snow and not a step she came back by.

She had gone away twice down the hill, I thought. She had gone away once the mother we knew who sat for us in the window. Then look on her heels came the other. Here came the one from before the boy we had forgotten was hers to ever be or ever was ours to know.

I liked to think of it—that she could walk herself out away from us from what we did or did not do, she could call herself out on the road going out going out in her boots in the unbroken snow that we would know at the last we had lost her.

And yet the tracks quit.

She would find Goose in the barn she thought. She would see him she thought from the bend in the road see what we had done to him who sat at her table after and ate the meal she cooked for us and slept in the beds she made for us and so she quit well shy of it and came away back to home. She walked herself back up the hill to us walking backward her back to the wind to keep her boy from the snow.

The snow climbed in the trees in the fences. A night would pass a morning time and soon Pa would set upon her again and break what eggs I brought to her that the hens before the rooster quit still had in them for laying. After that I did not bring the eggs. After that they did not lay them.

The rooster went from the field and back to sit the broken back of the couch stood up in the ice of the pond. No thought in his head to rooster. No eggs to bring for Pa to break for Ma to fry for supper then even should we want some.

I thought I would not want some. I would break an egg in his socket, I thought, let the yolk freeze bright and round. Should Goose lie down.

And then he lay down—the night of the day the wind came warm and the thaw set in the sudden melt and the birds appeared and bickered and swerved in the steam twisting up from our farm.

We hitched the trailer then. That we might use him. Sell him off quick on the hoof down the hill in the warm while we could move.

I had kept Goose's tail in a braid for him and kept his head in a hood for him so the wind could not eat at the socket. The last of our sorry apples dropped I had kicked to him in the field where he lies where he pawed at the snow for what grass there was and picked the leaves he could get to yet from the beech the oak the whippy trees at the edge of the woods that held them. What he did not eat the deer took to and to the cobs of corn I brought and his coat grew thick and ratted in the wind and his hipbones stood out from him.

We kept our heads down. The cold had deepened. I tramped a path past the coop the failing hens the rooster would not when the cold had come leave the pond to rooster.

I thought at first our rooster would ride with me out in the pail with the corn to the field. And so I stopped at the bank to cluck at him. He turned his tail to me. I brought his prize hens to the bank to see and scratch to spread to tempt him. Before the pond was skinned with ice I ferried him back through the muck the weeks yet never once did I see him eat nor seem to think to rooster, never once did I pass the crib to climb the hill to the house to Ma but that he hadn't flapped back out to the couch to announce what we had done.

This was when the freeze augered in, this was in the thaw.

In the thaw of the year when the water rose Pa's bird seemed to walk upon it.

I WENT THE while before the thaw before the hillsides snicked and steamed and then the once thereafter after Ma had gone. I knew to call to him, picking my way once the creek froze through between the spindly boles of trees the needled limbs of the buckthorn there where yet the small dark berries clung the beads in rimpled clusters. I shook in my pail as I went to him the corn I was not to bring to him. I brought cigarettes and sugar cubes crumbling apart in my pockets.

Hope hey. Hope hey. I meant to tend to him, to swab and slowly doctor him. To sweep my thumb through his socket. A day came I came upon Goose there forgetting myself to speak to him and stood upon his blinded side and he swung away and kicked me. I let him kick me.

Then it was easy. Then I could quit then.

The field was hidden. I tossed my pail back to the back of the crib and the rats there shied and scuttled out and trotted away to the barn.

So it was easy. The cold had deepened.

I went the once Pa sent me out when the thaw set in to fetch him. I saw his head rise up to see me. Otherwise I went no more.

WE SNUGGED IN when the worst of the cold had come and fashioned a room with the blankets we had with the tablecloths she kept to spread should a guest appear should Christmas. I rode on Pa's back to drive the nails to stand in his hands in the stirrups he made and hit at the few ruined crooked nubs the old people left to hang them. We brought our sheets our pillows in and ate and slept in what warmth there was from the fire we nursed and prodded.

Ma ripening in her gown. Our shadows should we sit in quiet there yet flinching against the walls.

Ma kept her eye fast on her boy. Sitting her silk chair.

"Time was I thought the milk teeth came to make the women stop it," Pa said. "Let them rest a time—for the next to breed. Give a man his chance abed. Time was."

She set the baby down on his feet at her feet. Should he squall she swung him up again.

"But it makes your ma keep at it, same with that boy as you."

Her boy. Him lolling yet at her bosom.

We woke for months to snowfall the curling drifts the wind banked up to pin our flapping door. The hedge disappeared the leeward fence cow Maggie walked out over to find her way to the barn. No school for weeks no place we went our tractor left with the broken plow on the road where Pa sprung off from it come up on him and over until all but the lip of the high-side tire the wind picked clean seemed gone.

Then of a night a velvet wind and foreign swept our farm.

Pa legged me over the windowsill. He heaved me out in my mukluks onto the slope of snow. The slabs of snow of thickened ice already in the pooling glare crept across the rooftops. I took my list to go by: cigarettes, sardines, D-con, cheese.

Barn and barn and crib and pond and on the pond Pa's rooster—spun—our grudging weathervane. I think he thought to crow at me who never crowed by morning light and so I waved my cap at him and waved as I went at his baffled hens, sunk to my peep in the snow.

"How you?"

They had lights at the store and the woodstove burned and the wind flown hard in the blackened pipe sucked and moaned and tumbled. I gathered my goods and bagged them. The girl held out her hand for the money she knew my pa would never send me with and quick I turned for home from her, the thaw sunk deep upon us.

Every stone and matted leaf and fence and sloping fallow steamed. The ice on the pond broke soft when I passed and soft the newts the spotty frogs the dull fish frozen in. The barn the mossy pond I smelled and in the wind the flowers bloomed where it had crossed to reach us. It came on.

Ma went back in her blotted gown to the back of the house she had happened from and found her hat her dungarees her chalky split galoshes. So quick I went to fetch Goose. He lay in the field on his blinded side in a patch pawed free of snow.

I let him stop for a time for the apples that dropped and palmed him the last of the treats I had kept the months for him in my pockets.

We took the path past the crib. I knew no other way to go so as not to pass her. She would go on. Her boy in a bunch in the wheelbarrow. She had her bag at her knee her hat on.

I led him along his hood pulled free him lathered in the sudden warm his brisket gaunt and heaving. *Cricket you Cricket you.*

It would not be long. I knew as much to look at Ma her flicks and starts and sudden flush her voice like something burst in her should she gap her mouth to use it.

I went on. I led him up between the barns where Pa had drawn the trailer up and stood the high gates open.

Ma turned back the once and once again to bring herself to go. We stood on the road and watched her. The road black in the wet in the sudden thaw in the steam that dipped and gathered grown so thick to squat upon our pond that it seemed not our rooster there but the air itself yet crowing.

Stay. Stay. So go.

I gave Goose his head to lunge at Pa to beat the air to strike at him should Pa swing past where Goose could see else think to speak or touch him. To see if she would tend to him. But Ma was going on.

She went up through the lopped and pollarded trees I kept as she went a count of. Pa's dogs at her heels since the barn. Good dogs.

I leant against Pa's legs with them. I licked his pants when I was small with them with him not looking. Quick.

"You get."

Pa toddled off for his gun.

Goose scraped at the road the rilling stream with the shoe those months he had not thrown that I would pry for luck from him and clip the braid of his tail from him hung fat with the mud we had hauled him through, the slickened clay and loamy sweet and thinking I would go there yet where Goose had lain in the sun and moon I found a tree a buckthorn near and deep against it hung them.

I blinkered him to calm him.

I walked into the trailer ahead of him and we could hear Pa coming back, I was backed against the trough with him wedged away under the bars from him and Pa swung the creaking gate shut and Goose went back to thrashing. I felt my head flung back. Pa stood up on the running board and the shaft of the gun pushed through.

So it was Pa shot him.

It is for my sake Pa shot him.

I was in the stall beside him and the trailer shook and ringing quit and the blood of my face where Goose opened it ran free in my mouth and warm.

ENOUGH FOR ME. No matter.

Ma looked back the once and went on.

All that she had left to us and what is yet to come to us the oaks on the hill the lightning hits the fox in the field in the weeds I keep gone red to gray come autumn—it is enough for me. No matter.

I will sing Pa her song the getting up song she sang to me in the morning time when she leaned to me to nudge me and the baby was in her hair.

I could smell him from her hair.

I SLIP THROUGH the muck the gone-by weeds the flattened grass the dogs bend down and think *if I could run from him* else think *I never came on him* wallowed up on the couch in the green suppose Cricket supposing.

We sat on the shore and watched him. I did not know in myself what to do for Pa nor what there might be in tending him to call so even gently. To say: *I tend him gently*.

Pa would have me poke at him. He would have me pinch and twist at him.

Yet to say: *I tend him gently*.

And ever in the dusk in the sinking light I knead his feet his withered legs to move the gout and feed him.

Am I not his girl Cricket?

Enough for me. No matter.

I sing Ma's song to him.

Our blessings count.

Enough for me to keep our Goose and in myself the truth of him and the dogs grow fat and eat of him and by the silken sweet of glue we spread across our palms to peel the skin I feel him with me and feel of the seeds that split in me and of the living harvest, shell and hide and cloven tongue and of the fruit and fowl we strew the yolky eyes the deer we cull the great whales flensed for blubber.

Ever so. Ever so gently.

I lie in the field and picture it. Who have come to be one to picture it. How long it was Goose hung there. Such a time it was he hung there pawing softly at the stars.

CHUPETE

HE DROVE CARELESSLY AND THE SUN PASSING THROUGH the window looked to melt his hair to his head. His eyes were shining. His hands were chalky and raw.

One hand, he kept on the steering wheel and the other let slump between them. A blackened thumbnail, a knuckle bloodied. He made his living with his hands. Like Jesus, she thinks.

But this man is younger than Jesus. His shirt is on the seat between them. On his chest is a lump a parasite makes eating its way toward air. He circles the lump with his fingertip, as if stirring. As if making a doll-sized stew.

The sea was heaving, a mirror that showed back nothing. The town was falling behind them.

She can't see it—how one sack is going to do. She should have given him two, she thinks. She gave him money. He gave it back to her. He took a shirt from her from her country—two—the ram's head of a sporting team, a soaring modern god.

Her shirt was—but that was his shirt. Hers stuck to her from the heat of the day and the engine heat pushed through the dashboard.

Her shirt was becoming transparent, she thinks. And thinks: what a funny way to say it: make a living with your hands. Make a life.

In the back is a sack of concrete, a tongue of fine gray dust. He has a daughter—there is that. And his god—there is that. And the work of his hands she gives him.

The road was ragged. It was underway. So much in this country was underway. His boy—she supposed you could say that: in the oven: underway. Nearly ready. Some months.

Why the oven, she thinks, and not the sack? Baby in the sack. In the stew.

The sea ate at the roots of the palm trees until at last the tide, when the moon was right, dragged them away. They fell softly and without noise, the wood soft and shallow roots drawn out of the loosening sand. Beyond: islands. Soggy unbroken swells.

She brought shoes from her country to give to him, tiny as a doll's. Now she would keep them. That part of her life was over— years of nights of waking to find her children in their beds. *They are the sons and daughters,* she thinks. *And Jesus died and was buried,* she thinks, *and on the third day*—was it the third day? And she began to write the story in her head:

He needed money and I had money. He needed concrete to make a coffin with and he didn't have money to buy it. Just a sack was enough to make a coffin with. He didn't have the little money to spend on a sack so I gave him the money to buy it. He just needed enough for his baby. They didn't have money for a hospital and when they got there, the baby was dying. The baby was being born and dying across the river all at once. I had money so I gave

him money. I gave him a ride to where he lived with his wife. I had
a truck I could borrow from Tulio that didn't have doors and the
windows were cracked and he had taped them back with packing
tape and that was what we drove. He put the concrete in back in
the rusting bed. He had a girl and a dying baby and we drove along
the sea in the sunlight until—

AND SHE REMEMBERED the baby when her boy was born that
went on tossing inside her. She had a real living baby on the outside and another baby knocking on the inside, saying: *I am still
here.* And she thought of the baby as it was being born and dying
all at once and of what it might be doing, why—what it groped at,
what it pushed off from and clawed at—to get out, to stay in. Of
what it might know, what it knew of what was happening to it in
the minutes it had to live.

And she thought if the coffin were hers to make, who made
little with her hands, that she would begin with a coconut, a heavy,
sturdy, hollowed-out seed to pack the mud around. To keep the
dogs off. A seed inside a seed inside the concrete. You might want
it to float but it wouldn't but a seed at least gives a body room.
It will rattle in its pod like a pea, she thinks—and wishes she had
never thought it.

But if he packed the mud right against the baby wouldn't the
concrete burn the baby or pull it apart as it dried? That seemed
likely. Nobody wanted to think about that but *he* was going to
have to think about that who made his living with his hands. The
blackened thumbnail, the knuckle bloodied.

He drove on. She could not think quite what she had seen in him, what she was seeing now. The lump in his chest. His Halloween teeth—like the teeth of the dead she finds walking. Teeth and bones and burying beads. Still—something. Some old durable hunger.

She had given him a *chupete,* of all things, a lollipop, a knob of candy on a paper stick. Now he tossed the stick out the window. He reached around to smear a clear patch in the dust to see through the glass to drive.

A butterfly snagged against the windshield and the wind the truck made moving plucked iridescent dust from its wings. There were thousands of butterflies like it flying above the sea, dipping to leave their eggs on the water. They arrived for days, a living cloud, and she remembered the summer her daughter was born that crickets had made their way into the house—by the dozens—by the hundreds—a great abundance. And sang all night with their knees.

His skin was seeping where the *bicho* pushed against it and polished from being stretched too far. And she wondered in a dream of his baby he might have if the baby like a god would burst through his skin and, once and again, as the *bicho* did, keep blooming in his blood.

That seemed likely.

He needed money and I had money, she thinks.

She thinks, I had it all along.

She had the baby all along and it moved in her and it would bloom as when the rains came and burst out through her head. That seemed likely.

Life longing for itself.

And the baby would be the size of a beetle, how it felt. And on one face would be her father's face and on the other the face of her mother. And wings like a bee. And little snelled feet. And a great booming voice like a god's.

PERIHELIA

SHE HAD BEEN SICK FOR DAYS WASHING CLOTHES IN THE river so the witchdoctor came with his gunnysack and his parrot clinging to his hat. The parrot was skinning a grape, turning the fruit against the blade of its beak with its purple tongue. The girl was pale as a cloud and cold. Unmoored. The witchdoctor pulled off her shirt. From his sack he drew a leafy bundle of stalks and beat her across the back. He had a stew of sticks and leaves in a jar and something fat that floated. This he filled his mouth with. He spat the stew with terrible force against the girl's narrow back. Archipelago of bone. Faultless, her skin. His mouth was leaking. The witchdoctor drew two eggs from his sack. He rolled these as though in orbit over the litter of leaf and bark and the sewn-over drift of her spine. He broke the eggs into the jar. Spun them. The girl cried out from pain or fear and the parrot mimicked the sound she made and the skinned grape dropped from its mouth. They should never have come. What kind of mother? The girl was radiant, beyond human. Fever had lacquered her eyes. Snakes in the trees and dinner arrived bungeed to the back of a motorbike, a river fish, battered, fileted on the floor with a machete. *Ojos*, said the doctor, looking up at the mother. The eggs hung in the murk: a doubled sun. The parrot with great patience repeated the word. Someone envied the girl. Cursed her. Someone had sickened the girl with her eyes.

QUERIDO

A SEED CAUGHT IN HER TEETH THAT MOVED WHEN SHE spoke. Her son was killed. She had tattooed into her arm a dragonfly to summon him by, the glassy wings, the obscenely quivering body. A water creature once, millennia ago, flown into the hinge of her elbow. Angel beyond life. Beyond mercy. Wingspan wide as an owl's. The seed swam across her tooth. The sea kept coming.

CUERNAVACA

THERE WERE THREE LITTLE GIRLS WHO WERE SISTERS named Sparrow and Phoebe and Wren. Wren was the father's favorite. One day he watched a bird in an airport flying from chair to chair. The bird flew into a window and dropped to the floor and for an hour lay stunned at his feet. In great anguish the father knew Wren had left him. She had fled to Cuernavaca. Here he found her, and dragged her home by her hair.

BOULEVARD

THE DAUGHTER HELD THE GATE OPEN FOR HER TO walk through to the field. Against the fence were the horses. Where the horses were inclined to stand, there were bald spots in the field. A fine dust kept falling. At night, the dust disappeared and the bald spots appeared to the daughter like small clouds sunk down. In the dust, the mother's footsteps were as soft as if she had not worn shoes.

It was a night you could smell the river. A hard rain had come from the north and—saffron to the riverbed—enough water for all the fields.

There were laws about the water.

You were only allowed water certain days, certain times.

The daughter brought the chain around to pull fast the gate and the horses shied at the sound this made, and snorted—circling in a slow, breaking canter around the dry field. The fence leaned from the leaning of the horses. Walking the fence line away from her mother, the daughter jostled each post with her hand.

"Candysara," said the mother, "Lady Jane," calling to the horses.

The daughter watched from the mouth of the ditch the horses mill around her mother; only the one mare let her mother come near.

"Candysara," said the mother again.

"MOTHER?" THE DAUGHTER had asked. "How do you spell O-H-I—?"

"Why?" the mother had said.

"How do you spell *Ohio?*"

THE MOTHER STROKED the mare named Candysara in the hollow of her throat and the mare, as though her head were a thing to be carried, gentled her head against the mother's coat. The mother kissed the small white star that marked the face of the mare. In the mother's coat was a deep square pocket the mare had learned to muzzle into. This was why she was called Candysara—the mother's favorite—she came with a whinny to the leaning fence anytime the mother came near the field.

"What are you doing?" the daughter asked.

She could hear her mother talking to the horses.

The daughter's horse was Blue One—a white mare, speckled gray, a mare named the name of the color she had turned when rain fell on the field.

The mother walked out from the horses. Past the bald spot where the horses stood, roots clumped where grass had been and the ground was brittle where rain had dried in the deep prints of the horses. Above the ditch that traversed the field, the sound of the leaves of the cottonwoods turning above the daughter was the sound to the mother of water running into the ditch to fill.

But the daughter had not remembered: the gates ought not be opened fully, but opened at once. The ditch behind the gate had filled and water so pressed against the gate, the daughter could not raise it. The gate was metal and cool with the coolness of the water that had run down off the mountainsides into the Rio Grande.

They worked the gate from side to side, their shoes pushing into the slope of silt washed from the river bottom. The metal edge of the gate cut into the bend of their fingers. When water ran out under the gate and tugged at the cuffs of their jeans, the mother said, wanting to rest, "What's this about Ohio?"

The daughter shook her hands out, copying her mother.

"Is there an ocean in Ohio?" the daughter said.

"Why?" asked the mother.

"Is there?"

The daughter patted the water with her shoe.

"We've got to get this thing open," said the mother.

She felt the brush of a weed, the small tapping touch of a stick passing beneath the metal gate in the quickening water. The water's smell, the mother knew from years of snakes in coffee tins—she had let her children keep things—a broken-winged dove the dog brought home, a ringwormed cat. Her own smell, she thought, was of something kept, an old smell, something hoarded.

THE DAUGHTER HAD cut the tail of the mare who had blued when rain fell on the field and carried it to her mother, a tail they would pull through a nylon stocking to bend into a drawer to save. In the drawer was the braid of the mother—fine hair banded at either end—a girl's—still flaxen as the daughter's. The daughter's braid had been so long she had threaded the loose ends of it through the back belt loops of her jeans.

Cut short—*pixied*, her mother said—it swung into her face when she bent to the gate again to work it open.

The daughter reached around from behind her mother saying, "Guess," her fingers cupped over her mother's eyes, saying, "Who is it now, Mother?"

She nickered—a low, caught sound in the daughter's throat, a sound that no longer seemed practiced.

"Lady Jane," her mother guessed.

"Nunh-uh."

"Bubbling Fancy."

"Now?" said the daughter.

She stooped into her mother. They were almost as tall as each other.

"Guess!" the daughter cried. "You're not guessing! Guess again!"

She stamped her foot in the water of the ditch, blotting her lips together.

"B-L-U—"

"I *know*," the mother said.

She had thought as a child they would come to her in the underwater tongue of leaves—words—how many she could not guess
of them nor how they might be said—a spell, a plea, she was certain—you could walk out into them. They would sit like birds on
your shoulders. They would light on your hair as they fell.

She heard the slow steps of the horses. The air was cool against
her back where the weight of her daughter had been.

"MOTHER?"

Her mother had said those were mare's tails, but what did that
mean? She had said they meant rain coming. When the rain came,
the mare had blued and the sky blued when the sun came up, but
those were not the same colors. Those were colors named the same
name but they were different colors. Her name was Melissa—a
yellow name, her mother said; she said every name had a color.
Different names had the same color and different colors had the
same name and mares' tails meant there was rain on the way—
high, said her mother, serious clouds that streamed above the
mountains. The mountains were named *Sandia*—watermelon in
Spanish—because that was the color people thought they turned
when the sun went down in the desert. The daughter had not
thought you could name a mountain for the soft inside of a fruit,
so she had thought of the color of a watermelon's rind, which was
the color of the name of her mother.

WAS HER COLOR like that inside her?

She had not seen where her mother opened.

The sound of the mare, she could make with her tongue, a wet, almost popping sound of pucker and slack, spittle the stallion had tasted. The mare had pushed against the paddock fence and the daughter had leaned back into the fence, helping, holding the mare, saying with the mother, "Whoa, Blue," pushing the fence back into her mother saying, "That's a girl, now, easy."

It was the skin of the mare that had blued in the rain; her mane and her tail had not. Her tail had lifted over her back and the daughter had seen her winking, the pink clot of flesh as bright as the turned-up lid of an eye. Her father reached under the stallion, helping, guiding him, walking on two legs.

Was that her own smell, a smell not the smell of the mountain color or snakes that swam in the field? Was that the smell of her mother?

"LET ME REST a minute," the daughter said.

She could not see the water, but the slow shape of her mother raised up and the water was louder then. She said, more loudly now, "I get so worn down."

"Me*liss*a," the mother said.

"I do," said the daughter.

The gate trilled against its brace, opened but for the bottom edge the water curved past swiftly. The mother leaned into the rush of the water.

"Pumpkin," the mother said, "what about the horsies? If they cut off the water before we're finished, what will the horsies do?"

"I don't want to," the daughter said, "I get so worn down."

She was watching her legs, pulled along, hop and bob in the water.

"I hurt my hands," she said. "See?"

When she let go the weeds on the bank of the ditch to hold out her hands to show her mother, the water pulled her down into the ditch to the waistband of her jeans. She giggled. They leaned together into the current.

THE DITCH CUT the width of the field and past that was the boulevard and then came mountains. The water ran back to the mountains. Snow fell on the mountains and ran in the spring to the river and the river ran into the sea. In spring, the snow got smaller. Some days you could not notice it, but that did not make it not so.

Unso, the daughter thought. Some of it stayed on the mountains—patches of white the daughter watched—to speckles, a shine in the eye—then nothing but the blank of stone. It would not happen if you watched it. One morning you would wake and see and it would be unso.

SHE WENT OUT along the ditch ahead of her mother, walking with the water. The water pressed her jeans against her faster than she wanted to go.

Weeds that had come from the riverbed, pulled free in the flash of rain, caught on the mother's legs as she walked; the weeds that grew in the silted ditch broke loose and floated—mustard, the mother knew, and ragweed, goat head and loco. Her coat sleeves pulled long. The mother dipped her arms in the water, netting weeds with her hands. The skin of her hands looked blue to her. She had found them, waking, beside her, on the sheets in bed.

"Come on," the daughter said. "We've got to get these things open."

There were half a dozen smaller gates to let water throughout the field. The mouths of the gates were narrow. In the weeds the horses would not eat were the webs the yellow spiders built. The daughter could not see them, but she beat them down with her hand.

WATER HAD BROKEN inside the mare. It was different water—not like water for the field. The field water broke on stones as it came down the mountains. You could not hear a mare's water breaking.

They had brought the mare to foal in a clean stall in the earth-walled barn—at night and in the rain also, for the rain, it seemed to the daughter, weakened the mare's skin.

She had said, "You can see right into her."

The mare's milk veins had swelled blue in the rain or not, thick as a rope used to hobble. The daughter had slept out in the feed room, so close she could hear the mare eating—sweet feed and warm bran mash, select flakes of alfalfa. It would only take keeping near the mare to know no harm would come.

Yet it had not surprised the daughter—that you could drown as the foal had drowned inside your own mother.

Hand and elbow, up to where the muscle hooked into his shoulder bone, the father had reached up into the mare to yank the foal out of the mare pinned against the paddock fence the daughter pushed back into.

She was the daughter.

The places there were to go were the sounds of their names in her hand.

OHIO.

Armathwaite.

Wetumka.

Canarsie.

THE WOMEN ARE still walking.

We expect when they reach the gate at the border of the field, something more will have happened. Something more should have been said.

ARMATHWAITE.

Lady Jane—a gray name.

Canarsie.

BLUE ONE WAS the name of her and—where the dead mare winched by her pasterns lay—a grassless place the horses, for whatever reason, stood. She was the sound their hooves made striking the dry field. She was the dry field.

"Uh-oh," the mother said.

They walked stoppingly, held against the push of the water. Behind them was the spoor of weeds they had netted with their hands.

"Penny," said the daughter.

"Afraid."

The dark shapes of the horses lunged out in the thudding field.

"Afraid?"

"I don't know," the mother said.

The daughter whinnied.

SHE CANTERED TO school in the morning, practiced dressage in the courtyard.

Horsie, horsie, horsie.

WHEN THE HORSES ran, in their bellies you heard the break and slosh if you rode them. Her mother said that was not water. But it was a sound like water, a place to have tea parties in, a sound where toads at night froze into the gawk of swimming. You could wrench through water, pinch and suck and poke at it; it would never save in it the places you had been.

THERE WILL BE no words, Sister—but shape notes to sing out over our dead, over muddied fields and boulevards, shopping malls and hospitals our mother left for coffins. Oh, what snare of scars we claim of our mothers' bodies, what wounds we have stitched ourselves into. Blame us, we beg, forgive us, all thanks and grateful blessings due.

We are coming, Mother.

We will be there soon.

She will know us by our voices, our wild manes, by our splitting hooves.

JERICHO

THE ROOM WAS HOT AND DARK AND THE CHILDREN were sitting eating with their hands. The air smelled of rice and diapers. The children sat in chairs made for children or kneeled on the dirt floor. The floor was freshly swept and the lines the broom left in the loosened dirt still showed.

Rice fell from the children's mouths as they ate. The old señora who cared for the children would sweep out the room when they had eaten again. She would put the collar on the blind boy again who had pulled it off and dropped it.

He was always pulling his collar off and dropping it and he fought her when she cinched the collar back on but he swung his head loosely without it as though he had no bones in his neck. He had a skinny neck and the bones showed. His skin was the brown of an egg. If she let him swing his head, he would begin to dance and soon the dance became wild and fast and took up the whole room. The dance frightened the other children. So the señora would have to fight him.

She was old and she did not like to fight but the younger women had jobs in the town and the mother who was the blind boy's mother had gone off to Guayaquil. She was fifteen and nobody blamed her. The boy had been blinded inside the mother by the medicine that saved her life. Nobody blamed her. She would have a life now. She danced at night in the discotheques and had her eyebrows tattooed on.

The señora sat in her chair made for children and watched rice fall from the children's mouths. She was as big as a boy of ten. She wound a sash about her braid to keep tidy.

SHE HAD BEEN a girl once with her father in the city of Guayaquil. Her father bought sandals for her in Guayaquil with tiny beads and sequins, and when she returned to the town all the other girls were jealous of her for a time. The beads were the eyes of flowers, luminous and blue.

Some things should be beautiful.

The bowls the children ate from were beautiful. At the bottom of each bowl, the señora had painted a fruit that grew in their yards or on trees near the town—*chirimoya* and *maracuyá*, guava and *tomate de árbol*.

She painted the face of the mother on the bottom of the bowl the blind boy ate his rice from. Of course he would never see it. Even if he waked and could see by some accident, he would not know it was the face of his mother who had gone to Guayaquil.

"*MAMI,*" SAID THE boy, and held his bowl out to say that he was hungry.

The señora kept very still in her chair and watched the other children watch her. If she moved, the boy would know where she was. He would stand on her feet and twist her skirt in his hands and say *mami*.

The other children liked to play at being blind and swung their eyes up so the color didn't show and bumped into things and stumbled. The blind boy only stumbled when he danced. His eyes were the creamy blue of the beads of the sandals the señora's father had given her as a girl in Guayaquil.

She held herself very still. She had one dulce in her pocket.

The blind boy came at her, as she knew he would. She had his collar in her hands. The collar was foam and dirty. She caught him under the chin with it and when he went to his knees as he always did, she cinched it at the back of his neck.

The boy clawed at the collar. He rocked from one foot to the other. The señora said something soothing and the boy made a sound that was not a word but a sound like a cat or a monkey. He pulled the collar off and his head swung free and he began his little dance with his bowl held out.

"*¿Que haces?*" the señora asked him.

There was no more food and he knew it. There was never more food after the first bowl and the children knew not to ask.

The blind boy's dance grew wilder. He slapped his arms against his sides. His head swiveled on his neck. He rocked from one foot to the other and spun until he stumbled. He fell against the girl who was the smallest girl and she struck him hard and cried.

The blind boy went on dancing. He was always happy, dancing. He danced until he could hardly stand and when he stopped he wore his beautiful bowl like a hat and stood with his legs far apart so he could stand and the dark shapes swam in his eyes. The dark shapes were all in the world he could see and he only saw them when he was dizzy from dancing.

The señora let him be. He would be happy for a time. She would not have to fight to put the collar on him and he would go in his collar to the corner where he slept and the señora would have her chance then to sweep the rice from the floor. She swept the rice out the door into the terrible sun where the children jumped rope and ran.

HE SLEPT WITHOUT moving, her little *ciego*. He made his long sounds like a mule.

She had one dulce in her pocket. She knew by the shape and smell of it what flavor it would be.

When she had washed the bowls and stacked them and wiped down the chairs and swept out the rice, she took the dulce from her pocket and gave thanks for it. She gave thanks for the children and for the fruit in the trees and thanks for her good broom, too.

She unwrapped the dulce and the blind boy waked. She said his name and he came to her.

Jericho stroked the tops of her feet with his feet. He smelled the dulce in her mouth.

He would be patient; he knew to be patient.

He heard her tug the sweetness from it.

Jericho found the señora's face with his hands and drew her mouth to his mouth and waited.

He mustn't whimper, he knew. He mustn't ever brag or move his feet to dance or tug at the señora's clothes. Jericho mustn't blame his mother.

His mother was beautiful, they all said so. She had her eyebrows tattooed on.

The señora pushed the dulce to the tip of her tongue and she let him with his teeth pull it onto his tongue. Only Jericho she let do it. Jericho was such a good boy is why.

HUNGER IS THE FIRST EMOTION

THE GIRLS BRAID THEIR HAIR TOGETHER—BLACK BLONDE black; blonde black blonde—and drag the water trough into the pond. It is a farm pond clogged with frogs' eggs, salamanders, slime. They clamber into the trough and row out. It is the pond one girl's brother nearly drowned in, the pond the wheezing goat drinks from. It is summer. It is autumn. The cold is closing in. They will be eighty together, rocking on a porch in the sunshine, even the grandchildren grown and gone. For now they are girls on a pond. They sing to each other, their foreheads touching, their braids hanging slack between them. One girl sings of her wheezing goats, the other of a bird asleep on the wind dreaming of a country far away.

FIRE FEATHER
MENDICANT BROOM

HERE WAS A STONEMASON WHO WENT BY THE NAME of Hawk who, until his mother died and left him her home, had scarcely owned a thing. His mother's home was not a house but a trailer on the outskirts of a big eastern city Hawk detested and he lived there with her dresses and jars of cream, with her radio tuned to the station she liked, and her book still opened on her chest of drawers to the last of the pages she had read.

Hawk would rather have slept and passed his days in a hippie van or a pickup truck but he owned neither and never had. He arrived to work holding his broken-down gloves and soon these sprawled among the stones at his feet—a nuisance, he thought, and frivolous, though every finger of each glove was eaten through and the thumbs were mostly gone. He liked the feel of the rock in his hands.

Hawk's work was slow and meticulous. From the rough gray schist of the region, he built a stone egg that stood on end amid milkweed and goldenrod and the glassy bent grasses of a meadow.

The egg was his most beautiful and difficult work and he carried a picture of it in his money clip, the way people carry pictures of people—daughters, sweethearts, sons.

Hawk had no children, no wife, no mother now, though the idea of his mother was everywhere in the trailer where she had lived.

He brought his hand to his mouth to feel his breath come and go in the room where she had passed her last days. He was Hawk for the shape of his nose like his mother's and the unnerving flicker of his eyes.

HAWK. A NAME like a revelation.

So he wandered, but a boy—setting out by morning, by nightfall looping home. Home was a house on a rubble footing then. Hawk a boy in his feral glory, a truant who had buried his shoes. He learned the trees of that place and birdsong and ashen tatters of skin; tooth mark, claw; the habits of bees; the smell of a thing afraid. Here a doe slept, here a fawn. Here the ledge tilted skyward, glittering schist, and beneath it a fieldstone wall ran slumping through meadows to keep cattle and sheep in an era when the woods were cleared. Here morels grew, here were berries. Ginseng, psilocybin. Sap pulsing in the trees.

The place was enough for him and then it wasn't and soon he was said to be elsewhere building a house of mud. He baked bricks on their sides in the reliable sun, brought the walls to his knees and walked away.

He walked from Tucumcari to Reno, across the great divide. He walked from Reno to Winnemucca and there found a cobbler in a dusty shop who taught Hawk to cobble his ruined boots and sew his own clothes and carve wood. He made a pouch from the tissue of a buck he had killed and from the bone of an elk he made buttons.

Stew of raccoon, of squirrel.

Roadkill should he come upon it.

When his boots went to shreds he left them standing in the road facing where he had been. And walked on. His feet grew flat from walking, and calloused and gray and wide. He walked from the Black Rock to San Francisco and from San Francisco to Truckee and on to the Hood, the Missouri, the Milk, great northern wind-blown plains. Crow country; Mandan Sioux. For years little was known or left of him but the cairns of what rock he came upon as though he meant to be found.

Hawk sent word from time to time to his mother to relate some next fascination—a beetle walking out of its luminous shell, out of the barbs of its legs. The orderly ways of elk herding up; moonset while the sun lifts, too.

Once a picture arrived of a cave of ice Hawk had chinked some indecipherable thing into—how, she could not say. By wing, by rope and harness.

No word, ever, of a woman. Her son said nothing of where he had been nor where he was going now. A rumor reached her of Patagonia, great palisades of muttering ice, Hawk traveling with only a rucksack in whatever way he could. Tierra del Fuego, land of fire, people of fire in scant guanaco hides they moved to shelter their sex from the wind. The wind incessant. The calamitous past recorded and calving into the sea.

Here rabbits clipped the grasses and trees grew hunched and low, turned from the wind and twisted. Gray seas battered the shore-bound rock and, green in the face of the lifting wave, the ice swam, brief and lethal. Heavy, hissing, frothing tide—it spit out the ice and moved on.

Green of his mother's dishes; shattered glass of the gods. A place that was like a painting of a place.

A gray mist, and Hawk's hair turned, and when his skin appeared gray he walked north again—blasted, brilliant, vacant days, pampas and tidy vineyards and flamingoes in shimmering pools, uncountable iridescent flocks like something from a dream he dreams still.

By his hands he is known and recognized and by a picture of the egg he still carries. By his flickering eye.

Hawk.

But something leaves him now. He is like something dying in a cage.

Traffic moves without pause beyond the window; headlights approach and swing away.

If he had a place for her things—but he has nothing. He sits among them. A neighbor boy comes to hear tales of Hawk's travels but soon the boy's mother forbids him to so much as walk down the block. The days are lengthening. The tin of his mother's trailer ticks like a clock in the sun.

He saw a condor dead, a few alive, rising, the sky immaculate. He saw gauchos in flimsy slippers standing on their horses in the blue. A lamb in a box. A spoonbill.

A mobile home, Hawk thinks. Ridiculous.

One night he sets fire to the withering grass, standing in the dark with a garden hose poked through the chain link fence.

She lived for years like this, sequestered, he cannot begin to grasp why. His mother was waiting; she ironed bedsheets; she was polishing the stove. She raked the grass each day as if it mattered—ugly little patch the dog pissed in—until the morning she tripped and fell in her kitchen and called out and no one came. A stain spread where she lay on her buckled floor with her small dog chewing her hand. The radio played, the singing, the talk, and in pencil in meticulous letters she composed a list for herself: New broom. Ammonia. Bicarbonate. Bobby pins. Chicken.

Hawk sets to work trying to lift the stain from the place his mother fell. Ammonia—his eyes are streaming, and his hands, his hands are from another animal, huge, like paws, like slabs, torn from the rock he built with. He has worn his fingerprints off and his thumbnails are gone and the skin is thready and raw.

The stain comes back by morning. Always as something new. It comes back in the shape of a toaster. A pony. The shape of a sleeping dog. Hawk crouches above it, scouring, gloomy and consumed. *At last,* he thinks. Still it comes back. Now as a dress she favored. Now as fire. Feather. Mendicant. Broom.

SWIM FOR THE LITTLE ONE FIRST

HOW NICE YOU COULD COME TO VISIT. SEE OUR HOME, how we live, how the leaves sweep down. The fields green still.

We turned our clocks back. I brought squash in, tossed a sheet across the withering vines. We're to expect a frost once the wind quits, wind from the north, flurries. A chance.

We'll move the rabbits in in the morning, light the stove. Chicory in your coffee, honey how you like. On the radio the news.

Dark falls and the wind comes up and leaves flock out of the trees. I tug windows shut and yet, inside, doors keep sailing open. Leaves shore up in the kitchen. The floorboards buckle and heave.

These old houses. Every wall leans toward the south, toward you, your modest hills, your clemencies of weather.

It can't be easy. It is a distance. Our stairs are steep and narrow. You will never make it up them; you would never make it down. We would have to keep you, as eccentrics keep their reptiles, captive in a tub.

We have the dog you gave us. We have reasonable jobs in town. Sick pool, personal time. Time to travel. I took a lover from the tropical regions once who washed my feet in the sand. Children loved him. He owned a shirt he never wore. He danced, with keening grace, with my Isabel, who has lived so far to be five.

YOUR ROOM IS freshly painted. Your bed is your bed you slept in in Kentucky when you were a boy. The sheets are the sheets Mother monogrammed when she took your name when you married.

If you need anything, if you are up in the night. There is the wingback chair to sleep in. Whiskey in the pantry. Pecan cake in the breadbox—your father's favorite, the cake your mother made you.

Our house is yours, naturally.

You need only ask.

I am awake in the night in the yellow room at the top of the narrow stairs. Tap your cane on the stairs—I'm sure to hear it.

WE KEEP OUR boy with us in our bed. Our boy looks like your boy, like my brother. We gave him your name you gave my brother, the name your mother gave you. He is the third Frederick, a grandson at last. Papa, we named him for you.

My lover's name was Artemio.

"*Quieres tomar mi leche?*" he used to ask.

He danced beautifully, in keeping with the custom of his people. Isabel bent her back across his arm and dragged her hair through the sand.

My brother was Frederick the second.

He skied out of an avalanche that caught you—we've told the story a thousand times. Your ski swung around and put a gash in your leg and, by this wound, Freddy tracked you. He skied you out of that chute on his back. You were knocked out; you waked in the hospital.

Remembered nothing. You remember nothing of it now. It can't have happened, you insist, even now.

He was weak, your boy, he wasn't like you.

The second Frederick.

WE SHOULD HAVE named our boy Jack. Jack the first, Jack the only.

Manuel, we should have named him, Carlito. Gordito—*little fat boy.*

You should have said, *Freddy, thank you.*

Instead you said, *It can't have been you.*

IN SLEEP, MY brother, my boy at my breast, makes his visits, too. He is not himself but I know it is him. He is not the boy who set the house ablaze, not the boy who sawed the heads off snakes and skewered mice with a pitchfork. Freddy stands at the door until morning, waiting to be seen. He sees nothing. He has no eyes, no mouth, no reason he can speak of to be here.

The trees thrash in the wind. Apples shake loose and drop to the ground—a sound loud enough to wake me.

PACHEW, YOU SAID, and aimed your cane at my girl.

YOUR CANE IS wound about with electric tape. The shaft is splintered—you fault the dog. The dog was digging at your peas, *how many times?* You broke your cane across its back.

Pachew.

You will have peas at Christmas and pecans and cabbage in your garden still growing.

Here, snow will heap past the window sash. The bears hunker down and the rabbits, and the frogs endure the season frozen solid. Ice pries slate from the rooftop. When snow slides off the roof, and ice, all at once, the house thunders, and quakes on its rubble footing. The dog gnaws at the door, and Isabel cries out.

My girl sleepwalks, so you know. Isabel talks in her sleep. We mustn't wake her—only follow at her heels quietly until she makes her way back to bed.

Isabel is likely to walk to the church next door and swing from the rope in the belfry. The bells startle her—but she can't wake. She is afraid and calls out for me—but she can't see me, she can't hear. I have to hold her to keep her from looking for me as though I am nowhere near.

I AM NEAR, Papa, not to worry. Only tap on the stairs should you need me.

You have sight in one eye. One leg is shorter. Your joints swell and wear away and you are older of a sudden, eighty soon, tomorrow we'll mark your birthday.

Your boy killed himself on your birthday.

At dinner your wife fell from her chair, asleep. A long way to come and you are tired.

You don't sleep well. You ache in the night. Your friends are dying. You wake with your hand thrown over your face not knowing it is you.

It's your hand, Papa. You can't feel it. Your hand lies across your eyes. You can't move it. It won't come to you what it is.

YOU MAY HEAR birds in the chimney in your room. They often catch there. Their feet scratch the flue. No harm.

You'll hear the wind scrub the hill we live on.

You'll hear me. I sleep lightly, I am up in the night. I am in the room above you, awake when the baby wakes hungry, carrying him across the floor.

His first curl is on the shelf and his umbilical knot in your room where you are sleeping. I buried his afterbirth in the garden deeper than the dog likes to dig.

I keep Freddy's old teeth the tooth fairy left. I keep the lamp Mother made from your ski boot that Freddy dumped the blood you lost out of when he brought you down off the mountain.

You bled wildly. By the blood from the wound, Freddy found you, by the stains on the snow, the blood pooling in your boot. That was lucky.

That lamp made Mother feel lucky. Mother drilled a hole through the bottom of your boot and ran a shaft up through it and filled the boot with cement she threaded wire through.

Funny, what you keep, what keeps at you.

I keep a feather I found in Freddy's pocket.

I keep an acorn I kicked the morning Isabel was born, out walking on the dirt road, my water streaming over my knees.

I keep a satin bow from the attic of the house where we lived when Freddy was alive.

YOU PAID A bounty on birds when Freddy was alive, on pigeons and the obnoxious grackle; a nickel for every rabbit trapped, a dollar for the brazen weasel who ran across your shoe.

He killed to please you. Freddy got rich trying to please you. He drowned mice by the dozen in a bucket and a mother raccoon in a wheelbarrow and the last sorry runt of a puppy your bird dog dropped in the barn. The pup wouldn't amount to much—you had him kill it. Freddy blasted the daubed nests of swallows with their spotted eggs inside.

You taught him what to kill, what to run off, to save.

What Freddy killed he put to rest with great ceremony, with flute song, in a common grave, quietly, secretly weeping.

Spare the songbirds, you taught him, for their pleasing song— the plain and faithful phoebe, the thrush and homely wren. Spare the heron, shoot the goose. Kill the cuckoo bird that hides its eggs for other birds to raise.

We ran skunks off. We brought a fox home to save and you shot it.

He needed toughening, you always said so. Freddy needed a keener eye.

My brother was pretty; he was beaten in school. He had been born too soon. His lungs were weak. I tried to be your boy—so Freddy wouldn't have to be your boy. Wouldn't get to, I think I should say.

FREDDY SHOT A housecat once, out hunting with you, the first and last time you took him with you.

"He's a hazard," you told Mother.

And gave her the geese it was her job to pluck and the pheasant and the dove. Birds are stacked top to bottom in your freezer—pinkish, yellow, their feet still on, more birds than you will eat in a lifetime. Mother plucked the birds on the bottom of the stack and stacked on these are the fresher kill, the birds your next wife plucked for you, bright mallards and drakes, their heads loose on their necks, their feathers carried off by the wind.

MY LOVER CALLED me *la flaca*, the skinny one.

I liked the smell of him, and his mighty arms. I like a little how easily he will accomplish nothing.

He had a scooter we rode around on on sand roads, through tiny towns. He rode me out to see a tribe of monkeys. One stole my necklace. One unlaced my shoes.

Those monkeys were the greedy kings of that town, the *pendejos*, the thugs. They chased dogs off. They stole wallets—stole mine—snatched anything loose.

"Why did you bring me here?" I asked him.

"To teach you to live, *mi flaca*, with nothing."

HE LIVED IN a lean-to of lashed-together palm fronds. The floor was sand. He had a bucket and a bed. He had a rag he dried my feet with. All night, I could hear the sea.

All night, certain nights, I knew he would kill me. He had strength he wasn't using.

He would scalp me, pretend to be me—my mind blasted clean, ecstatic, swinging my yellow hair.

HERE IS HOW Freddy went about it: he made a blow dart with straight pins and bamboo and climbed, wheezing, into the hayloft. By dinner, he was hivey, dripping, blotched. He couldn't eat for sneezing.

You've forgotten this. It wasn't so, you say. But, Papa, it was.

For hours Freddy lay in the hayloft waiting for the pigeons you hated, waiting for the kill. I liked to watch him. My brother was patient. I saw a snake go over his neck once. He was good at keeping still.

Freddy gave me his stuffed dog you hated—dingy and matted— old Snoopy dog. He gave it up to me for your birthday.

He didn't need it: he wasn't a kid anymore. He loved it foolishly. You were sure to take it from him; he took it from himself. The dog's big head flopped and caved in on itself: stuffing drifted out through its neck.

It smelled awful, my husband insisted, but to me it smelled like Freddy and the bed that Freddy slept in in the house where Freddy died. And so I kept it.

I KEEP THE satin bow I meant to give you.

I keep the shell Artemio gave me.

He gave me little; I asked little. He wanted money and I gave it to him. I gave him a shirt and shoes.

He has two shirts now and one flimsy bucket—to wash sand from the feet of his women he brings to his lean-to to bed.

NOTHING STOPS YOU. You hunt and fish and travel.

You are buried by an avalanche and your dead boy digs you out.

You keep moving, marry again, keep your hair, your pornography, it can't be easy but here you are. Come to visit. Come to see at last your grandbaby, a little man to carry on.

He is Freddy but not like Freddy—this one is loud and plump and strong. Not a quitter.

Don't be a quitter.

"Where's my mister?" you say.

"Where's my water?"

Sit tight: here it comes.

Here comes your boy to save you, digging in from above. You won't even need to thank him—only lie there. It is all you can do.

Bleed, and maybe he'll find you. Breathe. Except the heat from your breath melts the snow against your face. The snow freezes to ice. It makes a mask of ice. That's what kills you.

EXCEPT IT DOESN'T.

You live to be eighty. You could live to be a hundred and eighty, your grandchildren buried, your new wife dead, sitting in a wingback chair.

Carry on, is your counsel. *Don't be a quitter.*

You stashed food for a year in the basement of our house, taught us to divine for water, to forage for windfall apples under the ice and snow. You taught us the stars to go by and which snakes were safe to catch and how to gut and skin. How to read wind and cloud for weather. How to make an arrow true.

We needed toughening; you meant to toughen us.

We lit fires with flint how you taught us. Learned our roots and berries. We'd snare rabbits, shoot geese. We'd know mushrooms, cache food. Train a pigeon to carry messages to Mother.

MOTHER, WE LIVE *in a tree house now the phoebes are happy in. We have water. We know a cave very near and kill rabbits. There is plenty here to do.*

CHIPMUNKS EAT AT the walls of our house. A bear rubs its back against the clapboards: that's how it sounds. But that is only the arborvitae, Papa, pressed against the house by wind. Not to worry.

Of course you worry. You stop breathing in your sleep. You find your hand across your face. Your wife has to wake to wake you, so spent she falls out of her chair.

You wake gasping. Your mouth is grainy and dry. Your feet are such a long way from you, bleeding into the snow: not yours.

They are too old to be yours. You can't feel them.

Papa, sleep.

Let yourself rest. We'll have a party for you tomorrow, a nice meal. I'll spend the day in the kitchen.

Isabel wants to hang streamers for you and have a water slide and balloons. She wants cupcakes and rainbow sprinkles. All her bunnies can come.

WE WILL TAKE a walk when you wake.

I'll show you the fort my Isabel built with apples and yellow leaves. Our apples were sweet and wormy this year; all but the last have dropped from the trees. They lie in the grass, two tiny bites taken from them. Into two soft apples, Isabel pushed two sticks to stake her rabbit by. I'll have to show you. Her rabbit wears a collar like a cat. She gets him tied up, the apples at his sides, to watch her, *you have to watch me*, jumping rope in the sun on the church steps, singing jumping songs, singing *rabbit*.

FREDDY BROUGHT YOU a bird at a party once. He was blotchy and proud. "Here I got one, Papa."

"You dummy," you called him, it's true.

You held the bird by the neck to show the others, the silver pin still in its breast. Everybody had a good laugh at my brother: he'd killed a mourning dove, not a pigeon.

Freddy whacked that bird against the side of the barn until its insides were coming out.

Freddy killed every bird he could get to after that, didn't matter, every beetle and snake and rodent, and brought them to me as a cat does, and with him a stick to hit him with. Freddy wanted all the wrong things, I knew. I hit him. I did what he asked me. I hit him until we both felt better.

I HELPED HIM light a fire with his socks. Because he had lost his coat. This was later. You had bought him a new coat and he had lost it and we were afraid of what you would do.

So we lit a fire in Freddy's closet. We would say the coat was burned up in the fire. It wasn't Freddy's fault. His coat was hanging right where it was supposed to hang. There was a fire, we'd say. We were in the barn, we'd say. We didn't know the first thing about it.

HERE IS HOW Freddy went about it: he fed the ladder through the open window.

It never mattered to Freddy how hard a thing was once he had the idea.

He used the apple-picking ladder, tapered at the top for going up among the limbs and wider as you went down. He climbed a ladder with the ladder on his back—it would never have made the turn on the stairs.

I went up there to look for a bow for you for the gift I had gotten for your birthday. I wanted a yellow bow. I wanted paper with purple dots. I have no idea what I meant to give you only how I meant to wrap it.

There were paintings tacked to the rafters of that house that Freddy and I had painted: volcanoes the lava spat out of, a black and white smiling cow. He painted lightning, pyroclastic flow.

The sun blazed in the attic windows. Flies knocked against the glass, stupid in the cold that was coming. The cold made a fringe of ice on the pond and the last apples swung in the wind in the trees and rotted in the bent-over grass.

He had no shoes on. I thought: he has lost them.

His feet were red from the cold from coming through the grass to feed the apple-picking ladder through the window. He didn't care how hard. Freddy was stubborn. He had a feather in his hat. He lashed the ladder to his back to use his hands to climb—no way could he have made it up those stairs.

The geese were moving. The bears were drunk on apples.

The sun made buttery squares at that hour against the chimney where the ladder had fallen. Freddy kicked the ladder out when the time came. It had rained and his feet were muddy and the sun threw his shadow against the brick.

I stood under him. His foot crossed under his other foot like the feet of Christ in pictures. He sort of turned in the wind. I thought to hit him. I was wearing my pleated skirt.

I sat a long while at the window up there with Freddy at my back and looked out. A few apples hung in the trees still where the limbs were too weak to climb. The trees were young still. We had to go to our knees to mow under them.

That became my job, a boy's job. The sky heaped up behind me. The storms came in from the west in that house over the fruit-ful hills.

HEAR THAT?

My husband laughs in his sleep. He wakes himself up laughing. Otherwise you can forget he is here.

ONCE A COWBIRD flapped out of the chimney in your room. Its wing was broken. A cowboy bird, Freddy called it.

It's funny what you remember, funny what you forget.

Once a bear came and ate the bees—left the honey, ate the bees. Pulled the bird feeders down, drunk on windfall apples.

I GET OUT of bed with the baby and carry him across the room. He nearly glows, looking up at me, his face so plump and pale.

My husband has left his shoes in the middle of the room. It has been raining and his shoes are muddy.

He goes on laughing. The owl starts up in the orchard. The leather splits and the toes turn up. He doesn't sound like any man I know.

Count your blessings, Mother always said: he doesn't wake himself up screaming. He is a happy drunk; he dreams funny dreams; you can forget he is even here.

THAT OWL. WE have barn owls, horned owls, eagles. Owl is a funny word.

That's a barn owl, calling across the field. I leave our ladder stood up in the tree the owl likes and, nights I can't sleep, climb toward him. He holds himself very still.

If he has flown, I won't know, you can't hear them. I could knock right into him. Sometimes my knees give out. It is unnerving: to be seen so clearly by something you can scarcely see.

PACHEW, PACHEW, PACHEW, you said, and aimed your cane at my children.

FREDDY WAS BAREFOOT; his feet were muddy. One foot went over the other as if to stand in the air on himself.

After my brother died, a redtail attacked you. You were riding your spotted mare, who threw you. The hawk went after your eyes.

You had a redtail stuffed and the head of a moose. A turkey, a small bear. You had hooves of elk made into ashtrays with a skinny fringe of hide. You had a pair of geese hollowed out and stuffed, lifting off, friends for life. A gift to yourself on your birthday.

Your boy killed himself on your birthday. This is punishment enough for many lifetimes. For this, you don't need me.

I'LL MAKE A fresh cake. Corn pudding, how you like, and collards. I'll soak a ham. Maybe I'll polish your shoes the way I used to.

We'll sing a pleasing song—your wife and I, and Isabel. That's the trick: sing a pleasing song. Dress yourself up pretty.

Let me know what you hope for for your birthday, Papa, something small, a watch, a wallet. Soap on a rope—the old standby. A gleaming golden cane.

Only ask for it.

If there is anything you want—someone will get it for you.

My daughter will. Your wife will, or I will. Somebody always has.

MATRIMONIAL

DRIVING WEST TO BE MARRIED, YOU BROKE OUT IN hives. We blamed it on the shirt I had bought you—stiff, never washed. That night we ate rib eyes in a dusty arroyo and dug a hole in a cliff with a spoon. Lighted a fire to burn sage in. The hives reddened and spread. You couldn't sleep for itching. We gave up sleeping. I stood behind you. Together we made a shadow of one body, four arms, thrown against the cliff from the moon. Raptor. Two-headed worm. And went at each other until sunup: *What if, what if, what if?*

PUT ON YOUR CROWDED BODY

T IS HOT. IT IS HOT AND I CAN SCARCELY BREATHE AND you cannot quite see me. I am standing beneath the stairs in sunlight. It is afternoon. You have been gone a long time. Years, even. You could be my brother—you favor him. My lover. You favor him. Everything we did together we could have done together in a week. Instead I saw you by addition, by love unspent, by remembering somebody other. Of you I had little to remember—your mighty arms, the bird moving over the muscle. You smelled of wood, of feathers. For a moment now, the briefest glimpse. I stood beneath the stairs. Frightful.

WHAT BEGINS WITH BIRD

START THE BULBS IN THE WINDOW THE DAY SHE FLIES IN from Mississippi. I stand them up in the bowls of gravel I scraped with a spoon from the driveway—hours ago, when the ground still showed. Now the yard is a blank of snow. The crocuses are buried and broken.

The bulbs have gone spongy or peeling and split from sitting in paper sacks too long. I should have planted them in October, picked a hole in the pebbly ground. But back then I had things to do yet, things I could do, and I can't now. So I force hyacinth on the sill.

I sit among the brocade chairs and wait for the smallest changes: his lazy eye to open, a sound at the name in my mouth. We have named the boy after the city we succumbed to marriage in, in a storm as freaky as this one: wind from the north for Easter, our sky a pink velour. Our trees are as black as shadows of trees, pressed flat in this light and moaning.

Reno, Reno, Reno—without thinking, when we thought of his name, what a trial they are, those Rs. *Weno*, we know. But we didn't know it then.

My sister will call the boy something else, no doubt, as soon as she has seen him, not sweet pea, nor pumpkin (I do), but by her weekly sweetheart's name, or somebody lost or dead. They die off early, turn up their toes in babbling sleep, down where my sister lives. She will arrive with photographs, mangled faces, folded into her pockets.

Or it could be the snow has stopped her, turned her back for home. We call it that, all of us: home: it is a family habit, this turning away, a lie we began her lifetime ago, gathered over her, immobile: a lump, for months, in her crib.

My sister lives in an institution. The place is built in the dusky bottomland of the Mississippi River, among stands of trifling hardwoods overrun by the South's Great Vine. Even in winter the trees bow their heads to that gray roving appetite, a great hunger—acres consumed by the pestilence of kudzu.

Nothing grows as quickly here. The ivy is slow and civil. Our trees bend their heads for hours, a week, then toss off their burdens of snow. This can't last. A day of melt and the goose will be back to jab at the grassy patches.

Only the rabbit, in the surprise of cold, keeps to her routine: brazen creature, fixed as stone at the foot of the leaky birdbath. Frost has split the concrete bowl, parted the fluted column. These rotten New England winters. But everything else is calm: our one raccoon, the fat goose in our yard most mornings.

I tap at the glass. Not a flutter. Even the rabbit won't scare. She will keep to her place at the birdbath while night comes and day again, waiting—who can say for what? Instructions, I suppose, a murmur, a nudge, from her sack of eggs.

Small as he is my boy trumpets, stiffens his back a little. These are *my* instructions. But there is nothing I know to do for him, nothing to do but cluck and drift and wait here for my sister. We pass such liquid, unmoored days, no sleep, and only outside the seeping beech, the rising snow to mark time by.

Love, love. I want nothing.

My boy draws up again inside me, nights, small body rocked shut, sweet thrill—to feel him pitch and tumble. The sea at night is yellow cream, a tongue from the waking shore.

Too soon—to be asked to speak, to rise and walk. They are slow, my tribe, by habit, to come (it is a birth, after all, not a funeral)—but even so this is too soon for me. I am still jerking awake at night and dressing for the hospital: the chalky, sudden sky, the gray road, salted, gritty, slush hissing from our wheels.

Still bleeding, the stuff dropping from me in great gobs.

I say none of this. What use? We are found out. There is no saying no to my sister. I hear her grinding her teeth over the phone, heels dug in, and her father, ours, our father has bought her the ticket to come. So we ready. I start the bulbs in the window—something more to watch for; I buy wrapped chocolate eggs. My turn—it has been decided, and there is no getting loose from my father, either, even from afar.

He calls ahead to say to me, "They say she's been funny lately."

"Funny?"

"I don't know."

We move on to weather because this is also our habit; I am given the nationwide report before he asks about my son.

"Our Mr. Sun," I say, when he has embellished the heat in the Middle West with stories of rotting bodies, the elderly done in by stroke in the tenements of Chicago. This is when he seems to remember—that he ought to ask, to have already asked. We are both quiet, quietly breathing, and then my father plunges ahead.

"So how's the baby? Baby okay?" he says.

"Yes, yes—" he must be, though I wake him as so many mothers do to be certain he is still breathing. He grins in his sleep—these are dreams, I say, and startles. An arm flaps up. The lid of one eye heaves open.

Dear lump. I could round his pointy head, work the flat patch where he sleeps on it, the notched resilient plates, the bone still spongy as the bulbs I found to force in the gloom this morning. But I don't; it won't last; I leave him be.

I leave the plastic band on his wrist where Nurse Jane wrote my name—how strange, that you cannot at first even pick out your own from all the other babies. Mine has eleven dimples—dimples instead of knuckles and one on each side of his nose; in the fat of his leg is a pucker the color of pencil lead, a stitch drawn deep and tightly and tied off at the bone.

I knew him in the dark this way. I felt for the stitch in the dark of my room where the big windows looked at the Merrimack, the viscid fenced canal; I watched school children pasting up paper eggs and tousling in the hall and, once, one boy swung his lace-ups up to catch in the branch of a tree. They dropped, and the other boys spat and hooted. I kept it dark inside in my room for him so that when they brought him to me, I knew him by his smell. He smelled of lanolin, clean and old and animal and bitter to me then and now and I knew him then as I do now by the feel of the stitch in his leg, not a stitch, nothing that will heal.

There is this, and the plastic band I will leave on his wrist until Sister has come and gone, my name, we had not named him yet, and there are too the ways in me to say as I do *mine*:

The cut in me, seeping still, the grinning stapled mouth: proof that he has been here, proof that he is gone. Here is where they found him, red and bawling, lifted him plumply out.

My belly skin a lizard's, shrunk to shimmering and scale.

And here—this dimming streak, gray as ash, that marks me thatch to sternum; this line drawn through my navel that darkened as we grew. We grew, we grew.

I WOULD HAVE carried him in me for years.

And yet here in my face is the vessel I burst trying to push him out. Too late—by then he had already outgrown me, grown into me, a leggy, dogged stalk of boy left to bolt to seed. He left in my forehead the fine mesh of roots that living things send out, the paths, the swerving abruptions of blood, the friable clump in the floor of a pot, as though I had needed first, to birth him, to tear him from my brain.

I do not try to hide it. I obscure no proof, no possible claim.

I am claimed in the old animal way—the tails of my shirts, my thick brassieres, hair and neck and cupping ear: give him air and the spigot is on. All's well. All the lights green for Reno, his penis a plump blue cone. I roll it in its sheath between my fingers, gap the bloody pinprick he pisses on me through.

And if he pisses on Sister? She will *skrauk* like a crow and giggle, wince, and I will be near, watching over, looking out for her as I used to do, as I look out for snow that slides from a roof, and listen—for the strained-rope sound a branch will make before it tears from the head of a tree.

Who could trust her?

I am watchful these new days anyway of anything that moves—small dogs, a fat goose, his own father.

And my sister is always moving, even when she means to sit, or we are, one of us, the rest of us since Mother, we are moving her around. Giving her instructions, keeping her out of the way.

She has a way of making her absence felt. You know better—you should not have let her go. But she is bored, nervous, sullen. She grows weary, quickly, of family, needs somebody new to love. She comes to you for a visit and next you know she has disappeared. It is a monsoon, or a blizzard; you have made your nest in the desert, earthquakes coming, or it is the year of the romance of slums. Scarcely matters. She will wander out into anything, take up with anyone, drift off with the nearest miscreant to look at his tattoos.

I am like her in this; I move away. Even an infant finds safety in motion.

I never settled for years long enough for my father to send her to me, to track me down with news. But he is a good tracker.

Give him time, he finds you, elated some: some twister gouged the riverbanks, floods in Tennessee. The dying bees all summer. All preamble, priming, the news delivered first that you can do nothing about. And then, *your sister*—calling her not by name of course but by title, binding clause. The slippery possessive. *Your sister.*

My daughter. Under what condition does he call her that—her, I think, or me?

It used to be we tracked down a new place for her every few months, every year. Our father's house, the YMCA—disastrous. Some school near here in Boston that packed her off in a blink to the loony bin. A problem of climate, my father decided. These dreary New England winters. The desert was next, saguaros and sun, the sobriety of a mineral landscape. She burned down her apartment, dropped a lighted cigarette into a heap of dirty laundry. That was Phoenix, and she was pregnant, a condition nobody noticed until she was six months along. Then the family engaged, oh, oh—moved in for the crisis. We are a family that loves a good crisis. Birth control? I'd have thought that you . . .

None of us had bothered.

Our father found me, enlisted me; it was a time in my life he could find me, when he could *call in the troops*, as he said. He flew me out to Phoenix first to see if I could persuade her. My father knew of a clinic not far from him, convenient to him, in Atlanta. I was to fly her back over the country to him, to the house we left our boxes in, in the town we had once called home. He had his

TripTiks in order. He had his prim new wife. He had mapped out places to show to his wife on the drive to the clinic in Atlanta.

On the flight west I had my soothing, brief heroic moment, or the thought of one, the big idea. Nothing lasts with me. But for a moment I thought I would take her in, be her good big sister— quick, quick, before Daddy comes. Six months. By then a baby is swallowing; it is opening and closing its eyes. It had begun to hear, to know her voice. It must have turned toward the light as mine did, as I felt him face the sun.

ANY LIGHT, EVEN this gray gloaming, my boy turns his head to see, though he still sees nearly nothing, no distance, mostly only we keepers, mostly only me.

She stays put now, my sister; the grounds are fenced and gated.

Another bellow—raspy and prolonged. I am beginning to know the difference—between hunger, say, and fear. I lift him to me. I am dripping milk. His mouth opens quick as a bird's.

My breasts are stiff, prickly, lumped. He is rooting, and then uprooting me—that's what it feels like. I feel the tug in the wing of my shoulder and in the ball and socket; he is drawing my ribs together, cinching the narrowing slots; he is dragging silt from my bones.

All's well. Night soon. Above us, the snow ticks down. No distance. No lapsed horizon bleeding pink beyond the flattened trees.

Little raccoon, funny monkey. He drinks and drinks and dozes. Yawns, and the trough in his wrinkled palate shows, slender and deep for sucking. A blister fills on his lip again, the skin of his first mouth already shed, the pale strips frayed and loosened.

Our rabbit flickers her ear. A squirrel drops out of the gingko tree at the far gray rim of our yard. Everything in its place; a place for everything. A patch of dirt for the sickly elm, a barn for broken china, rake and nail and rusting plow, a crib he will soon grow into.

IT IS ALL always too soon for me, the crib in the wings, the coming melt, the year's slow resurrection. The steadfast family wagon— my sister fetched from the airport—yawing into the drive.

I lay the boy down in his wicker tub and wheel him away from the door, from the surge of cold when it opens and damp and the squalling of crows in the heads of the trees and the plows groaning out on the highway.

Ready? I think. *Ready?* Because it has already begun.

My sister is out of the car and running at us before George even opens his door, all teeth and arms and flagging hair, a sidelong lurch and stutter. It is motion, the infant's comfort, mine, which gives her away. When she stops in the doorway and holds out her hands, waiting for me to come to her, nothing seems so wrong. She is pretty, and she has mastered the phony, square-bottomed smile taught in better homes: clean gums, corrected rows of teeth.

I move to her to see what I already know, cannot—would not— keep from seeing: the tremor, the scars, her bitten lip, the puddles of shadow around her eyes.

She stamps the snow from her sandals, standing wobbling in the doorway, the cold still streaming in. She hugs me, knocks against my chest. It always feels to me that her heart runs rough, won't idle, wants to race and quit; it is worse every time I see her and tells more clearly what is to come. They come mildly even now to me: days I cannot stop shaking. Another family habit—inherited, her tremor, worse with age (what isn't?) among the women in our tribe.

She keeps holding me so I stand there, stroking her hair, feeling her shudder against me. The first hour or two is an act with us, as with the early weeks of love. Easy enough, early on, to be sweeter than you are, to keep your few good secrets. But give a girl time, weather, meals. Quit closing the shithouse door. Pretty soon, this is me, I am chewing my tongue just to sit in the kitchen and listen to her, to the squalor of her feeding.

Those shoes—skinny, strappy things—and the snow some inches deep by now and she has left our George out in it, please, to gather up her bags. "It's like cream of wheat," she says, too loudly, "mercy."

It is a game they two have been playing, I guess, passing the time from the airport.

"It's like walking through frozen beer—" that's George's, and he laughs, and water pools as he walks in his footsteps and slops across the porch. He tips his hat.

"Hello, rabbit." He kisses me. "Hello, mother. Made it."

The trick must be in knowing who to be afraid of, what.

Our spotted dog, pent up, neglected, pokes her nose around the corner, suffers a paroxysm of joy—somebody fresh to love.

"So how is it in Mississippi?" I ask.

"Nice. Very nice. Flowers and such. But cold at night. Mercy."

She shakes the wet from her head, teasing, at the dog who quivers and blinks at her feet.

"So where is he? Where's that baby?" She throws her hair back. "C'mere, young'n. Come here."

SOMEBODY FRESH TO love; somebody new to harvest.

I am watchful, and sick in my heart to see the boy calmed in even his father's arms. What use, to see it coming? Bed down one yellow afternoon when the tide is in your favor and you begin the long moving away. Months pass; joints soften, slip; veins give, the blood in you doubles and quickens.

And yet this was not the feel of it—not of quickening, not to me, but of paths begun to silt and pinch, to slow, and, slowing, close. My neck swelled; my lungs rode up.

I fell into myself calmly, besotted and sufficient.

I was sufficient and am no longer, will not be again. Any mother knows.

The body remembers, seems to insist—there was something it meant to do—to lose him, to birth him. To finish what it had begun.

I wake, and find the boy beside me in the ripening bed, my bed, I keep him near me, the nightlight on, the barn beyond the window gone tossing out to sea. I drag the sheets back. His eyes are sprung open. His skin is twisted on him, rubbery and slick. He is not mine, is not the real baby. There is one yet still to be born.

There is everything still to go through again—my belly a stained translucence, the doctors in their starched blues.

Stupid, I know, to think it, want it. But even now, these weeks gone past, the small hard snaps of milk in his chest—witch's milk—dissolved; his lazy eye, the slackened lid, begun to draw up and quicken, so soon: I would go through it all all over again: the idiot howling, blood sliding from me in hot strings. Hours of this and then nothing, the needle pressed into the spine. The limp pale drape someone hung at my chest to keep me from seeing.

His little face had tipped up, watchful.

Somebody whistled somewhere in the greenish bright and quiet and someone was asking, *Ready? They've already begun.*

I felt nothing but that they moved me, crudely, my sloppy haunch, hardly mine—the drape seemed to hang to mark the place where my body detached at the sockets.

I listened: this was his being born.

This was the sound of a hand wedged in, and then the small bent head popped free, quick as a tooth you are losing. This that I felt backed into my throat was the body shoved into the cage of my ribs, brief, and how surprising: the rest had seemed so distant: a ditch cut into a distant slab, spongy and geologic, marsh, a bowl of softened bone. Then the baby, the bawling sight of him; then the staples driven in.

NOTHING LASTS, BUT nothing is finished, either. The brain boils and cools, same as many things, heals with the slickness of scars. Nothing's lost; no grief, unspoken, forgotten.

Yet we hold our tongues. Not a word, these years, about it. Hardly a word between us, even then, my sister and me, the very

day, those hours, the long before and after in the back seat to
Atlanta, after Phoenix, Daddy driving, after Mother, I think it
pleased him, the look of it, his girls, his new wife neatly beside him.
He wanted to stop and look at things: Chickamauga, Antietam, the
cannons in a row.

Of course I think of it—how it must have been for Sister, closing in on Atlanta. In the morning, plain tea. The righteous out in
the early heat, their foetuses wrinkling in jars. Our father moved to
her to take her arm to steady her along. She seemed to straighten:
he had noticed her being brave. Had she seen the fluted columns,
he wanted to know, the Corinthian scrolling above? She looked up,
we all did, and listened, he spoke so little, and spoke of Sherman
that day as though they were friends, as though we had him to
thank for it, my father, that the building still stood, Georgian and
grandly columned, spared—handsome, I remember thinking it
then, he was as handsome as when we were girls.

We needed so little from him. To be spoken to, to be steadied,
that was extra, that was gravy. Because here already was bounty, I
thought, her own crisis, here was her chance to be Daddy's, to be
brave, to be seen being brave, being ready.

Here was her act of love.

The worse the march the better. The righteous who strained
at the roped-off yard, rattled their jars, a child on a hip, how
lucky—something more to endure. Half a year's neglect endured,
the wiggy pitching months of it, and now, this late, late as it was,
the danger, the night's long labor ahead. The toddlers in the leggy
grass, writhing, moaning, *Mommy.*

The day a blaze, the early heat. The bodies yawing sweetly in their lettered jars.

They did not hurry. They were solemn, the two of them, processional: a girl on her father's arm. There was something of a lilt and quickening, something graceful—vaguely—supple, fierce, something punitive and bridal in the way she moved to the door.

She had worn her heels, our mother's pearls. She had worn the dress our mother used to dress for parties in.

I held my tongue; this much was easy. I began for a time to feel it, too, a queer sort of pride in myself: I had gone to Phoenix and fetched her home and here we all were with him, quietly, soberly walking. To what, walking to what, it seemed all at once not to matter. What mattered was that we were doing as our father asked. He made it easy, provided; he gave us our instructions.

I FLEW OUT. The desert bloomed. I was to fetch her home.

I withheld him, the threat of him, the name in my mouth, to try her. But nothing else I could think of in the days I spent in Phoenix, not love—I trotted out every homily I had heard of the family romance, sacrifice, devotion, the kindness of a kindhearted man (my mouth: I was moving between lovers, snorting junk in the sumac behind the corner store)—her own unreadiness, it did not move her, and not the ghoulish stories I knew of babies grown in wrong—the ones who lasted, babblers, maimed, stood up, shipped out to Mississippi.

MY GOD, THE lavishness of her Mississippi. Any outrage I could think to relate was an insult, a pittance against it. But I did not know so then. Mississippi was years to come—bodies dropping in the viny woods, *hula hula*, somebody new: a curdling, lunatic glee. We held our ground, the field in bloom, the gate swung shut behind us.

A gate swings shut behind you, going in, if you go, coming out.

They came to us over the open field, toothy, threnodic, multiplying as they moved.

"THE BABY'S FINE," she said. "It's going to be fine."

I said, "That baby grows in you."

We roomed for days in a motel in Phoenix, a dry wind scratching the door.

I said, "I was in the airport. I was on my way here to you."

It was something I had heard in the Ladies', talk of the boy, women tipping toward the mirror to slide their lipstick on. I said I had seen the boy, coming to her, his hand in his mother's skirt, a blinker of flesh hung over one eye, eyebrow to nose, the skin crusted and thick and frilled. I went on, I could feel my voice rising—his eye yellow in its socket, wild, what I saw of it, who saw nothing, and the flap as brown as potato, gouged, stiff hair hatching from it.

None of this moved her at all. We drew the curtains, hardly spoke, and watched daytime TV. When the day came for us to leave Phoenix, I said what I had been saving to say, to have it on me, to feel that I had convinced her. It was easy.

"Daddy's on his way."

DADDY HELD HER arm, to guide her, to keep her on course for the door. Sister reached behind her back and fluttered out her hand and I—I think it must have surprised me: that she had thought to reach for me, and then that she had not. I took her hand. She drew me up from behind her to walk along up the walk with them, on Sister's arm, Sister on our father's arm, the new wife trailing behind us. I had not heard her. I had not likely listened. I was hearing, I think, the rest of them—the fathers, daughters, churchly men, the sisters hissing scripture, a vast unholy throng.

I saw her face then: I saw our mother's. I saw her face in the face of another mother gone to her knees in the uncut grass with her baby hugged against her chest in the litter of all they had brought there.

They had labeled the months, the stations: Here is your baby at three months, here is your baby at four months, here is your baby at five.

They were reaching in under the rope strung up to keep them off my sister, to keep them away from me. They were snatching at the hem of our mother's dress. I kicked at their arms, their faces.

"Mother—" she said it loudly, and let my hand go.

I thought she had meant it: Mother.

I heard Sister all along, I know, walking along: "Mother." But I had not thought of it. This is how I came to think of it—it made it easy, easier for me: we were sending her baby to Mother. There were not enough babies among the dead for all the mothers to mother.

Sister turned from me; she fluttered her hand behind her back, teetering on her heels.

They bent their heads; they were kneeling, rocking on their knees. I thought maybe they meant to drink from the jars, maybe they meant to sing.

I thought, going on—I knew better: I understood it, the news of it, the reason they had come—but then I thought they had come in need to her; they had come to her to be tended to—it was stupid—to be answered—I knew I was being stupid—to be dropped to their knees and saved.

I saw they had saved out a jar for her.

She began to throw them coins.

"One more."

She touched a forehead. She tossed away a ring she liked. She kissed a boy they offered.

"One more baby more," they said.

I saw her knees give; she was turned from me. She was reaching for the new wife's hand, calling the new wife: "Mother."

And this surprised me. It was nothing, it was the way of things.

I fell behind some. If it had been me. She tried to lie down. I might have let her.

She was to let them cut it out of her, the easy way, who can say now, what she thought of it, what I had brought her back over the country to do, what Sister thought she was meant to be doing?

He got her moving. Daddy was gentle. I could see Daddy meant to be gentle. He had her by her hair. He hauled her up some. He had her by the braid his tidy wife had made of the mess of Sister's hair to keep our Sister nice that day, to keep our Sister tidy.

You think it's easy?

The way she tries you. The way she—listen. You think it's easy? You think she means to make it easy?

Sister, Mother, holy Joe. To be our father? To keep her moving, swung to her feet and gone?

MY GUESS IS they gave her Pitocin, a drip, same as what they gave me. They give you your fishnet panties. Then they send you to wander the halls in your socks until the contractions begin.

There are other mothers out there: it's insulting: that it is not only you. But it must have calmed my sister—to have somebody new to talk to, to lap the nurses' station with.

In time, I talked, too. Stood in the gaggle in the yellow glare rubbing the drum of my belly. Not because I thought I had to (talk)—decorum, no, nicety, not then, not yet again. This was our blessed respite. Nothing decorous about it. Only lassitude, rapture, a flaunted animal pleasure. I'll go on, I went on, I have never been quite so sweet on myself, and talky, in time, and shameless—avid, giddy, apart. I might have told anyone anything. I think talking made me hope to prolong it, stop it, hedge some way—I wasn't afraid, much—the table, the curtain drawn, not even the room, the stirrups, the blank chill of the day outside, none of this really shook me—not the pain, quite, the prospect of pain: I thought,

Come on, come on: What is the pleasure of what does not cost you, hurt you?—no, the room, I think, thrilled me, the wide belts, the tools, the dim medieval look of it.

When he was in me—that was when he was easiest to love.

They let me blather on, the others. We all of us mothers did. We scrutinized, amazed ourselves, the hearts we grew, the milk, the bone, the ax to wield; the father, yes, come in, do, gently— there—helpless there, supremely: remote, absurd, refined. Our faces swelled, our eyes withdrew; we spoke our old lost tongues. This of course was later; this was the fabled room. We were lucid at our station, patient in the yellow glare, divulging in our mea-sured tones the blanching gape of cervix, vying some, even then, predatory, preying, somebody's sticky plug spit out, somebody's bloody show.

Had your bloody show, dear?

Yes, yes—then nothing. Instructions. Nurses, nurses, somebody always grinning from the corner of my room.

I lost hours; they might be years. The grasses sang. The river-banks shrilled and buckled. I know I wandered. I saw a white horse burning. I saw my mother sleeping in the bend of a yellow road.

Pieces missing, syllables. The living thinned to shadow, droned, busy at my knees. At what?

But who could know?

Even now I worry George to recall to me the day's events; I want orderliness, a story, the discrete before and after.

And after, before the room, the wide window over the Merrimack, dark then, the coming dawn, before they brought him to me—these are the questions that flare in me, petty, absurd—I had not seen him but to see him, plump and bawling, thrashing in the sick light and in whose scoured arms? Who is it who went off with him? What surly, immigrant nurse, mistaken for a mother, bathed him, while I in my decorum lay in the cool with the curtains drawn chatting with the postmaster's wife?

What difference? And yet I think of it.

Ought to think instead of Sister, yes, be a good big sister. Easter in the morning. Ought to bundle up in the morning, stash my boiled eggs. It being Easter. Since she is my sister.

Sit her down—she claps at me—show her how to hold him, show her what to do.

Her own, she could have held—a guess—in an open hand, small as that, if she wanted, if she was lucky, if the nurses were on their rounds.

Of course I think of it.

I hardly think of it—except that she is here.

I think of us in the blaze of heat and of the room where we waited, the chairs we took, side by side, the row of scaly bucket seats bolted to the wall. We tipped our heads back. People do—and there were years of people before us, drooping in those chairs. How lucky: a single salient detail: the plaster worn smooth behind us, stained: years of hair, the press of heads, oily, elongated patches. We were resting, had been, those of us who came to help, to fill out papers, if help was how you thought of it, who waited there, dozing, until we were certain the job was done.

It was done—this is as much as I know or want to. Do not know or ask so much as even was she on the potty, the sheeted bed, the floor? Was it dead or living? Did she have a look at it? I would think you would have to look at it—see was it a boy, a girl, have a name to call it by, count its fingers, toes. Or maybe this is me. Or maybe I don't know. But I think I would want something from it—a thumb tip, a twist of cord, we keepers, not to have nothing at all from it, anything small to show.

She turns her palms up. Supple as he is and weak—what harm? And yet she is my sister. And yet she is my sister.

And there is the favored wingback, stout of arm, of wing, of foot. I pass him to her. "Watch his neck."

"I know, I know, I know."

HICKORY, GINGKO, WILLOW, elm.

Sweetpea, wicker, junior mint. Little man, I call him, honcho, buster, sugar boy. Almost never Reno, sometimes kid Reno, buckareno, buckaroo. She calls him Binny.

Heeey, Binny. It's your Aunt Kathleen.

The bird dog she calls Honey Gal and, before long—because much of the time we call her Snoot, for her snoot—my sister calls her Snout. This gets us laughing, George and me, helplessly, until we are falling out of our chairs.

"NOSE," SHE SAYS, and touches his nose. "Ears. Cheeks. Chin. What's this?"

She spreads her hand on the crown of his head and gives it a turn to show me. "Look."

But it is only the scabbing rash he has had, yellowish and common, thriving between where his eyebrows will be. "And this, what's this?" on the slope of his nose, the puggish end, the hard pale knots of acne. "Uunh."

She lets his head tip back and fingers his neck and it is in my mouth to stop her but I am thinking I understand it, suppose I do—the hope of finding a flaw in him, some lasting crimson blemish. Even a terrible wrongness, I think—it is not such a stretch to think of it: she is hoping to find her mark on him, evidence of kinship, even if, or especially if, it is the kinship of the maimed.

I stoop over her, look to see what she sees: there is vernix still, I have missed it, gray and ripe and gummy, lumping up in the folds of skin. My sister draws her finger along a crease and the baby squawks and gags. "That's enough."

Too much for me already.

I gather him up. Remember to kiss her. I remember the place at the bend in her arm Mother used to rub before Sister slept, to help her sleep, and I touch it.

"Love you great big," I remember.

Then make my slow way to bed.

MY BED IS the bed for winter. I sleep where it is warm.

I wake backed away to the foot of the bed, our boy grunting and snuffling against me. Else I cannot find him—he has pushed off from me in his sleep as I sleep: he has crept into the cold with George.

George sleeps out in the summer room where we used to sleep before the boy, in the wind and sun, in the trees we liked, the sickly elm, the willow, the branches bent to shade the barn we keep our boy's things in. He runs the fan for quiet. He makes a tent as boys do of his blankets to read by flashlight in.

Three long walls are windows. He wakes in the cold and trees.

Nights I wake to find George here should he come to me from the summer room, the room the late-summer gold of corn the afternoon our planets crossed, the day I made my harvest. The baby is between us, or I have laid him briefly, near, in the wicker bin beside my bed.

I reach in sleep for him: I reach for the baby. I pet his face, his tender belly. He pulls me to him. I feel his penis stirring softly in its patch of hair.

Boy, my boy.

But what years I have slept. He is weathered. He is bony, bearded, grown.

THEY TOOK HIM off from me, to keep him safe from me, early on, while I drifted.

I came as I drifted to a dazzling sow, a slot chinked in her back for coins. In my back were names I'd forgotten, welted loops and straightaways I could make out with my hand: PRIM SUE, PEPPER, GLORY: the animals when I was a girl.

I'm a dwirl, I'm a dwirl: my boy scamps through the house—in a heartbeat, shall, the brief day gone. *Sthla, sthla, mbla*, he learns, and swings to his feet in the crib.

I had them roll me in my bed against the window: *let me drift.* I went willingly, unafraid of the cold, my hospital gown with the stamped-down name lapping against my back. The river whinged and gurgled. I skirted the ice at its weedy bank, a selvage poorly sewn.

The baby kicked in me. He would throw his foot through the cut in me, flail through the ragged mouth.

And then? And then?

Instructions. My father in velveteen robes. Presiding, intent on a girlish descant: how to love and hold your tongue. Above him— no cloud, not a tree for shade—I watched my life, a plains bird, circling. *Hello down there. Hello.*

My boy appeared on the riverbank. A dull kite snapped in the trees.

The sow would make her way out through the thicket, I knew, a pig-pretty face, glistening, and drag up the stairs on her hooves. It was the way of things, the way they come at you, I heard the coins tinkling in her belly. She would come at me with her snout.

WE STOLE THE bedsheets, a towel, the hospital gown, anything marked we could carry. The fishnet panties, they gave us, and Q-tips to dab his umbilical with, and the bottle with its hooked spout.

We waited the month and then some and by and by George came to me from the summer room in his slippers. He lay the baby in the bin beside the bed. I felt him push at me. He was eating his way back into me. The old story. You want to creep back, creep back, feed at the spangled shore. My stomach fisted. Seized, contracted. I breathed, a pant: the huffing the nurses teach you. The body going on. He kept on, the good George, so patient, so brave, I felt his brain beat in my knees. I felt him tire. I held him to me, the baby crowning, folding apart on his tongue.

SHE CAME ON, the sow, she blapped through the door, rearing. She was tall as a man and grotesquely smooth. Her breasts were a pinkish girl's.

I lit into her with my umbrella; I beat her about the head. I was blazing, vile, a blinded heat. Still she charged, charged again, rutted at me with her snout.

It took hours of beating to kill her and when I had killed her I hauled her out and threw the bolt on the door.

Still she lived. She clawed at the door and simpered. *A cigarette, dear*: her last request, her voice a child's. I softened. I crept the door open.

The sow was swaddled in cellophane and wearing a bridal gown. Her eyes were sockets, sooty, gone—the soupy mass flushed out. Her breasts were lumped and spitting milk. She would never die. She would die at my door forever; she would wait me out.

WE ROCK FOR a time and I lie with my boy and listen to the talk downstairs. The good George. Sister telling of her weekly sweetheart; she has had a belt tooled with his name. And what, George asks, do the two of them like to do?

"Goof around. Eat popcorn. Listen to music," Sister says.

One day, she says, they will marry. They will have a big house and a horse in the barn and their children will learn to ride early. And dogs, oh, they will have lots of dogs, and too many cats to count or name, and geese and such, and heaps of corn, and her children—mercy, let them, fine, she isn't going to fuss at them if they want to play tag in the garden.

She has brought me two spores of kudzu to force in the windowlight through the trees. "From home," Sister says, morning then, the coming melt, *hooome*—a drawl, a diphthong, our lie. A little something, a little green in our house when the cold has come—from the heart of Mississippi.

Seeping, cloistered bottomland. The spores loosen. Look—they are dropping through the trees.

You would have to burn down the delta to stop it.

And do what—to stop our Sister?

She makes her way in with a sickle, hacking at the matted vine. The spores shake loose—a sack of eggs, a thickish rind, a warty bulb that roots, divides, in the loam where it touches down. They find Sister fallen to sleep in it—in the broad, sweet leaves, the ghosting, the heads of the trees grown over, grown into, disappeared.

Hearsay from Mississippi. We make our few brief visits.

I swear and swear to do better, and Daddy does, and Daddy's wife, and doesn't Sister have her vocation meantime, her piece work they give her to do—bagging dirt, sorting screws, packaging tobacco? Tasks for the able of body and mind, for the residents who stir from their chairs.

The boy I remember best doesn't. "He's gone by—" this is how Sister will say it when I ask. "He went on by last week."

He is spindly, pretty, his mouth licked clean, a boy grafted to a shabby chair. He sings, and drives and drives a Matchbox car across snapshots of his family.

HONK AND THE gate glides open. A pond, a rolling green. A hatching of beds for flowers, the crepe myrtle in bloom.

And then they come at you, falling out of the trees for you—flapping arms and twisted, torpid, ruinous mouths.

They flopped themselves onto the hood of my car, shrieking, pleased, *hula hula*—somebody new, some mother, hawker, hapless holy Joe.

Some stingy sister. I sat at the wheel with my head in a vice while they battered and stroked the windows, my boy not even in me yet, my belly flat and still. And still it seemed to look at them would spread their sickness to me, saddle me with mother-dreams: ears knuckled stubbornly in the column of a boy's limp neck; hands like melted plastic, paws, paws, repeaters, spit swinging from their mouths.

YES, YES, WE will visit. Make our slow way down.

How better to feel lucky? To list my missed afflictions, his: no blighted limb nor burgeoned lobe, no purple stain: to gloat?

And yet I must know better. Things take their time to show.

Baby okay? Baby okay?

Just ducky.

I HEAR THE piggledy snoot in the loam. Then sleep—in the shallows, in the grievous sweetness of milk on his breath.

Before long they will mount the stairs, George in his boiled slippers, Sister hauling the dog. "Hey! What do you think you are doing, huh? Quit that. Gooood. Hey."

George is trying, gently, to hush her. It is like trying to hush the wind. "What did I just say to you? You stay. There. Hey. YOU. COME. RIGHT. HERE."

The baby stirs, and paws against me.

Outside: a growth of fog, a glaze of sleet on the windows.

I sleep again, pretend to, when George eases open the door. I watch him undress in the windows, fast, in the cold of the summer room—a boy with his flashlight burning, diving for his bed.

I go bed to bed, boy to boy, as I wish to, as I must.

BABY SWEET, SWEET night. Something nibbles, drags its tail through the walls.

They will come to me—days I cannot stop shaking. Burgundy at noon. He is toddling, too young for school, strapped into his seat in the car. *I hate you, Mama. My heart hates you.* I am driving. To keep him safe from me. Keep him safe from harm.

Sister turns in her bed, the dog nested.

The animals asleep in the barn. Used to be.

Used to be I whinnied. I was a girl who whinnied. Slept out in the field with the broodmares, springtime, foaling time, a stick at my side should the coyotes show, longing for the night's heroics.

Sister asleep and walking, used to be, water for the rabbits, a pot to scrub, the garbage dragged to the barrel where we burned. Her shoes buried. A stash of food beneath the bed.

My bonnie. My bonnie lies over.

We had a music box for our necklaces. A ballerina beneath the lid. Little cake top, little throwaway, mesmeric, smooth and pink and poorly made. Little glory. A life's beguilements. She sprang up before the mirror—endlessly, shamelessly spinning.

IF YOU WAKE her, you wake her screaming. Something you ought to know.

MONTHS PASS, WHOLE seasons pass, my boy caught, clasped to the bed, a clock hand, he turns, searching for me, his mouth pulsing—in the watery murk of a car swung past, the slow sweep, a dappled shade, the great leviathans circling.

Sister is singing, a few odd hollow wavering notes, out on the glistening shore.

I draw the bedsheets back. It is winter yet, I can hear them: the small, furred bodies in the walls.

The wind has risen. Ice crazes in the trees.

I find Sister down the hall in the bathtub, in a dusky wash of grime and blood, sudsing with the dog. She has got the candles burning. The dog whimpers when I open the door.

"Just checking," I say.

Well and good. Good enough.

"Good night, then," I say.

"I'm just washing her. She likes it," Sister says.

"Yes."

"She likes it. See?"

"Well, good night," I say.

"Where is Messpot?"

She calls him Messpot. Young'n. Binny. *See? I am right here.*

I see she has ground out her cigarette on the iridescent rim of our tub.

"He's asleep," I say.

"Like a baby. I gave him a soft good-bye."

The dog lunges, "HEY," tries to. Sister hauls her down by the collar, water slopping onto the floor.

"It's late," I say. "I'm tired."

"So you won't sit with me."

"No."

"I thought maybe."

Might have, yes, maybe—in the humming, the distant ward, might have brushed her hair, mothered her, a girl without a mother, laboring in a tub.

I swing the door shut.

SHE TRIED TO lie down. Daddy had her by her hair.

He had her things heaped up in the room Sister claimed in his house by the time we reached there. I was to clear her out, drive her south to Mississippi—withered fields, the cotton picked, the river dropped and chalky. *Home.*

I packed Sister's figurines for her, the pale little porcelain boxes she kept, the dingy china dolls, amused, their vacant breakable faces, their broken hands and shoes, their bodies cloth beneath their gowns, flimsy, durable, sewn. Our grandmother's sorry slippers, I packed, and the bundles of letters a boy had sent, some darling, new for a time, the ones I hadn't stolen from her that Sister was waiting to open.

A little something, baby. All I'm asking, the boy wrote.

Token, talisman, cake top, stone. Anything small to rub or suck, to hoard, a nut, a buckeye, I packed. A china doll, a Matchbox car: easily lost, renewably dear, something to grieve, lament at last, the breakables, perishables, bloody plugs and silken locks, the rheumy gristled button plucked, the newly born, the newly dead: first and last and only.

Send me a word or something, the boy wrote. *José needs a kiss or two.*

We kept the windows down—Sister healing, rank in the heat—and her hair, pulled free, was carried upward, out; a great bristly shank of it hovered and plunged above the roof of my car.

A day at the lake, a battlefield. And then the bright gates swung open.

I PULL THE door shut, move away down the hall.

The baby is waking, whimpering—quick! Next the trumpet, a sound like an elephant charging.

I make my way to him. Lie down beside the boy, against him, animal to animal, anyone would do. It is not lost on me, not lastingly: anyone would do. Nurse Jane, Nurse Jane, Nurse Alice.

I am food, heat, a smell to him; a teat in the dark, a plug in his mouth. No matter the claim, no matter what tenderness moves me. He moves to the smell he left on me, the mark he knows me by.

Little monkey. Little brain on a stalk.

How can it be he lives?

He is impossible, embryonic again in the simple dark—doomed, suddenly, mouthy, gilled, unready, misshapen, unmoved.

MY ONE.

Brain in my brain, heart in my heart. A dimpled leg, ten fisted toes.

I did not know mine from another's.

Yet he thrives, plump, deep in the gorgeous, ruinous lie: nothing lives but that he lives, too. Nothing stirs. Not a wind, no bird in the stippled wood—but that he cries out, that he sees.

Such a world. The sun sails past, warm to the touch. His body tethered, flown.

Now the moon.

What of the sea, the barn adrift? The fallen throbbing stars?

Try crying, cry out: a shade appears, a dolorous tide, darkens the window, swallows the sky. A mothering heat, a shadow bent.

Feed and she will vanish; cry and she appears. Not a rib, not a bang. Only whimper. Small god.

I AM EMPTIED out.

Shaken loose, how swiftly—George is coming to me down the hall.

He smells of Naugahyde, of ready food, the distant rude perfumey press and beery lure of airports, of bodies on the move. He drops into bed beside me, emits a gassy sibilant conciliatory whisper.

Then he is on me. The baby jostled awake, watching up, hairy papa, pleased.

I pinch my eyes shut, not to laugh at them, at how they must look to each other, how they look to me. George is wrestling my pilly nightgown free, rolls me, hurried, dogged, gone—but that Sister is screaming: "WHAT DO YOU THINK YOU ARE DOING, HEY?"

George stops a beat and we listen: she drags the dog back into the tub.

Two beats, three, another. Sister sings. The dog sputters and coughs. Poor panicked hound, slipped free, hauled back. A dog devoted, briefly loved, gone to the Post Everlasting.

Yes. Tell it, Sister. The gods shine down.

She is a Miracle, soon to be, a gospel girl in ribbons and pearls: a Miracle in Training. Cheerful Helper. Much Improved. Miracle in Training.

George rolls off me: he has remembered—where he is, and who.

Husband, father, suitor, son.

Resolute, a man in need. Thinks: give it a go. Hup, boy.

He takes his time for a time, he is easy, he is breaking softly into me.

I would stop it. Send him off down the hill, Sister in tow and the dog behind and every last goodly neighbor, everyone else who means well, everything else that needs.

Just the one, I want—shoeless, a girl, her tongue cut out—to slip food under our door. Not a peep. Leave me to molt and heal. I have bones again, I'd forgotten—joints—gristle, sinew, glassy balls drifting in their pockets. The lifted blue of my veins recedes. A man-sized thumb in my belly unmoors—a nudge at the hull, a nosing; a ghoulie, a ghostie, a bump in some fattened tube.

Buck up.

George turns me away, not to see, should I weep. "Stay with me."

Say *mine* again. *Gimmit, do.*

The rest of life before us.

Sit tight. Lie back. Lucky you, you feel it.

I have kept to my chair to feel it—what hook is set, what press desists, what frightened, woozy, ravening love bends its back against us.

"Where are you?" George says. "Stay with me."

Our boy bats at us, god of us—his blessed farce.

I say, "I am right here."

Here to please. A girl, a mark, caught again, my wrists cuffed above my head. George is working up to it, working slowly in.

I give in. It is my habit, my dodge.

He had me pinned, this George, another, pricked, Andy Petie
Billy Bob, the way into me dry and narrow.

"All your little friends," he said.

Pig-eyed boy, he smelled of hay.

"It's a matter of time," he insisted.

What isn't?

Soon—a plea, a girl spliced in: virgin girl on a spongy pier,
how you? what's your name? hardly matters, fly right, it's a phase,
call it that, a passage, Christ, what's it for if not? Little vestibule,
shrunken bloody windswept maw and why fuss after all, it will
knit, tell her that, little whisperings: sing, why not, something
plangent, try, to ease her: the cranes flown south, the murmuring
flocks; her name, something sweet, hang the sheet out: his: that's
his flag in my yard, his hand at my mouth, my brash little lollipop
of blood, and I am fifteen, the wind in the leaves, the brackish
lurid face of the pond, the birds circling. The dead horse gnawing the barn. Girly, look. There there there there. Say mine again,
our little sweetnee hushed, hooked on a tit, he swipes at me—and
yours and yours, keep your eyes snapped shut, your back to the
door, hip hey, little girly, look. All your little friends, girl, look,
you think you're what?—all your life, because it's nothing, hey,
we got babies red ones yellow brown, four of everything they are
making, Lord, scissors knife staple string, a nurse in the wings,
hup up. The dogs panted, frenzied, dodging him, a boot to the
snout, he kept his boots on, shy, he was kind, he meant to be
kind, conciliatory, pig-eyed boy, and what? this was what? half
your life since, bet, half your silly life ago, and he is going, gentle,

cautious, gone—husband, father, suitor, son. Christ, the stink of
it, the tedium, the final blind obliterating rut, and the dog cries
out, the dog breaks free, hysteric. She would drag the boy out
by the scruff of his neck, paw a hole for him in the yard, half a
chance; here she comes.

Sister blunders in, weeping, she is naked, "YOU," wet from
the tub, hot on the trail, like the time, like the time, our little tribe,
what a sight, little sweetnee boy, buckaroo, will you look, buckareno, pleased: little god, lucky life, lucky mama, lewd; heat; teat
and maw; the muscled sack, galactic. A mind blown out, the shimmering hoard.

I am cellular, moldered, spall. Dewfall, a pebble turned. Viscera
and brine. Oocyte, fiber, hind milk, fore. The body's yield and issue.

He cries: my milk springs forth. George laps it up in a rapture
and the dog dives under the bed.

THEY ARE RESTORED to their places when I wake again, the
room hushed. Nothing to hear but the baby, the jubilant, garrulous
moon.

I fetch the basket from the foot of our bed. A little something.
I think it is something a sister might do: bring a basket—grass of
tinseled plastic, a few wrapped chocolate eggs.

The light is still on in the bathroom, the water still in the tub.
A streak of her blood on the toilet seat, Sister's fingerprints on the
wall. And in the hallway: something soft underfoot, a lump, then
two, another. I think I am finding animals, deer mice come out to

forage at night and caught, our bird dog's habit. I pick them up by their tails, hold them up in the bathroom light.

It's surprising—how little you can tell. But I can smell them, a mineral stink, the legendary filth of menses.

The dog has worked at them to leech the blood, to grind the swollen cotton loose. They ride in her stomach, glossed and turned, grown slick before she spits them up and the color of tarnished silver.

I creep the door to Sister's room open.

She has her foot out. Our mother used to sleep with her foot out.

I pull the sheet back. The dog's lip twitches; she yips in her sleep. Sister has a hand hooked in her collar.

"Go outside?" I whisper.

I draw the curtain back, the sky in the trees a weak boy-blue, light enough to see by. I see she has a pile of the cotton pads I keep in my bra to sop the milk. The pads are shredded. She has found a bra, too, the dog tore up and a plastic diaper cover.

She has my gown on. On her pillow is the mangled snapshot I have learned to expect to see: the newly loved, the newly dead, a name in her hand across the back, the boy's name: Joe Young. She will pull it from her pocket and speak to it when George ferries her back to the airport: *I'm coming home, Joe Young.*

Her duffel's open. Two spores. Socks: one pair. The raggedy peel of an orange. She has brought her makeup case, my kaboodle, she calls it, locking, big enough for shoes. Cowboy music and a hymnal—so she can practice: make the cut, the bus.

They go by bus, the Miracles, mouths pressed against the window glass, plying the river towns. They wear their leather bracelets, tooled: W.W.J.D.?

The mark of the exalted. The innocent, the maimed.

Sister wears her bracelet in her sleep, I see—should she wake in the street, the rain coming down. Should you find her. She has wandered off, her house in flames. Her ribboned hair freshly curled.

W.W.J.D.?

Let it be a question.

What would Jesus do?

A LITTLE SOMETHING, *baby. All I'm asking.*

I try to think of something to take from her, to give to her, the towels I took from the hospital, mementos, what have you, the drift of things, the sock stuffed with rice for the suture, I think, to lay across it, warmed, a balm to me, a smell like buttered toast. Let Sister strew rice through the house, I think, and tattered foil and tampons, the shells of the eggs I have boiled for her, dribblings, her mark. The body's gluey excess.

Here. You got me here.

I will find her with the sock with the toe eaten out and pretend she has failed to be grateful where gratitude is due.

I slip her Jesus bracelet off.

Make a deal with myself, with Sister. I will teach her how to hold him, how to bathe him, what to do. How to tend the stump of umbilical, the pasty, toughened button. It is turning on its tether by the time Sister flies in.

You draw the nub back, the button. Take an easy sweep at the healing root with a cotton swab.

Don't be afraid of it, I will tell her. I tell her what Nurse Jane told me. Nothing to snip, to tuck or stitch. Nothing to be alarmed about.

Come light, first thing, when I am tidy yet, rested some, stronger then, scrubbed. The night behind us, breakfast on the stove. Sister will come down swinging her basket and take her place at the table.

Somebody new to talk to. Somebody new to listen. Sister, listen.

WE LEFT THE house first thing in the morning, I will tell her, salt on the roads, the blank of the day, a foot in the cage of my ribs. We crossed the river—once, twice, crossed again, for the feel of it, the sweep through the fog; for the time it took, the scrap of a chance to be ready.

I didn't know what to feel. What would it be to love him, to tend to him, never to be alone again, my own again, never to be without him? Still to wake and find him gone. A curtain tapping at my window.

This was our house when you were a boy. Here is the bed you slept in. When you waked, you shouted, *It's morning time!* and we lay in our bed and listened for you—coming to us, bright boy, running to us, for the sound of your feet in the hall.

She will sing to him, coo at him, bounce him on her knee, the baby palsied—her whole body going, his. "Whee hee hee. Whee hee hee."

Oh, don't worry, Binny. Don't you worry, Binny. I am right here.

Sister turns in her sleep, moaning. At her throat: our mother's pearls.

"I saw her sleeping."

I say it aloud, whisper it—to hear how it might sound to her, how it sounds to me. "I saw our mother sleeping at the bend in a yellow road."

They wheeled me off from him—swaddled, scrubbed, still as death in his Lucite bucket.

Nurse Jane who wheeled him to me. At her throat, a string of pearls. First light, white world, the blind at the window sprung.

Little bird.

The day clapped shut. The river turned and gurgled.

I thought I'd lost him. I thought if I never saw him.

They drew the curtain across my chest.

No moon. The light popped, the room stuttered out.

Maa maa. Want to jump on rocks?

I called out for a nurse.

Nothing doing.

I SLIP HER pearls off, her glassy ring.

"Little bird," said the nurse, "little keeper."

"Nurse Jane."

She lifted him out to show me, pleased: no X where there should be a Y, no extra smudge of either. No stump of gray, vestigial tail, no show of sticky bone.

No moon. Not a sun I could see.

YOU THINK IT'S easy?

I kicked at their hands, their faces.

I wanted to go out swinging, wild, and knock off their heads with my saber, bawling Sister's name. In the name of dumb heroics, of the bold Tecumseh's boys.

I will let her hold him. Tend to him. I make a game of it—of pretending she will not hurt him.

I make my offering: the band at his wrist, the name my name, a loopy, girlish cursive. Orderliness, a story. Something to think of us by.

"Nurse Jane tidied my bed, humming," I say. "She seemed to bleed from her ears."

I bend to kiss her. I kiss the bright patch above Sister's eye, a scar from when we were girls.

You will take good care of your sister? Mother asked.

Her children loose in the world.

No harm. All's well. Nurse Jane. Come light.

I'd have destroyed him—when he was in me, pod, stalk and sponge, not to have him be like her, not to be as I am with her.

Her mouth is open. I think to spit in it.

I think of us in the quiet, the blessed antiseptic cool. The nurse standing by to wait for her. You have to wait for her.

She draws her foot back. Such a pretty girl, our sister. So easy, for a moment, to love.

I bend to kiss her. I kiss her gently.

I think of how she called to me; she pressed my hand to her belly.

"See?" Sister said.

I said nothing. Nothing came to me.

Nothing comes to me now.

The baby kicked and swung in her. He was having a good hard romp in her before they got him out.

I stood and felt him. The nurses whistling, padding about in pneumatic shoes, music on the PA. Sister hummed a bar, how like her.

And then he quieted. To hear her. I swear I think he quieted to hear the bit of a song she knew.

I leave the basket. Get out before she wakes, I think, go down to dip the eggs.

And yet she wakes. I press the pillow against her face—to calm her. It has calmed her for years: to have something soft to scream into.

She thrashes and shrieks and I hold her, wait for her to twitch off to sleep as she does—on the instant, the disconnect, the body jerking free.

Then I go down to dip the eggs.

I DIP THEM briefly, pallid blues and yellows, enough to be seen in the snow. It is early yet, the plows have not come. The wind has not come from the sea yet and the snow is crusted over.

I pull my boots on, step out. The yard is shining. Everything is shining, throwing off light from the snow. The trees are bristling. The crocus are showing through. The first of the jonquils bloom and droop and the thrush in the trees come back to us out of the hot flat land.

I put two eggs in the birdbath. Another behind the gutter spout behind its gout of ice. I put a blue egg in the bottommost limb of our front-yard beech. The limbs are bent and glisten. The tips of the limb are cased in ice that rises from the crust of snow.

I bowl an egg gently across the crust so as not to leave my boot steps leading to it to give it away. Just the one I bowl. To make it difficult. The rest are easy.

I take my time some, the baby asleep, the plows groaning out on the highway. It seems to me a blessing to be out in the bright and cold. I bask in a patch of sunlight; wave at the good reverend passing, pedaling off on his bicycle bearing the bright calm lamp of his head.

I hide the last egg, open the door: he is screaming.

I find her lying in bed with the baby, my bed, a cigarette smoking on my bed stand, my gown in a heap on the floor.

"I was trying to—"

She can't talk right. She's got the nub, the gristled button, tucked away in her mouth.

I sweep a finger through. She was trying to what?

Don't ask her. She didn't do anything, she was lying there, she found it dropped to the foot of his sleeper. No use in trying to ask her: did she yank the nub loose or gnaw through the leash, take a bite of his hide, so sweet, so soft you scarcely know you have touched it?

I FEED HER—COFFEE, toast, get her out and away, searching for eggs in the snow. The dog by and by learns to carry the eggs, to hold them gently in the heat of her mouth. She bumps one along to Sister, bowls it along with her nose.

The snow moves in a slab to the lip of the roof. The barn is steaming. The grasses appear—in the sun, risen up, a friend to the earth, in the wind blowing in from the sea.

I keep her out there. I make her find the eggs, bored or not, after I have gone to the trouble of hiding them, before we go back inside. I found a cap for her, a coat and gloves. I'd have found Cinderella's glass slipper for her to keep her out of the house for a time.

George passes through the window with the baby. They are happy, drifty perhaps. The blooms perk up. The day slackens.

Our old beech groans and tosses its head. We hear the bristle and click of ice on its boughs—a squirrel has lunged and, sluggish, missed, and the body is dropping through.

WE MOVE IN. Afternoon. The dog dreaming. The baby asleep on my chest.

Sister takes a nap in the sunroom, ribbons in her hair, gorged on sweets, her cache beneath the bedsheets, the chocolate rabbit nested yet among the bright sweet beans.

I walk Sister into the pines when she wakes, the orderly rows, her fingers hung in my pockets.

No sun much, dusk coming on. No wind where we are to speak of. A thrush somewhere, silvery, sings. The boughs are still laden with snow.

And then a squirrel chirps, a clump of snow breaks free. The dog springs like a deer through the timber, squealing, demented, a grape-sized brain, Sister lurching after, the squirrel going limb to limb. Quick as that.

A great wet clump is falling. She keeps her face tipped up to watch it, watches it to the end.

The dog rears up and swoons as she does and hooks a paw over each shoulder, kisses her neck, her ears. She picks Sister's—George's—cap off, lopes away snapping the cap in her teeth as though it is something to kill.

By then I've reached her: Sister spluttering, spitting out the plug of snow. Her mouth is bleeding. Her face is the grotesque of a face, a soul in flames, some rung of hell, spit puddling under her tongue.

I sink to my knees beside her. The Keeper, the Tender: the cheap tableau. "Let me see it."

On her forehead, the abraded skin is grainy with blood. "Poor girl."

I bend to touch her. But she is up, what fun, lunging away, stupid thing, elated. She pounces at me, forgetful, or not—it's that I'm feeble still, tender still, careful. I have been told to be careful.

Sister pants: a dog. I never see it quite: who she means to be: monkey horsie walrus bear. She rears up and kisses me.

I take a swing at her.

It is the hour, the light, it must be—the sly animal weight of it, amnesiac, the seizing, the night sky clamping down. Fevers rise, hunting time, predators on the move.

I try to get the dog to come to me, come sit by me, I think maybe this will calm her, if the dog comes and sits very quietly, she is trained to, you can't know.

I know I haven't had my pills yet. I have taken the last of the pills I had that have been while I heal a help to me, in the evening time in particular, dark coming on, the flattened trees—to dull the ache, the progress, the healing meant by the mess I pass, the sheeny clumpy liverish ruin that is left of being sufficient, of having been, for a time, sufficient, for a time, I swear it, calm.

A body needs something.

Sister wheezes, pets at me. I stop and wait for it: her sudden chirping cry, her drawn-on cartoon mouth.

And then I hit her. She is the way she is and has always been and how she will always be. And so I hit her. I had forgotten. You forget how it feels to hit somebody like you used to when you were young.

No moon, dim world, the sky velour. A bird above us, circling. We make our way from the trees.

The reverend streams past, slush flung up. Gone to vespers, gone to God. Perhaps he hears her. Thinks not. It is the hour, the light. The wind in the trees. And yet it comes to him; he must think of it—crossing back, going home—to supper, sleep, to his wife, a dream—he must have seen it: the bloody trail Sister leaves, walking back to the house.

We cross the street, the welts of slush. The light in the kitchen is burning. The windows are steamed from the heat of something George has set to cook on the stove. Still we can make him out with the baby. He is sitting in the kitchen with the baby, looking out across the road.

It comes upon me—the old gone way we used to live, how we lived outside until dark came on, until Mother called, the dogs at our heels, the horses fed, hay in the rustling barn.

We pass the bed of slackened blooms to pass unseen through the window light to watch George sitting inside. I see Mother at the sink then also, Mother at her labors, at the washing, at the meals—young still, pretty still, laughing. I remember myself in the spindly dark, the lee of the hedge, the sweetened smell of the harrowed rows turned in the fall in the ripened fields. I spun myself out in the clovery dark; I felt myself thin and wobble. I lay on our land like a fog—upon every fence and creek and stone, every leaf and fallow.

I watch our George in the blaze.

"You know I saw you," he said. "I never meant to. They had you opened. He was spun in his sack and looking at me, lodged in the saddle of bone."

The dog whimpers. Sister kicks a pale stone at the barn. A dry hush in the limbs and a wicker.

A pine is down in the street. We see in the gray in the grainy dark the seepy luminous tear in the trunk that the head of the tree as it fell has torn—all trunk now, that tree, a hollowing snag, a

yellow gash that as the woods grow dark tips and floats and burns.
I swing the porch door open.

"Aren't you cold?"

"No."

"Not hungry?"

"Uunh."

Sister moves off, calling the dog out slowly.

LOVE'S THOUSAND BEES

THE BOY WAS BLIND AND FROM ZELIENOPLE. HE CAME among us as a bear-child might, such a slumber, the sow labors in sleep, from sleep heaves up, raving and newly mothered.

The boy had fattened at the taps, sucked from the trees was how he reached us, wise to set out in spring. Our nights had warmed and the frogs thawed and by day sun weakened the trees. Sap twanged into our buckets. To improve these notes, the frogs gave up their two favorite notes from the pools.

The boy added to this the wheezing a fat boy does to breathe, and the slur, as he walked, of one pant leg against the slickened other. He slogged through the pools and his galoshes filled up. He felt with his hands for trees. We didn't know was he blind or did the meat of his face make it hard to see. We looked for his eyes—they were bloody, shot into his head from afar. We saw his scalp creased under his hatband, yeasty and flushed in the stubble.

The fields were too wet to plow; we had snow still patched about. So we busied ourselves in the sugarhouse, sweetening in the steam. We sharpened our hoes and shovels.

Spring, and everything wants to move. The children wake at daybreak and beg to throw from the mound.

The boy was spotted first beyond the backstop. Daisy it was who saw him, lifting out of her trance on the swing. Daisy had clawed a ditch through the snow for her feet to pass through to swing, who loves to swing, the one among us, the better yet to see. She sailed down in her skirts and went to him. She heard a kitten, who mewed in his pocket.

"Who are you and why are you here? Don't you have school like we do?"

He lived with Mr. U, he said, except that he said *yived*.

"He yived in #3 with me. I yiked how he was soft to me. Mr. U was yike some sock to me. But I did never yove him."

"So you want to come be here?"

"I guess."

"Geese! Geese!" Daisy cried out. Two flapped low overhead.

"Yovye," the boy said.

"What is the name of that kitten?"

"Goose."

"Goose?"

"Goose," the boy said. "You can have it."

"Does it fly in its sleep?"

"Maybe," the boy said.

"Do you pee in your sleep like my brother? One night he peed on my head."

"Mr. U peed in a bucket. It was my job to carry the bucket through the hanging-down fence to the stream. One time I dropped it. It went out of my hands in the stream. I had my kitten. I had my yittle chick in my pocket that died so I walked over here to you."

"Can I see?"

The boy held out the chick. It was muddied, a yellow wad of down.

"You can have it."

One of his fingers was off.

"Yook," he said, "I yost a tooth."

This he gave her also, a little milk tooth, brown as a scab.

He was happy to himself. His face was bursting. They heard the school bell sound.

"Wait, he said. My name is Zach Syoat. I come from Zeyienople. My mother's name is Yenore. I have two sisters, Yenore and Yenore. I yive with Mr. U."

"Olly olly umpf," the teacher called.

Daisy waited still. The boy got out of his coat. He wore pajamas, slick and humid, a superhero's satin.

"Sweet," Daisy said, and pet him. The kitten smacked a fly from the air.

"I better go," Daisy said, and turned to go.

"Geese! Geese!"

The two came back.

"See you yater."

The door to the school bucked shut.

He had a tadpole, too, in his galoshes, he had caught, and a ball of goo, and a miniature shrimp, and to hold these, he made a bark-bucket for Daisy girl to find. The sap surged upward in the trees as he worked. His pajamas steamed from the heat he made. The jelly of his scalp melted open.

"Daisy mine," he breathed.

Love's thousand bees flocked to him, to draw the sugars from the heart, from the head.

ONCE I WROTE A STORY

ONCE I WROTE A STORY ABOUT AN OPIUM ADDICT WITH a self-driving car.

ONCE I WROTE a story about an ostrich.

ONCE I WROTE a story about a blind boy in superhero satin.

ONCE I WROTE a story about a hummingbird drowning in a bowl of cream.

NEXT I WROTE a story about an animal addict with a mule with two bitten-off ears. The mule was Notches. Ever gentle. Every night of her life, he told Notches good night until at last she drove him off and disappeared.

ONCE I WROTE a story about death do us part. Extravagant, the wedding night, such as nobody can afford. The bride wore sequins. They found her in the motel bathroom. Her husband had stabbed her in the dry bathtub, the sequins from the bed to the bathtub strewn like coins, like scales, like sequins. Iridescent, incandescent. Like a mermaid, like a bird.

ONCE I WROTE a story about a boy I loved who wrecked everything he had made for me and is wrecking it for me still.

ONCE I WROTE a story about a Jennifer and a baby named Lloyd and a Jew.

ONCE I WROTE a story about you.

YOU SAID, *What's it about?*

I SAID, *You.*

I WAS TRYING
TO DESCRIBE
WHAT IT FEELS LIKE

T'S LIKE BEING A BEAUTIFUL CITY ON THE NIGHT OF A biblical flood. A million bucks—all mine—already spent. Like a beach ball skipped out to sea. Baby, you show up on my avenue, baby, and buildings drop to their knees. I'm the flood I'm the flood that fells them. I am the zoo and animals in it and I feed you out of my hand. Eat from my hand. You have to let me. Every boy I ever loved peeled his face off and gave it to you. They're all you. It's your face instead of stars and stars on the move, arctic—and you're the tether. Christ's gaudy hissing crown. You make me loose in the middle and melted. I'm like fire but slow like rock. Like I'm the planet and you're the axis. Be the axis. You be the thing I turn on. Up in the igneous. Up in the rot. Make me a moon, moon-maker. *Woo.* Like that like that like that.

TIME FOR THE
FLAT-HEADED MAN

T HAS COME TO ME TO INTRODUCE TONIGHT'S READER.
My wife asked would I. She said it's easy, easier for you. She makes it difficult—to stand here, to open her mouth. It's a struggle, she says. I said, Yes, dear.

Yes hello, dear. Our director. There she is, everybody. Give a wave.

You mostly know me. What I mean to say—I know some of you from class, the ones I've been thrown. I see you out there.

I'm not ungrateful. It can't be easy. For my wife, I mean, not to seem, you know, it's very delicate. Still she has managed to throw me work. It clears my head some—to stand up here and talk to you in a grownup sort of way.

We have, as you know, the two children. The girl, a boy. They are thinking she is going to get better, our girl. Give her time, they say, some months to grow—

Yes, come in, come in. I'm glad you made it, every one of you. Blinking into the snow.

I was talking about our children. The girl, a boy.

I taught our boy to ride his bike. That was nice. He skids out, lays a patch, wants to show me. Shows everybody his scabs. *Lookit look*: a scab on every joint he can get to. Point of pride.

He says, "Our baby's name is Noodle and I like to suck her hair."

He sets his lips around the hole in her head bone and slurps in a satiny frill. I think she likes it.

How nice to see you. You few I know. You look lovely, really, you do. Hello, darling, up there. I like your muffler. I like your hat and shoes.

She missed the winters, my wife, it's why we came here. She missed all the different clothes—the heavy coats, the bundling up. You could pass your long life in a halter top in the town we came north to get out of.

The air velvet. Squinch owls and duckweed, pickled eggs. A pontoon boat with the radio on making laps on the nearby lake. Our boy was small there, he was a baby. You could sit him in his bucket on the lakeside in the sun. We had egrets. Once a wood stork. Peahens on the roof of the cabin—tatting at the nail heads, the pipe coming up. Anything bright they could get to.

She comes from Akron, tonight's reader. Akron by way of Toledo. By way of Mayor's Income. That's in Tennessee.

She writes poems. This is my introduction. Wrote a book of stories, skinny thing, lot of white on the page. She's got two kids same as our two kids. A good gig in Tuscaloosa, a lanky buckaroo in the chute. It's what I've heard.

You ever hear of the ones they break the bones on young to get them back set right?

And it works!

While they're small. Little miracles. Such a miraculous day and age with all they know and do.

Hey and look. They are spot fucking on with this weather—it's doing just what it's supposed to do. Good old wintry mix. Three feet on the ground and now it's—raining swords, our boy says. You've got to really run.

I said Akron, right? She writes poems. Said that. I don't get out much. I've half forgotten—what it feels like, what all I mean to say.

Our boy said, "Papa."

We were lying in bed and he was messing with himself, his little package, trying to make the hole bigger, he said.

"Papa, look." He stretched it up to show me. "Doesn't it look good?"

His *woowoo*, he used to call it.

"In a few days your woowoo will bloom into a thousand flowers."

He's got the skin on still and he forces it back and out comes this purple ball. It looks all wrong, it looks rotted.

He says, "When you die I hope you're a frog and I will catch you and I will keep you in my bucket."

I liked to think of him there in the heat where we lived rounding up snakes and frogs, growing up, fishing. Little barebacked nut-brown boy. Swinging through the trees on a strangler fig. I liked thinking of him being a man there sitting on an overturned bucket.

He'd have a pontoon boat. He could think there. He'd have a radio, a little old crackly transistor of the sort that hangs in a shirtfront pocket. A gentle man. A party of one, making his pointy rounds.

A simpler life.

Of course we're lucky. It's easy to feel pretty lucky. I think she likes it, my wife, this job of hers—all the details, all the many tiny important things a woman of our day and age has to do.

Plus a mother, don't forget.

Plus the baby.

She's not old enough, the baby, you can't break them yet, little rubbery bones. So we keep her stuffed into her harness. Keep our chins up. As per. We think in pictures. It's a help.

She wags her arms a bit, but otherwise—

I'll just say it. I'm not cut out for it. We're not. I mean men, I mean. We're cut to gather. Gather and hunt and think—I used to think, have a thought through in my chair. My chair! Shoved into the corner of my room.

I lay the girl down at the back of the house, pull the door to, steal away. Have a sit.

She has to lie there. She's just a nugget. I could drop her through the mouth of the woodstove, be done with her in a day.

Who am I?

Because who am I really do you think to her?

She's just little. She doesn't know me. Give her time, some months to grow, she'll point me out, say, "Bapa."

The ennobling moment.

The blow to the head. Then the knees go.

Like the heartbeat, first time, the first picture, her little face full on through the tissue, the fiber and brine, and she waved. *Here I come*, she seemed to say, *don't try to stop me.*

You do what you have to do. Burn through. Drop into my hands, big Papa's hands, and he flinches. I gave her up to her mother: glistening, blue, the cord in my hand still humming.

And her mother's first word? *Luscious.* Think of that.

They say it's easy, it is all she knows: harness, plaster, spreading bar. *Bapa. Hot. Brother. Dog.* All the little slings and pulleys.

Her brother drew on her face with a crayon, drew a face.

I was elsewhere. I was taking my ten deep breaths. As per.

You take a breath, keep moving. They can't move, you think you're safe, you think they lie there, okay, and what could come? Well, here we come. Bapa. Mama. Brother. Dog.

My wife busts through the door, "Come to Mama, baby."

The old egg clutch. The gladdened hand. She is spitting milk, she is weeping. Bringing the bacon home.

WHAT I LIKE?

I liked lying on the bed on the phone with her, nothing left to say.

I like a good outside shower, looking up through the moss and leaves. Our man in his boat, turning circles. Little lake.

Our lake was shrinking. It was dirtier every year we lived there, the water siphoned off. Lake Rosa. After Rosa.

It was storied. All the good stuff—rape and pillage, dirty Feds. Stills in the woods and sink holes you could drop your murdered through. Gothic excess. I always liked it. I liked the old gin joint sloughing on the banks, the desolated piers. Our boy was small there. Sit him on the slope in his bucket in the sun and the peahens would stroll down and gawk at him.

Then the rumors flared up. Something had killed a peahen, a fellow was missing his dogs. Two, and then another, and then somebody else, and pretty soon they had gotten a posse up and were combing the lake for gators. They came upon an ancient bull in the muck, bellowing and sluggish, and everybody had a go at him, and beat him on the head with pipes. They opened him up and, *lookyloo*, found a dew claw, hair balls, gizzards. A broken chain of vertebrae, a clutch of radio collars.

A boy bloodied to his elbows, sickened.

The pontoon boat run aground.

I'd say I liked that. The freakish tableau.

The penny in your pocket mildewed.

"PENNY?" SAYS MY wife.

Nothing to report. A polar cold. The wind chirrups.

Cheer up. Cheer up.

Forgot your hat! Now go on, little Miss. Look both ways twice. Don't let the door hitcha in—

Somebody else scooting out?

Nice to stand here. Talk to big folks.

Poems and stories, she does both, she does the colonies, the clusterfucks, lunch at the door, a little basket. Qigong, fêng shui, reps at the gym. Have a look at her. Stringy thing, she used to dance, flattened abs, the haunch on her, quite the hottie. But you can smell it on her: she's a mother. She's submerged.

Use your nose: she will have turned some. She'll have soured, that's a hint. Something's ferny. They're grown over, grown in. A flicker: then gone. You can't reach them. You can't console them. You touch them and they sink away.

What's to do?

I sweep the floors clean. I make the meals.

Our boy sprints at her; the baby wakes and cries.

The ravaged female. Our Lady of the Mount. Miss DMV.

Fresh from the stirrups. As if.

Really, it's nothing, she insists. It's just she's tired.

I'll give you tired, what the fuck. I'll give you nothing.

Sit down, sit down. You think I'm finished?

"I amn't finished," says our boy.

We'll make a night of it—the wide belts, the tools. The wonder, the stunt.

She's got her papers out, the dog-eared book. She'll get up here, find her page. Proclaim the miracle. Another living body in her living body yada yada yada yada nothing but give give give.

YOU SIT.

Let a man have a little fun, why not? Air his mind some. I amn't finished.

"I amn't going to hit you," our boy says. "I amn't going to kiss you. I amn't going to get a sword and chop you in two."

"Into what?" I ask.

"A zillion pieces."

My mother's dead now. Which makes life simpler. It's not a joke, it's true.

When my old man was away, he was away quite a bit, I used to go to my mother in her bed. I never asked could I. We never spoke of it. She wore a nightgown the planets were pictured on and I knew in the morning when my father was away that she would lie in bed and let me pick at the sleeve, at the small gray beads of cloth I came to keep with the hair from her pillow. I lay in the dark in the bed heat, in the wet bready smell of her, not moving, pretending to sleep. I was a boy, and then not, too old for it, a mommy's boy, and disgusted, and in my disgust it grew easier for me to picture my mother in stirrups, strapped in, laboring, gassed, while the waxy molten globe of my head burned through her.

I never touched her: if I touched her she would burst into flames. I lay away from her and felt the seed move in me, heating up, pearly, the flashing tails, the race to the sea. The bliss of sleep enmired.

I would sleep enmired in the puddle I had made, happy and ashamed.

My brother served us waffles each morning and we lay propped up with the TV on and ate them with our hands. I wouldn't speak to her. I wanted to throttle her. I couldn't stand it: to have a mother: to have grown my arms and legs in her, my cock and balls, gill and lung, every plug and socket.

I wanted to come from nothing, from air, a cloud, the heavens jeweled. The tinted distance.

SHE SWEEPS IN, my wife. *Hello, hello.* She's a special event, she's a goer.

I report on the daily doings, tell her what she has missed. The shitty baths. The scabs, some stunt. Some funny little peep her baby makes.

I say, "She spent the day on her backside, lying there hoping to grow."

My wife hovers, coos, soon to bed. She's spent. Asleep by the time I get there—dreaming, I guess, of you. Some one of you tamping burning coals deep into her nostrils. You've pulled her teeth out.

And her a mother!

Full grown. Pushing forty, my wife.

"Those are longing," says my boy, and he swats at her breasts. It's not a joke, it's true.

WHAT I'D LIKE?

I'd like a day on that fellow's pontoon boat, a radio, the white-hot marvelous sun. I'd lash the helm, keep her circling. Sun on my ass, blister my nose. Sit and drink some. Think a few gothic thoughts through.

We got fathers out there? You a father?

He's going, *Yeah. Fucking yeah. Sit and drink some.*

"I mean it," says my boy, "I'm honest. I'm just standing here, I'm honest."

He's at the bedside, the baby howling. His crayons poking out of his pants.

Sweet doll. Sugar girl.

He'll make it up to her. He'll saw at his trousers with a Lego. He said, "I'm gonna make these littler so when Noodle ever has a baby then her baby can grow into them. Wouldn't that be cool?"

He puts a dress on, very flowery, a lacy thing his sister will grow into, should she grow. "And what shall we call you?" I ask him.

He's sitting on the pot, thinking. "I'd like to be Glorious Angel."

And so he is, spinning through the kitchen with his dress lofting up.

And I am Claybrain, Hiccalump, Clumpfoot, Tuk.

A man in need. Could stand a drink. Stand to sit down.

"We lived in Florida?" he asks. "I was a baby?"

"Yes."

We lived in the land of the halter top. We snived in the snand of the lalter snop. Hip. Pop. Pifflewop.

How nice to see you. You're very tall.

I brought pictures. The boy, a girl. You see, they're lovely. We keep her dress pulled down to hide the harness. You can imagine— her little stirrups, our girl fresh from the womb. Her feet folded flat against her shinbones. She looks fileted even now, laid open, very clean. Little clean plump butterflied lamb.

But such a beauty!

You drut. Get out, get out, don't think you're sneaking. You and your sneaky friends. You, man. Up. Make tracks.

"Let's get a knife for ourselves," my boy says, "and run out there and stick them."

HA. The rest of you can stay.

Tell you what, here's a tip, we go to market. Take the baby when you go to market, boys, take her anywhere there are girls. Works like a charm. You let them pet her. I take the baby down to the pool. You get a daddy in the pool they're a swarm, *watch me,* little lunging strokes, the water frothing, they walk on their hands, *be a horsie, swim me where I can't swim.* I do, and they are kicking; they are breathing fast in my ear.

"And we lived beside a lake?" my boy wants to know.

"We lived beside a lake."

He's down to stories. Suspicions, omissions. A foreign view.

"And my mother took me out in my bucket?"

"And your mother took you out in your bucket."

"And my mother loved me very much?"

"You were her prince. Her angel. And she loved you. And you were all she saw or could think of. And she loved you. You said *adnee. Awoo.* And I loved you. Your papa loved you."

"And my mother set me down in my bucket."

Firstborn, boy-child, hoyden.

Mama, Papa, Clumpfoot, Tuk. We make mistakes, give us that. We're only human.

Man the fires. Sweep the floors.

They say a year, tops. That's consolation. They say, "It is all she has ever known."

I say she used to breathe underwater. She was gilled, webbed, a rock, a frog. Amphibious. She was larval. Boiled in the heart of a dying star. She knows plenty.

So they forget: What is that?

The child knows plenty.

He is lava, lightning, Black Bart, bear. He's a worm, torn up, a withered heart. T. rex and the woods are burning.

That's him in the tub, hollering—hollowing, he calls it, a pirate song: *hardee-eye-yay, hoodee-eye-yoo*. He's got his face bunched up around his eye patch. He is using his mother's diaphragm for an eye patch.

"For a boat," he says, "to kill Noodle with. Kill Noodle."

HE KEEPS US racing: *marks, get set.*

"You just keep getting faster and faster," I tell him.

He gives me a long sweet look and says, "And you are getting slower and slower, right?"

He wears his tasseled hat—which makes the wind blow—which sparks a lightning—which fells a tree.

His mother took him out into the trees one day. This was lakeside—heat and strangler fig, every manner of insect living. Great mounds. She can't get past it. Carried him out in his bucket, in the cool of the shade she could provide.

"Let it go," I say.

Of course she doesn't.

Well it's hard, it's hard. Hand of God, you could say, but she won't say it.

"You have to say I forgive you," my boy says.

Forgive me, dear. Shameful of me.

You see she's leaving.

I used to like that—the feeling that my wife was leaving. I'd hear her drive off, I wouldn't stop her. After a time I would find some picture of her and sit with it in my chair. Then I would speak to her, as though to her, a grown man, a fool. I could make myself feel very sexy, and wanting—I wanted her, the way she tucked her feet between my ankles when we slept, or slipped her fingers into my pocket. I could conjure the smallest sweetness, hoarded, call up the least gauzy scene—the near-blue skin of her ankle, nicked, foam on the polished shore. Like watching a dream of terrific precision. The skin of her ankle was dented and ribbed where the elastic of her sock had pressed against it—glossy, a ripple, as when the tide recedes, and startling—the glare of love.

I was undone by it, wished to be, easily, in passing.

I rubbed out the print, smoothed it away—would, I should say, I never have. Another missed statistic: the incidence of men in their kitchens goading themselves to tears. Sobbing in their rockers.

Come home. Come home.

It's still me.

Your prince. Dear old breadstick.

THEY OUGHT TO fix that door. We'll all have dreams of it. Hooked shut. Then the stutter and wheeze.

A woman embarked. Stealing away through the wintry mix, we can't stop her. Just as well. We'll stay and speak of her.

She wanted sunshine. The very best for her boy, fresh air for her boy, a little sunshine. Ions, photons, vitamin D. Wanted heat. To be limbered and quiet and slowed. Be his mother. His cooling shade, soft, becalmed. The slow marvels, she would give him, the glistening ant, the lizard's coppery pouch; mirage—puddled silver in our road, the box turtles gliding above. Her wild boy singing in a secret tongue, tongue of wind, of dog.

He'd have collections: beetles, coins, crisp skins of snakes. The beak of a bird, a tree frog. A june bug on a thread. The dream of a life she remembered. The owl in the mimosa, the armadillo asleep in the cool—you could smell them beneath our house.

She set him down. For an instant. Buzzing heat, lake light, the drowse. The wag of the brittled palmetto. She moved off, a thinking woman. Thought: sinkhole, felon, dengue, flood. Not likely. But what of the limb, the pebble thrown, the interstellar ice ball? She thought of the arc: velocity: mass: the mathematics of the cataclysmic. Perhaps the wood stork. The kid with a stick, the hand of God. The orangutan sprung from the zoo. All that.

Still she moves off.

He isn't far, she thinks, she could hear him. She can almost even see him—should he need her. It's just an instant, just a couple three minutes she needs just to think, she isn't far, really, just to think some, he's in his bucket, rocks a bit but the ground is soft, he may be sleeping, yes, likely, lucky for her, she can think now, counts the minutes—three, four, loses track—and so she milks it. She will turn back, should, he must be sleeping, poor child, the breeze from the lake, coolish today, the day pleasing. She hears an owl in the trees and she turns back—spooked—I never liked it, you hear people say they like it—the hoot, the trill, old owlers, out in the cold, a boy at your heels, and here it comes, the great swoop, quiet as a cloud passing.

She went back then. Her boy was shrieking, strapped in. Just a baby. She had set him down on a mound of fire ants. Just the tiniest things but they swarm.

She came sobbing home back through the trees to me, his bucket swinging against her legs.

We got him hosed off. You couldn't touch him. He stuck every place you touched him. Those little blisters everywhere broke open and seeped.

Fire ants, the heat of the day, you see the logic.

We got him strapped in and sedated. Bound for the icy north. Move along. That'll fix it. Build a rock wall; saw the trees down. Mop and mow.

The nights were quiet. Cold already and quiet when we came. Sundown, sunup. Not a bird, not a frog.

He crawled, he ran. He had a birthday. Said, "Papa, I am four almost. And after this I will be six and after that I will be ten and when I become fifteen I'll drive and I will drive so fast and then I will be twenty. Then I will have one leg. Old people only have one leg and then I will be dead, Papa, and you will come and save me. I will be in a pond."

We get out of the car, snow coming down, we're rushing. He says, "Wait, Papa. I want to feel the cold."

It is like a knife at your throat, to love them. It's like gathering leaves in the wind.

We want the best for them both, we're like anyone.

The smell of home, the dog at the foot of the stairs. Your wife asleep, your children. Fire humming in the stove.

We think in pictures. The dream of a life we remember and slept through while we lived.

The velvety air. The way the trees crooked down—how easy he would find it to climb them. All boy. I think of the lake through the trees where we lived, where she lived as a girl, old Angel Oak, the swinging vines, shrimp you could buy on the roadside. Boiled peanuts. Old coot in the steam on the median, his boy fishing the grate at his knees—a string, a hook, a giving stick—happy with that, horsing, and it made us happy to see them.

We could take a week, go see them. Get some sun on our bumpy bottoms, yellow in our hair.

It's been a winter, don't you say? I would say it. We came out of our house to come down here, our car was gone to the roof in snow. Still we managed, we two.

It's a distance. Quite a drive.

She pulls her eyelashes out. We keep our hats on. She pulls her hair out strand by strand. That's life, I guess, funny workings, not to fret. It's just I'm—

SIT DOWN.

We all have them—little tics and such, how our minds work.

I'm not an ogre.

Give a hand. You're very kind, you few, our small tribe, it's just us.

The last listeners.

A warm welcome. Come on, Amherst. I give you Akron.

I'm going home to my boy. He likes to lie on my back. You know the specials? We'll watch the specials: the horned; the frilled;

the mighty bird-hipped. Ornithomimus, Avimimus. The theropods, the thecodonts. The king tyrant, T. rex.

Boy, his heart really goes.

Allosaurus, Staurikosaurus. Leipleurodon—what eats sharks.

You ought to hear him.

Yangchuanosaurus, Megalosaurus, Tarbosaurus bataar.

Velociraptor: the swift.

Troodon: the wounding one.

All the old dead meat eaters.

BARNEY GREENGRASS

E IS A BIG RUSSIAN JEW FROM THE BRONX. HIS HANDS are enormous. He takes the pencil from his mouth, tooth marks in the wood, and tells her, *We have a psychic connection.* He takes her order and comes back with four napkins to write her answers on. *Now, look at me. Look away. Any city. Your favorite ice cream. Any word in the English language. Any number between one and a thousand.* 978. FLOTATION. CHOCOLATE. CHICAGO. *I didn't read your mind. I fed it.* The answers lucid and blocky and new.

VEGAS

WHEN DANNY AND HIS GIRLFRIEND OF MANY YEARS break up, she offers, by way of consolation, to do his dental work for free. She is a dentist. Or, works for a dentist. She puts him under. Danny is so far under, he remakes the scene of a boy devoured behind plexiglass at the zoo: the boy on a dare, the bear put down, cut open. There the boy is. His face is Danny's. The bear is a graying polar bear, the sky that crazy blue. Meanwhile Danny's ex drags every tooth from his head with that implement they use. By the time he wakes, she's in Vegas. His current girlfriend, revolted, makes short work of leaving him, too. What instruction might we glean from this story? What should our Danny do?

ABSOLUTION

ME AND HIM, WE'RE LOVERS. SURE, I KNOW, HE'S A CRAZY motherfucker. And I'm the Banana Queen of Opelousas.

They say I'm the prettiest since Luana Lee.

But you best clap your eyes on Jimmy—he is something, too.

If you saw Jimmy down by the dirty river in his shiny turquoise truck, you'd say, Jimmy Lucas, he's plumb got everything—a dog in the back, banking turns, his Banana Queen right close. He'd lift a finger from the steering wheel, tip his head to mean something mean. It's the way my Jimmy is. I've seen it happen, I should know, I rode with him a lot.

Nights at the No Knees we ride to, Jimmy sets me up on the long bar. "Just look at you," he says to me, his eyes wild and proud. "You boys come on, take a look at her. She is the Queen of Bananas."

PEOPLE KNOW ABOUT me and Jimmy.

Jimmy was the first, I swear it. When I try remembering, creosote comes back best—two coats tacky on the storehouse floor, black across my back and legs. Helps cure dry rot—don't I know? I slapped it on myself.

Oh, I'd have been down there anyhow, watching the boys ice the trains. I tell you, it's too hot for work like that here in Opelousas.

Those chunks were all of fifty pounds, nothing but hooks to hoist them with. Those boys, they were always bright with sweat.

I used to sit up in the big red oak, just sorting, my head lining up their half-bare bodies: Jimmy: Jasper: Isaac: Read. Jimmy: Isaac: Jasper: Read. Jimmy was the first, I swear it.

"Hey, Jimmy," I sang out, real soft like, just enough for me and the birds. "Hey, Jimmy."

He was a sight to see, standing splay-legged on the silver car, sweat running rivers down his back. A round, ugly fellow would come dawdling along, sticking bananas for safety's sake.

"Just don't seem quite right," he'd say, eyeing the mercury like somebody's momma. "Best load her up, she's hot."

After a spell, the peel he poked went black inside as a bullet hole.

Oh, bananas.

Opelousas is the banana capital of the universe—cars and cars, quick up from Mexico City. Good seasons, those boys worked all night, throwing ice down the loud chute. Jasper always did the last of it. He was the oldest and he'd been to prison. Mind you, I hardly looked at Jasper. I wasn't bad as all that. I've seen his black arms bare, though, veins standing out like hard-ons in church.

Momma like to drive me loopdy-looped as she is about Jimmy.

"My lover Jimmy," I say in front of her. "My man Jimmy."

She don't stand for it. He's a no-count. He ain't the hitching kind. He spits tobacco juice on her kitchen floor, no two words about it.

Oh, sweet Jesus, I know. Jimmy's got a mean streak an acre wide that puts up a fence around me, puts a little shiver in me like I just better be ready, like expect the worst, because here it's coming.

But I like it. I don't know. I do.

WHEN I STARTED in on Jimmy, Momma like to pinch my head off. I'd get my hair done up.

"How could you?" You could hear her across the county. "How could you?"

Lord, my momma can carry on. Some nights she's talking a blue streak upstairs, and I lie down, dying for the train—all those explosions right in a row, and the whistle like something to run from.

Maybe I'm a sinner to sleep naked like I do.

Some nights I dream of fire, running stark down Jefferson with the neighbors gawking. Some nights Momma comes in, pushes her hands around on me.

"Child of my heart," she says to me. "Sweet sugar child, don't go."

DADDY LEFT WAY back, took a liking to some Mississippi baby doll. Folks says it's Momma I favor. But Momma wasn't ever Banana Queen. She ain't the contestant type. She like to lay down and get run over when Daddy brought his hussy—that's what I call her—his hussy home.

I knew it already. One day, early from school, I spied them, out at the kitchen sink, her bent down like she was spitting up, red hair sprung every which way. Strike me dead if I lie. I saw Daddy sticking himself in her. It's the gospel truth.

I never told Momma.

But she knew, she knew. Daddy's hussy's got a swing any fool wants for his porch.

Momma don't say nothing. She just smiles sweet-like, slow in the doorway waving. Just like the Banana Queen of Opelousas. Just like me.

ME, I AIM to be remembered. That's why the Banana Queen.

You can't believe how it's transporting.

It hooked me Jimmy. I'd have set up in that red oak till *I* grew roots, hadn't been for this yellow crown. Luana Lee is milk soup.

Did Jimmy Lucas bat an eye?

But give me a crown appointment night, and Jimmy climbs up, clamps his hands on my face. "Ain't you something," he says to me. "If you ain't a precious thing."

Momma says it'll teach me vanity, being a queen and all. She says it'll make me big for my britches. I say, "Momma? Tell me something I don't know already."

Momma's crazy, I can't help it. Momma says when your life goes short, folks quit listening to you.

"How many times do we get to do this?" she says.

She says, "Fetch me a glass of water."

I CAN'T HELP it. I want to sleep in the woods in a queenly bed and lacquer my broken toenails. I want to dig through Jimmy Lucas. One day last summer, Jimmy set a stuffed doll astride a rail of fence. He took her to pieces, shot by shot, head first and feathers rising. I could see the inside of his mouth. The inside of Jimmy Lucas's mouth is a dark, vibrating place.

I know.

I don't look in Momma's mouth. She's got pretty lips, but she smells like dying. I bathe her in the mornings these days. I try to help her along. I set Momma down in her pink tub and she tosses her arms around my neck and whispers, "You should have killed me when you had a chance."

A couple years back, before I got to be queen, we were loading hay on the flatbed. This is what she means—that the Devil took hold, that I meant her to flip off the back of the truck, bales of alfalfa tumbling. Momma looks like that now, like she looked that day—shiny-eyed and barely breathing, a fuse fixing to blow.

Sometimes Momma wants my mouth on her breast, like when I was her child. I lay myself down beside her, inside the darkness underneath the spread. Sometimes I think it could do me in—our nakedness, that in my mouth, I can feel her old heart pounding. I try to help her along.

LIKE TO MAKE Jimmy wild, hearing this. "Don't you touch that old whore," he says. "You got to have a life of your own."

It is all of it new to me. Everybody wants something I can't figure. Jimmy wants a baby and I say, Why? The sense of it quits me. We could get us a trailer on the outskirts of town, a place where a dog could run.

I just say, "No, Jimmy, no, no, no. You know I can't, Jimmy, no."

He don't stand for it. He grabs me by my ankles and drags me around, my head knocking on the furniture. "Fuck you, you bitch," he says to me. "Fuck you, you cunt."

He drags me around. When he comes down on me, I must look like Momma, all sprawled out, my head thrown back like I am coming on.

JIMMY AIN'T COME around since Daddy come home, but he is all I can think of.

Daddy done run out of luck. We supposed he drowned in the dirty river when they found his old brown boots. But Daddy ain't been drowning, only getting fat.

"Where you been, Daddy?" I say through the screen.

He looks to me like some old boy I never knew in school.

"Oh, here and yonder. Best let me in."

But do you think I budge?

"What you been doing, Daddy?"

He gives a little shrug like *plenty*.

"Watching the grasshoppers spit. Come on."

Momma sits bolt up in back of me, spewing lynch-pinned to the flagpole and fourteen million dollars. She is Queen of Nonsense now, and that gives her the right.

"She ain't saying nothing, Daddy. Don't mean a thing. What can I do for you?"

He says, "I just come to set for a bit."

I say, "Unh-huh, Daddy. Ain't no reason to live in hell and have to wind up there, too. Why don't you just get along?"

He is nothing but a shadow against the screen, and from where I stand, flies disappear in him.

"You had your chance, old man. Momma's got a thing with God now."

IT IS ALL I can do to keep my hands from myself. Jimmy shuffled up, kind of hanging his head, making a ghost on the screen. I've seen it happen, I knew it was come.

"Jimmy," I say, "how them bananas?"

He says, "I had me a dream. I was looking for you. I was down yonder on the blacktop ridge, hollering every way from Sunday. You wasn't hearing a thing. You was down in the long valley in a little old house with a white light. You was all prettied up and your lips were red and you was just setting, looking at me, not seeing a thing, not listening."

Ought to be something for a girl to say, but my mouth refuses me.

He says, "Come on, child. I can't dawdle around. I got me a life to live."

"Uh huh," I say. "Tell me about it, lover boy."

"TELL ME WHAT it's like," Momma says to me. "Tell me what it feels like to feel like a queen."

"Momma," I say, "Kiwanis makes six hundred and twenty-eight pounds of banana pudding every year, and every year those boys come up from down the road a piece and to go to pissing in the yellow vat. It feels a little like that, I guess—like everybody's happy to have you, but you got some secret stinking inside."

Any time she finds sleep, Momma goes to smiling and kissing the air. I've got a notion she looks like me, practicing love in the glass. *Am I doing this right? Do I look okay?*

I been making ready since long back when, but—Momma, she can still turn me inside out. When she came up last night from some crazy spell, she took hold of my face like she ain't laid eyes maybe for years on me.

"Oh, my beloved child. I thought I was living forever in that green, tumbling place."

It was like I'd never seen her before, like she was the light of another world.

"Here," she said. "Put your hand here."

I rested my hand on her belly—my hand pressed under Momma's hand. "I'm all of me gone from here. Feel?" she said. "Do you feel it?"

"Listen," she said. "Don't matter nohow. It's God does the things that ever get done. God made them boys piss in the pudding, ain't nothing to do with you."

FATHER, FORGIVE.

If I ever flew, it would feel like this, like the earth is just something long gone. I got a big heart and can hold my breath and when

I go deep in this dirty river, my whole body disappears. I feel the water wanting me. I know it's a sin, but I open my legs. I shout Jimmy's name so it turns to music by the time that it finds air.

Oh, ain't it a shame, my sweet, sweet Jimmy. I could have loved you good.

FATHER, FORGIVE.

I lie in the woods in the heat for the train. The thing gets growing inside me, up in my gut, around and around my secret parts. It has a life of its own, and surely the hunger of a hundred horses. It is a thing of the flesh, child of the Devil, who split my momma's pretty lips and spilt himself in her. Surely now is the time for prayer.

Dear God, sweet God, pray God.

What's my momma ever done to you? You listen to me. Ain't no kind of life you're lending her. I got the skirling sound of a train come smack between my ears. It goes, *Take me. Take me*, it goes. *Take me, take me, take me, take me.*

Do I have to do all your filthy work?

Have you spent up all your amazing grace?

You think I know better, but you got me wrong—I ain't afraid of you. You can have this no-count soul to keep.

Suit yourself. Do what you will. Tickle me pink.

I can't use it.

Glory be and to the Father, and to the Holy Son. I would let Momma sprawl on the shimmying track.

You got your doubts.

I'd say, *Go on, go on. Get on with it, Momma. Let's be done with this thing.*

MUSIC OF THE OLD

T IS DARK ON THE ROOF AND A SEAGULL PASSES LIKE something that swims in the eye. Cold. He wants a fire he can hold his feet to. Maybe he'll toss his skateboard in he has carried up through the parking garage, hoping to work off the feeling, drive it out with the speed, the thrill. Like skateboarding down a corkscrew. He feels dizzy, and the shadows keep whispering to him, his mother's voice, his sister's, and parked cars slide off without anybody living behind the wheel. The living drink whiskey at the Elks Club, shuffling to the jukebox, but he's a kid and they won't let him in. They'll call the cops on him or his mother. So he listens to the tunes from the rooftop, slow, dull, music of the old and the birds going past. He is hollow-boned himself and feathered and the seagull keeps swooping weirdly, wanting to put out his eyes. He has his toothbrush in his shirtfront pocket. If he had to say why. But he'll never. He is never going to get old enough to walk into the Elks Club for whiskey. The thought nearly stops him. He will wait for the song to finish. Then he'll lift off; then he'll fly.

INSTRUCTIONS FOR XU YUAN FLYING

OR

THE LIFTING FORCE LET GO

CHILDREN MUST UNDER THE CUSTODY OF ADULTS USE. Should choose the option open. No fire ban in areas, the tall building the floor. The airport ten kilometers from flying. Kong Cross wire in the side of the field against Deduction Presses. A person light take up a loop; another ignite the four angle. Wait for the heat enough light has when the lifting force let go. Xu Yuan light rose slowly the sky, do not forget Wishing oh. Xu Yuan light are on the rise, that of the flying cannot a long time fall, and flight not to append the Foreign Body.

SERENGETI

THEY SAT AT A RECTORY TABLE, FIRE IN THE STONE hearth burning. A pilgrim's feast. Neighbors. Autumn—leaves driven against the house. He put food in his mouth with the food in his mouth he hadn't chewed enough to swallow.

"I could go out tomorrow."

He leaned into her.

"I could find somebody next week. A companion, people seek company—to eat with, read the newspaper with, whatever we do, this is natural. Someone to talk to. Poor Beryl can't do it. Past a certain age, you can't argue this, women—of course it's sad. Well, *I* find it sad."

He poured wine for the girl and the firelight, thrown, hissed and shattered in it. The glass was dipped in gold—a golden circle—buoyant, living.

At last he swallowed; this seemed to hurt him. A tremor kept moving through him and through everything he touched. One shoulder sloped low. Years on the mound. The joy of it.

"Maybe not everywhere but certainly here," he went on. "She has me, naturally, but when I go?"

Shaking, all of him. And the windows shook and wind in the trees and the first bright scraps of snow.

Halloween. Talk of costumes—the children's, the grandchildren's. Someone was going as mulch, somebody else as a stop sign.

"I'm going as who I used to be," one of them said.

THE GIRL TURNED back to him.

"That face," Phillip said, "is not attractive."

She had been tearing skin from the fat of her cheek, tatters of it,
to swallow. She was sorry. Why was she sorry? Now she was sorry
she had said she was sorry.

"Please," Phillip said, impatient.

His wife was three chairs away, laughing. She was absolutely
silent when she laughed. Good breeding, she called it, indignant.
Her father had brayed like a mule. He had struck her once with a
pitchfork—her husband had. For something. A lost key? A broken
cup? Unforgiveable. But she forgave him.

"Poor Beryl. It doesn't matter that she used to be beautiful or
that she's smart and easy to talk to. Beryl is stuck with me and
when I die, Beryl will be stuck alone. That's the way it is. Who
wants her? You reach a certain age and nobody—nobody wants
anybody, really."

AFTER DINNER THEY gathered at the larger hearth and listened to
the wind in the chimney. A deer approached and watched them, standing in the dark field. The first the girl had seen. The deer were dying—
a mite of some kind. They fell sick and walked madly in circles.

Leaves struck the glass of the windows and lay, one upon the
other, in a fringe around the house. A glassblower's house. He

was talking. She was in love with him but he was married. He had hair like a cherub's, like a painting of hair. Firelight was on it. His hands—she couldn't explain it—he caught her watching them as he moved. He had had them insured, he laughed, for thousands. Tens of thousands, even. They meant that much to him.

THEY DRANK BRANDY and he kissed her in his kitchen, a surprise. Not a word. He turned her to him.

Now she slipped into the hall where the heat didn't reach and made her way to his children's room. His girl was named for a month in summer, his boy for a tree that grew nobly on a continent far away.

Beryl, the girl thought. A mineral. A pilot flying in darkness over the far Serengeti.

She lay down with the boy above the covers. You could love children and nobody stopped you. You were allowed. And they were let to love you, too.

PEOPLE WERE ALREADY putting on coats by the time she came back into the room. She had fallen asleep in the boy's bed. The deer had come closer and watched her, the girl dreamed, its breath fogging the glass, fever glazing its eyes. A springtime deer, it couldn't help itself. The spots on its hide still showed.

She would name her children simple names. *Meriwether. Linnaeus. Hidalgo*—no.

Sam. Jack. Jane. Just names. Not the names of stars or places. Not trees.

So many trees in these hills. She would never leave.

He studied in Venice. He liked Venetian glass.

Florence: no.

Simple. *Bob.*

The glassblower's name was Bob. He kept tabs of acid in a candy tin in a drawer beside his bed. In Scotland once he had fallen asleep, tripping, in a field of passing flowers. A flock of sheep closed in around him. *Bob,* they said. They said, *Bob Bob Bob.*

Dell.

Rain—no.

Maybe *Wen.*

Beryl will live to be a hundred and marry again, and the glassblower will go off with somebody else, a girl, not this girl, not a farm girl, a plump and sullen Venetian girl, and Phillip will be dead in days. An old man, nimble, in swimming trunks. A Halloween swim, his custom. A last act. A passable dive. The fallen leaves still burning.

MILK RIVER

THEIR FATHERS HAD TAKEN TO CALLING THEM *MOTHER.*
They had brothers in the war; mothers dead. They had
lockets of hair in their lockers at school; trouble at school; chores.

They filled pillow sacks with pole beans. The girls milked and
pickled and doctored and cooked and kept the hotrod running they
were too young yet to drive. Still, they drove it, nights, on the
county roads, the headlights off, throwing back a veil of dust.

They would marry men from faraway places.

They would find where Crazy Horse lay. The white man came
like water then—Blixruds and Wenderoths, Crarys and Dahls and
Otters. Coming, coming, coming. Yellow dust in the Black Hills.
Red Cloud, He Dog. Looking Glass and Sitting Bull. The girls had
studied them all in school.

"You're a pretty smart cookie, for a cookie," Franny said.

Hoka hey, she said. *Wasichu.*

IN THE DUSK of the month of the sinking grass, the girls lay in the
fields where wheat grew. They dribbled dirt on each other's faces.
The dirt was silver, amended, a chemical ash.

The night was warm. The fields were shorn. Chickadees fattened upon them. The girls lay on their backs against the stubble

of wheat, the sheared-off hollow pegs, dispersing their weight as they had been schooled to do when caught on ice that is breaking.

Crazy Horse had not been crazy, they knew. He was touched. He had been laid to rest, left for the birds. Crazy Horse was near and far. His blood ran in the birds, in the antelope; it ran in the fish of the river. They had found a cloth he wore. They found his tooth in the silt of the river, one summer when the water warmed.

WHEN THE WATER warmed, the story goes, when their mothers carried the girls in their bellies, two fine feathers, glossy and black, came to them on the wind. Which is to say: their babies would be girls. They would keep to home when the wars began, when their brothers leaned from the windows of the car, tossed out their kisses, and waved. Good boys, gallant, each with a foot in the grave.

The boys had written for months to their mothers, who were dead. Now the boys wrote to their sisters. They sent treasures to their sisters: a broken shoelace, a dimpled stone. The cellophane wing of a locust. For every boy in their town who had fallen, they sent a pinch of dust. *Be good to Poppy*, they wrote. *Feed the dogs.*

The dogs, too, had fallen—the one dog mauled in the thresher, another gone by in sleep. The girls' brothers knew nothing of this; the girls kept the news to themselves. For months, they kept the news of their mothers from the boys: they sent only news of the living, the newly living, the pups and calves and foals.

They kept—in a coffee can—in a time capsule—every last little thing their brothers sent them. They kept the key to the hotrod there, and a scrap of hair or feather or hide of anything slaughtered or fallen. They kept pictures of girls—goofy mall shots—their brothers had kissed and sworn themselves to.

If they married, these girls, or rode out to the buttes with boys too young to enlist, too crippled or scared, the sisters would burn their pictures. They would push tacks into the faces of dolls they had named for their brothers' sweethearts, and bury the dolls in the barn.

THEIR MOTHERS HAD died days away from one another, days the cold made jewels of the snow. Their mothers had been girls together. They dressed up in the ruffled dresses of the pioneer women before them and rode their ponies sidesaddle through the door of the one-room school. They roped gophers, and shot them through with arrows, and sawed off their tails as an offering to the chiefs they mostly loved. They loved the peaceable chiefs and the savage, the deliriums they could dizzy to when they spun in the remnant tepee rings on the bluffs above the milky river. They gave thanks in the four directions, from which the white horse and the dappled surged, the red horse of the springtime rains, the black of the east loping six by six over the darkening plain. They were girls. They would come to be wives together—too soon. Too late to marry Looking Glass. Too late to marry Mort Clark, wavy-haired golden boy, blasted out of a cloudless sky in the last world war.

"I'm him," Franny said, "I'm Mort Clark—" her mother's love, high school days, a golden boy, she'd seen pictures. Franny rolled across the stubble of wheat and kissed Magdalena without knowing she would on her open mouth.

"You poor, poor boy," said Magdalena.

"Franny," Franny said, and her throat burned.

She was Mort Clark speaking to her mother. She was a girl in a field in autumn. She said, "Nothing ever happened to me. Nothing ever will."

FRANNY HAD BEEN her mother's name. There were Blixruds all through that dry country.

Hoka hey was a greeting.

Wasichu was a name for the buffalo when buffalo were everywhere and next a Sioux name for the white man when like water he came and came.

It went wheat and wheat and canola now, advancing on the backbone of the Rockies. To the east: the white bluffs where Crazy Horse lay. Their mothers lay beyond that, in the burying ground above the river, with their heads to the rising sun.

The mothers tapped at their daughters' windows still. *Have you written to your brothers?* they wanted to know.

Blanched the beans? Don't forget. Mulch the rose.

The cold, after all, was coming. The girls ought to shove bales of straw against the skirts of their houses now, before the wind grew teeth, before the snow blew. Already the trees were picked clean. The scrub had turned the russet of potatoes.

THEIR FATHERS HAD taken to calling them *Mother*; they had taken to their chairs. They slept sitting, holding their heads in their hands. The skin of their hands was dappled, lovely as the bark of the sycamore, as a field of wheat in sun the wind moves the clouds out over.

The swans, too, were moving; the geese were going, gone. The girls lay in the dark beneath them. They pulled their shirts off.

"I dreamed," Maggie said, "of an ocean, and the whales rose up from below me and rolled me across their backs."

Their mothers lived still. Which is to say: the girls felt them drawing near. Their mothers stood in the fields and watched them.

Live, little chicken, they said, *live.*

Their mothers sang in the lee of the shelterbelt in the wind that bristled through the caragana.

Skippy the giant, they reminded, *keep away from him. I saw him steal a dollar from his mother once. He crushed a humming-bird, remember, in his hands.*

Their fathers slept with their heads in their hands. They wintered over. They had wintered over since earliest green, through tilling and planting and harvest. They slept in their chairs with their boots on. By God, they would die with their boots on, as their people had before them. Their people had come to this country in wagons, dragging a rope to keep to a straight path across the unbroken plain. Hearty stock, pioneers, blood in every step they were taking.

They made good, proved up. Came to this.

To this!

THE GIRLS DRIBBLED dirt on each other's faces, dirt on each other's necks. A marsh hawk glided above them, drawn to the flapping of a sleeve. The wind lifted their hair and dropped it. The hawk swooped, seized something small, a vole, a shrew, carried it off in its talons. It was a sign, but the girls did not know of what.

They knew snow would shore up in the shelterbelt, in the caragana and the olive trees, the whistling Lombardi poplar. Shut-away days; a gnawing wind.

A day would come the wind would quit and cold would make jewels of the snow. That would be the day, come around again, that Franny's mother had walked to the river, climbed the wide dappled sycamore tree, and on the rope her boy had swung from, summers when the water was warm, let herself down to die.

Let me die, she prayed, *before him.*

THE GIRLS PULLED apart their old Barbies, and hung their heads in the trees.

They painted each other's toenails. They took turns with each other's hair.

"Do you want to look like you, or me?" they asked.

They looked like sisters. They could look, with effort, like twins, as their mothers had before them. They could dream the same dream, they swore it.

They turned cartwheels. They walked on their hands underwater, months when the water was warm.

They knew birdsongs: *chickadee dee dee. Who cooks, who cooks, who cooks for you?* They knew one hawk from another, and how a marsh hawk's head, in flight, tips down.

They knew Sitting Bull was murdered. Crazy Horse was murdered. He was Curly, the years he was young.

Would that they had lived when Crazy Horse lived! They would have been a sweetness to him, little fierce Ogallala wives.

DARK SETTLED ON the plain and, with it, the nightly thimble of dew. Franny's goat appeared—she was a milk goat—she had been her brother's goat—her teats were leaking. Her brother used to lie down under the goat and squirt milk onto his tongue.

Now the goat went where Franny went, as with the little lamb of the song. It stood above the girls in the wheat field.

"She needs milking."

"I'd say."

"Poppy's hungry," Franny said, "he must be. What if he's bumping around in the barn?"

"He'll dream that horsey dream again. And then he'll thrash you."

So they stayed. Or: and yet they stayed.

They dribbled dirt on each other's bellies, spelling out the names they were given. They spelled out the names of the animals they had lost since their brothers went to war—Bonky and Marmalade, the old tom Hopsalot.

The mother cat, they lost to the weasel—easy pickings. The weasel was fearless, the girls knew, a great hunter, a great mouser. It killed for fun.

Their brothers killed because they had to—like their fathers and the fathers before them. Except they liked it. The girls could swear their brothers liked it—the hat, at least, and buttons, the snappy, glistening shoes. They couldn't stop swiping dust from their shoes.

Never mind that the town nearly shut down to watch them rocket off in the hotrod. Forget the women, their swallowed pitiful tremolo; forget the goofy bump of a hug their poppies tried to give them, to see them off, *g'luck, son:* the boys were swiping at their goddamn shoes.

Shoes in a shine you saw yourself in.

When you were a little boy, their mothers kept saying, until something in the saying snagged them, sent them off into the barn among the horses to sob until another mother brought them back.

It's hard, honey. But you've got to.

And the kids, the littler ones, whipped each other with Twizzlers; and the men drank Pabst from sweating cans; and the goat stood up on the table and drank from the good glass punch bowl.

The day lasted—hot and blue. The horses whinnied in the barn. A mother set out a sprinkler the littler kids bumbled through. August, and the hoppers had come, and the wheat was ripe in the fields.

At last the boys set out. Saying, *Love you, Mother. Quit now. Mother, mind the goddamn shoes.*

YOU COULDN'T PREDICT it: the weasel would kill every chicken
in the chicken coop. Partridge, it killed, once a coyote. It killed the
mother cat and left the kittens alive for the girls to save and mother.

The kittens were toothless still and tiny; weepy-eyed; their ribs
showed. The girls fed them out of an eyedropper—milk warm
from the goat, from the cow.

Maggie rolled onto a kitten and crushed it where it had crept
into her bed. The hens blinded another. Franny carried the rest in
the sling of her shirt until the close of school.

The girls walked home together, bumping hips, the kittens
mewling. "Show you something," Franny said.

They stood in Franny's kitchen. Franny dipped her fingers in
a pitcher of milk and bunched Maggie's shirt beneath her chin.
Franny's head swam. Her mouth went dry.

She went by feel, not watching, and dabbed the milk at Maggie's
breast. She held a kitten to her, let it root and mew. Their breasts
had puffed up—just enough, and the buds were like satin, and the
kittens latched softly on.

THEIR MOTHERS HAD been girls together; the girls were little
mothers together. Their clothes smelled of the barn, of the animals
fed, of the milk goat freshly feasted on whatever trash it could
find. The goat followed the girls to school one day and stood in the
playground bleating.

Hicks, they were called, and *lesbo cows. You stink of cow. Bet
she stuck her arm in a cow before school. Yeah, yeah, yeah. And
the other lesbo licked it.*

The girls kept to themselves at school.

They kept a box of crickets in their lockers at school to remind them of the time that would have to pass before they would meet again. They dropped a cricket in a shoe or a pocket, to sing the little song it harbored—the weakening *hurry hurry* it sang, slow in the cold, in the sinking grass, sounding the song of its kin.

"How long is the life of a cricket?" they asked.

"Not very, not very, not very."

THE MARSH HAWK came back.

A star burned out.

Maggie heard it, the star hissed as it fell; it whimpered. No: "That's the goat, silly—" Franny's milk goat was squatting in the dirt to pee.

The goat had lived twice as long as it should have, eating snuff and the hoppers of August.

The goat stamped its feet. It wheezed at the girls.

"We should go."

"I should write to Billy."

"The chickens need fed."

Still they lay there. "Go away, go away."

"Go to Bismarck?"

"Go home."

"He'll thrash me with that stupid rodeo belt he won when he was a boy," Franny said.

"Your poppy was never a boy," Maggie said.

"Boys," Franny said. "Good God."

THE GOAT FOLLOWED them, butting them, home.

It was the tinging of the bell around the neck of the goat that waked Franny's father from his dream. He was dreaming his dream of horses, the one from when he was a boy. Except now the dream happens in a corn palace; now when the horse comes at him, he has a whole corn room to move.

Except he can't: his boots are filled with quarters.

He was a boy on a dare, a greenhorn creeping into a stall. An only boy, a mother's prize—a boy whose claim to courage was the mangling, once, of frogs. He was terrified of horses. He was terrified of frogs.

He crept in from the sun and the stall was dark. The other boy, a neighbor boy, slid the lock to and watched him over the wooden door.

The horse came at him. It wheeled, reared, struck him. It had a blaze of white that veered wildly over its whitened eye.

This, some half a dozen decades ago.

Still, night upon night he waked shouting, not knowing where he was. He was alone, he remembered, crippled up, an old man dropped into sleep in his boots in a dead dry country.

He rose, shuffled into the kitchen. It was night yet, he saw, for the stars were out, the moon was smoothly passing.

He called out, "Franny."

He was a boy, else a dog, or a man, newly loved. He was not himself, waked from a dream, seeing his daughter in the lemony kitchen. He saw instead his wife—a girl. *Franny, Franny.* There she was.

She was turned from him, her rope of hair. She smelled of the dirt of the fields, the shit of cattle and horses.

She would wait for him. She would come to be his wife. After the war, years ago, she would come to be his wife. She would wait for the war to be over, as she had, as she would, then as now.

She was turned from him, at her chores.

"Whosoever shall," he mumbled, "whosoever shall—" but he had lost the words that follow.

He stood behind her with his hands on her belly. Franny's father had the hands of a milker. His fingers curled, he couldn't straighten them.

He bunched her shirt up, lay his mouth against her neck. Franny twisted away and he followed her as a dog would, or a goat. When she stopped—to dry the dishes, to stir the soup—he came behind her, shuffling in his split-apart boots, and leaned against her back.

A good girl, strong—she would look after him.

"Go rest, Poppy. Lie down."

He never lay down, night or day anymore. He slept where he could see, should he sleep, holding his head in his hands. He saw the yard, the barn, the path his daughter walked to school. He saw the girls bump at the hip when they walked, as their mothers had before them. They sang in the dark of the haymow, where the light pressed, in bolts of gold, between the boards of the barn.

They made a joyful noise—singing songs their mothers had sung, in their mothers' plain, thin voices.

It was a trick: you couldn't tell between them. They were elated; they might be grieving. They might be one voice, or four.

His head was roaring; he couldn't hear her now. He couldn't see into the barn.

If only she would let him see her!

One last time, he thought. His wife was singing. He would go to her. He tried to stand up. The dog was lying on his feet.

What was the matter with him? Hadn't he seen her, a day the sun burned on the snow, lowered into the grave?

Yet he lived. This was his house yet, his chair. His yet: the sun in the trees, the sinking grass. He had wintered over. He was dying, this much was clear. Yet he lived—an old man in a dead dry country. Widow man, cripple.

He pressed the great slabs of his hands hard against his ears, not to hear her.

He stood in the doorway, so to hear her.

His wife was singing him over to her, hesitating on the great divide.

FRANNY'S BROTHER FROM the war sent her a shoe worn by a child he had shot (a mistake) a seepage of dust from the desert. Into the toe of the shoe, he had folded this note: *Dear little sister lollipop, you will not see me alive again.*

Franny wrote: Poppy sleeps with his boots on. He does not want to die in his socks.

He doesn't talk much, but he remembers to go out and milk the cow eleven times a day. He thinks I am Mother or, some days, a girl he has never seen.

How old was the girl you sent the shoe of to me? What color was her hair?

I put the shoe in a time capsule.

The dogs are fine. The kittens' eyes are open. I learned a new card trick to show you.

Remember the time in the schoolyard when Mother ran with you with your kite you made on a day of no wind until night fell? I found the kite in Poppy's closet behind his high-shine shoes. He wears the same boots every day. The soles have come free and they flap when he walks. His sleeves are too long. He is shrinking. Holes are burned through his shirts from smoking.

He will flame up soon, he says so, and blow the hell away.

SHE WROTE: I found him lying in the kitchen with a bread sack stuffed up against his face. He had the gas line unhooked that goes to the stove and he had poked the end into the bread sack. It was a colored sack, for Rainbow bread. Sun came yellow through the frost on the window. It was pretty. It was a good day to die, I was thinking. I shouted for him to move. His shirt was off.

I am sorry to tell you this, Brother. I was only just home from school. Our poppy was lying on the floor in the kitchen. I shouted at him. If I touched him, he would sit up and bite me. It wasn't so but I thought so.

I couldn't touch him but then I did. I thought how I carried the dog that died and the stillborn calf and the foal. I thought of the Sioux at Wounded Knee carrying off their dead, and of the baby

Black Elk tells us was nursing from its dead mother. I thought of
Mother in her tree we swung from.

You have got to please come home.

I pulled the sack off. His skin was warm from the sun. I carried
him out to his chair. I could carry him! Poppy is tiny.

I went, *pops poppy lollipop, little sister lollipop,* talking to
myself.

His skin is spattered with scars from the embers that fall and
burn through his shirts when he smokes. He snatches at the air
when he sleeps.

Maggie and I like to watch him sleep. He looks like a boy catching fireflies like in August when you were here.

Oh, but, Brother, I need to tell you. They got him rushed down
in the ambulance, Brother, and Dr. Gene brought him back. So he
is back now. They brought him back without his boots on, which I
tore up the house to look for. He goes barefoot like an Indian now.
His toenails are curved and yellow and the shit from when he milks
the cow is stuffed in underneath them. *Bring me this,* he says, *bring
me that, I can't move for the dog lying on me.*

But he can still milk the cow, I told you, elevendy-leven times
a day.

PLEASE YOU SHOULD write to me, Brother, and let me know that
you are fine. It is a long time now since word came. The leaves are
all down and the snow blows in. The wind gnaws at the house,
you remember.

She wrote: Maggie hardly comes to the house any more. She is too afraid of Poppy.

I have started skipping school. Poppy wants me here every day now to iron his good shirts. He wants to look nice for the street dance that comes before the rodeo you remember on the Fourth of July.

Remember the once that bull rider got flipped over the fence into Mother? Poppy remembers. He remembers the float like a pirate ship and the veterans in a cage of barbed wire with their banner that says *Thank me*. It has been the Fourth of July for a month now.

Even so, even with me home ironing, Poppy wants to iron, too. Today he left the iron flat on his shirt until it was black and smoking. He irons Mother's clothes I never moved from their place. He holds the iron to the bottoms of her shoes. *This will keep her*, he says, *from walking*.

He says he will do it to me, too. *You better quit*, he says.

I need you, he says. *Don't you ever go away*.

STILL I GO at least to Maggie's, when the snow is soft to be quiet. It has snowed every night for a week now so in the morning my tracks are gone. I go to Maggie's and we listen to music very low and she lets me brush her hair. She gives me all the peanuts from her Cracker Jacks.

We ride out in the hotrod with the lights shut off to the bluffs where the tepee rings are. The rings are gone underneath the snow but we know if we are standing in them. We spin until we fall down and the stars smear wild and blue. The crows are black on the snow. The town sleeps at our feet. I pretend that I am Crazy Horse and Maggie is my pretty, young squaw.

REMEMBER WE WENT to the Bearpaw that time and all the little trails the Indians made to where Looking Glass fell and the women in the swale dug themselves in with their hands? It was hot and Mother made us walk. The wind came up, it was a hot wind, and we didn't want to walk. And we saw a deer in the rushes.

We knew the speech Chief Joseph spoke when they had come so near to the Medicine Line after months of flight and fighting and no help came down from Sitting Bull because the messengers were killed. Mother knew the speech, too, and we said it: *Hear me, my chiefs. I am tired. My heart is sick and sad.*

Remember? *Looking Glass is dead. Too-Hul-hul-sote is dead. The old men are all dead. It is the young men who say yes or no. Hear me, my chiefs.*

I cannot remember all of it. *It is cold and we have no blankets.*

We stood at the stone with our hands high and the sun burned down on our faces. I felt the wind lift my hair; it was a hot wind. It moved your shirttails. You stood between us.

And we said, *It is cold and we have no blankets. The little children are freezing to death. My people, some of them, have run away to the hills. No one knows where they are—perhaps freezing to death. I want to have time to look for my children and see how many of them I can find.*

You were between us. We turned away from the sun. And you said, "Yeah, but I'm still going."

We watched that dirty poodle, remember, squeeze out a stool at the foot of the stones that stood in the sun where Chief Joseph stood?

Mother kicked at the poodle. And you said, "Yeah, but I'm still going."

And that night all night in Minot, Mother sat in the tub in the hotel and we listened to her cry and cry.

AND NOW YOU are gone and no word comes and Mother hanged herself in the tree. And now I cannot go to Maggie's.

Poppy is like a dog. The snow came on to hide my tracks and I went in the night and quiet and it was quiet yet when I came home and Poppy was in his chair. I slept, and when I waked, the sun was up and he was standing over me. He had the iron in his hands.

How he knew is we never have Cracker Jacks and he could smell them on my hands, he said, and he said my breath stank of them.

Poppy sat on my feet and the iron was hot and he touched it to my heel. He touched first the one next the other.

Now he won't let me go to school. We are here in this house just the two of us and the snow has come and come. Still he thinks there will be the street dance. He will go there and dance with Mother.

He has hung a good snap shirt with a bolo tie on every chair in the house now. His high-shine shoes—every one of them is out there in the snow.

When I go to the barn, I hopscotch not to step in the shoes he used to wear that serve to mark the path now between the house and the barn. She is sleeping in the barn with the horses, he thinks.

He will catch her there one day soon.

ONE DAY A stack of letters tied with a string will arrive for me from you. It will be a day like the movies. Let it please come soon.

SHE WROTE: Is it true where you are that water appears and you walk and it goes away? I would like to see that.

I would like to see a place where no roads go and wind takes your footprints away. The hills move in the wind. They are nothing but sand. Nothing holds them. I would like to see what grows there. I would like to see what lives.

I see no one but the animals and Poppy, and Poppy's shirts and shoes, and Poppy's trail he has worn going barefoot to milk the cow in the barn. His feet are cracked and bleeding. I rub salve on them that is for the horses' hooves but they are foul to smell or look at.

Poppy could walk on coals, he thinks.

My feet are too awful soft, he thinks. He says, The river of fire on the great divide—how will I ever cross it?

"I will have to cross it with you," he says. "I will carry you on my head."

He crosses to the barn and comes back with a dribble of milk in his bucket and his feet are red and raw.

"Don't they hurt you?" I ask him.

He can't feel them. He only feels that the dog lies on them, he says, so he says, "Bring me this, bring me that."

But, Brother, I am sorry to tell you. That dog is dead going on a year now and buried behind the barn.

Poppy's shoes disappear in the snow every night. He shakes out the snow in the morning and sets them back on the path for Mother. He says Mother has her nose to go by, too, by the bloody seep his feet leave fresh in the sun in the fresh fall between the house and the barn.

He hears her singing in the barn, he says. But when he comes near, she is quiet.

He says, "When I was a boy we went quiet to the pond in our socks so the frogs wouldn't quit. But they quit," he says, "they always."

You ought to quit, too, and come home, Brother. You are hiding in your shiny shoes, Poppy says. He says you should never have gone.

He says, "*Widow*, we say, and *widower*. But what is the name for the mother of the boy who gets himself killed in a war? What is the name for the father?"

God willing, you will come back home. You will ride in your hat with the high-shine bill with the pissy old men from the rest of the wars, and the widows will throw you roses, and you will think always: *Thank me*.

I would thank you always, Brother. I would thank you to come straight home.

WE HEAR THAT Earl is dead and Dr. Gene's boy and Looks At The Stars from the rez. Carol Ann came home from the corner store, who can neither speak nor hear. She sits in a big chair shaking.

Maggie's brother is killed; we have heard it. I am here and cannot go to her, but I know the word has come. She wears her hair over her face now. Her poppy makes her go to school.

She still walks by our house and waves, Brother, on her way to school. She left a cricket for me from under her bed and a note that said *your Suzie*. Your Suzie is going with an eastern boy, so I pushed tacks into the doll of her and buried her in the barn.

This is the news I know of, Brother. Poppy says you can't hide from it all.

You can run, he says, but it always.

Poppy says you put a noose around Mother's neck and ran away off to the war.

POPPY POUNDS AGAINST the windows. He shakes his fists at the trees. He is like something in a cage with the door standing wide with the cold and the snow streaming in.

Send word.

She wrote: I would like to see sun so hot and soft it looks to melt out of the sky. Camels, I would like to see, with rubies hanging down from their halters. The camels kneel in the sand. The sky is burning. The sand is the color of my skin that you sent, so hot you cannot walk across it.

POPPY SITS ON my feet in the night, Brother. He is small but I cannot get him off me.

He hums a song our mother sang to us when I was asleep or pretended to be and she carried me over the field.

By God, he says, I got you.

He touches the iron to my heel. I cannot get him off me.

I try to slap at him. Poppy smells of the barn. I scratch at him. It is like scratching at a fence post, Brother.

But for the dog that lies on our poppy's feet, he cannot feel a damn thing, he said so, from the brisket down.

SHE WROTE: I would like to see Mother at my age sitting in a tree with Mort Clark with her bare legs hanging down. They let their legs swing. It is summer. He has painted her toenails red. The river is slow and milky and the branch our mother sits on makes a shadow across the water. The shadow grows long and longer until it darkens the other side.

SHE WROTE: I made my way out to Maggie's.

The sky looked like snow but it never did snow so easy you saw my tracks going out and coming back again. We went to the bluffs where we found the cloth, remember, that Crazy Horse once wore? We were keeping the cloth in a time capsule with the things that Maggie's brother sent and the things you sent to us, too. We mixed the dust of the plains and the desert. We laid a coin someone left for Looking Glass in the heel of that little girl's shoe. We had a jewel each from each of our mothers. A button we had not sewn on. We had the hooked toe of the badger you shot and forgot to take to keep you and bring you safe back home.

Maggie said, "Remember we scratched our brothers' names in the window glass with diamond rings our mothers wore? We should not have done that. We should have buried their diamonds with them. We should have worn our brothers' clothes every day and kept a black rock in our pockets and a scrap of our brothers' hair. We sailed a feather down from the rooftop—we should not have done that. We should not have touched the hotrod our brothers set out in. And not the toothbrush. Nor the tin of snuff. Nor the gloves our brothers left in the jockey box, worn through from stacking hay. Our brothers left money in the ashtray we spent. We should have spent it on them. We spent it on ourselves."

Maggie lay down in the snow. She made me cover her over with it. I packed snow against her face how she said to until nothing showed or moved. Still she breathed and her breath, the heat of it, melted a place in the snow. And the snow came to ice that held the shape of her face and, when Maggie stood up, it was there. Her face was pressed into the snow. The ice held it.

And I thought of us, Brother, on the lake that day when we lay on the ice with Mother. The ice made a sound—*like a bear,* Mother said, *like a rocket, busting in from far away.*

We had our faces up. My braid stuck to the ice. We wore mittens. It began to snow while we lay there and we thought of the goose we saw stuck to the ice and the time the car quit in the snowstorm on the highway near to Bismarck and by morning time was buried and we didn't know was it night or day.

We lay there. You are happy, it is said, when you are freezing, and begin in the end to cross over.

The snow twisted down onto our faces, onto our coats and legs. If the ice broke, I thought, or we stuck there, only Poppy would be left to grieve. The snow came down all around us, around you and me and Mother, and we saw in the ice when we stood to leave the darker shapes in the white of the snow that showed us where we lay.

SHE WROTE: RED Cloud gave up the land, it is said, when the white man found gold in the hills. You couldn't fight them. There were just too many of them, come flooding across the land.

So it is that Crazy Horse went quiet. He brooded, walking alone for days. You could walk back-to-back across the buffalo still; the great herds darkened the plains. I would like to have seen that.

Before the sheep came, and the cow, I would like, before the plow that broke the plains. Looks At The Stars. Sitting Bull. Earl. The grizzlies way out on the prairie. Neither wheat nor wagon nor wire, I would like. Before Wounded Knee and Bearcoat Miles, before the Crarys and Dahls and Otters. Before the little men from China came to lay the track over the plains, I would like. And the pioneers came. And the prospectors. And the gentlemen from St. Louis, it is said, who shot the great herds by the thousands from the windows of the passing train. For fun, they shot them.

But, Brother? Remember we had our lassoes, Brother, to lasso the passing train?

We wore clothes from flaps of leather, and we slept in the bluffs in burlap sacks with feathers in our hair. We smeared our faces red. You were Heavy Runner and, some days, the Great Goose of Doom. We raided our fields for horses. We lassoed Mother, and got her up on the yellow mare, and carried her away.

CRAZY HORSE FOUGHT and was captured, it is said. It is said that when the soldiers killed him, his people carried him off to hide.

His blood runs in the fish and the antelope, Brother, in the marsh hawk that dips its head as it flies. In the swallows lifting up without number, it runs, in the east in the brightening sky.

I am a fool, Poppy says, to believe any of this. There is no telling where Crazy Horse lies.

Poppy calls me a fool to write to you and to think you will find your way home. They have already killed you, Brother. This is what Poppy says. Poppy says they will send you back to us and we will have to burn or bury you with your head to the rising sun.

The ground will have thawed to dig then, Brother. I will help our poppy with you. Poppy says I have to. *You can run*, he says, *but it always*. They will send what they can find.

BLUE ANGELS

FOOTAGE OF THE MACERATED BODY. THE AIRPLANE crash of decades ago still live on the findable screen. So we find it. Play it again and again. A fuselage in flames. Then the loss of control, the tilt of the wing, the pilot turning earthward. Hoping to bury the nose behind the grandstand. No. Umbrellas for the sun. Glass blown to dust. Bodies torn rags across the sagebrush. Blue angels, faultless in the unblemished sky. Great wide American open.

SINEW

THE BOY MAKES A SHIELD FOR HIMSELF AND PAINTS HIS face black and makes arrows with the pointed rocks he finds and secures to the good straight sticks he finds with fake sinew his mother brings him from the craft shop. He cuts his father's suede coat into a loincloth and goes out across the shortgrass prairie. August. The boy white-blond, blonder even than the grasses, his bottom so pale it is luminous, the alabaster haunch of the gods. Does he suspect his mother watches from the window, that the pronghorn sees him coming, that the badger regards him from his den? What can he say, what does he know, of the savage history he enacts, the ancient, exultant longing?

HOME IMPROVEMENT

ERE IT COMES. SLOW ASCENT OF HER FATHER ON A ladder she has been told to steady. Girl of twelve. Time to whiten the siding. He had a bucket and a sponge, a yellow glove, his elbow spotty from bleach. Bleach fell against her face, the ladder blackened her hands. Her father grew short, shorter, one of the tricks of perspective. One leg was shorter than the other: no trick to that. Gimpy. And now the ladder, grooved and silver, comes swinging away from the house. Her name in his mouth. *Forgive me.*

LUCKIES LIKE US

ON THE NINTH DAY, THE MOTHER PUT ON HER SCRUBS
—not the clothes from home the father had laundered for
her but the uniform of her doctordom, the getup of a savior in
starched and leafy green. He brought her the soft, loose clothes of
the daily, clean, in a shopping bag she never looked in. She scarcely
looked at him: she was a doctor, he saw she was occupied, she
would look at him when she wanted. Speak to him, he knew, when
she wanted. He was to stand until then at the foot of the bed with
his hands folded over his zipper.

The skin had yellowed where the skull had broken and anywhere a tube, his daughter called them straws, anywhere a straw
slipped in. He tapped the boy's foot, which was cold. He took the
liberty of drawing the sheet across it, drew the sheet to the boy's
blunt chin. The IV was backing and filling with blood and the boy
had blood in his ears, did she know? Had anybody noticed that?

He turned away from her when he asked it, as though to check
something beeping, a blip on the screen—he was grinning, a stupid
hopeless grin, he knew, at how ugly she was when she bristled, the
little doctor, the tendons flinching above the collar of her scrubs.
Her face looked chapped and patchy. The vein that marked the
middle of her forehead flared, dependably: she had heard him. He

could read in her face what she thought of him. A man, just, a father. A donkey with a hammer and saw.

She went about her work pushing buttons, fussing with valves she rolled open and shut, nurse's work, filling in. He backed away from the boy to give her room to move and she moved between him and the bed. Her scrubs made the breezy important sound of somebody in a hurry. The boy whimpered. She let something of a mimicking whimper out, a mother sound he had heard her make in all the days before.

The news was worse on the ninth day. On the seventh, they unwound and patched the boy's bowels and stuffed them back in again. On the ninth, his brain was bleeding.

The mother pulled the sheet to his chin again.

In a moment she would turn, ask the question. This was not the father's domain but he could read it: the etiquette of the bedside, the arithmetic of delay. Let him wait. Let the loved one prepare to be grateful.

He didn't wait well. He lived by motion—plank and nail, joints cleanly held—rough work, not finish, a wall going up, work you could see you had done.

She was right: he did not even know the right questions. The building made him weary and sick to be in, the abandoned wings, the weird quiet. The smug, clubby ways of doctors made him sick, and how she tipped her head like a bird. (Now she would ask it.) "What was your—?" (He would slug her if she asked it.) "What was your question again?"

"I said—" and he asked her again. He saw her start up the little assessment that would tell her what to do, whether to answer or not, check the boy's ears or not, and he counted time on his fingers. It was a doctor's assessment, and a wife's, a guess, and he knew it was half-concluded. It was swift.

He went through the questions: Had he been—in the past—grateful?

Was he ready to be grateful again?

THE FATHER KEPT away when she put on her scrubs—for days at a time, in the house he had built. He kept away with their daughter, playing checkers, eating cheese, sliding on the lids of dog food cans down the hillside in their helmets. He dressed his daughter in flowers and plaids, in dots and the splotched animal pants in vogue with the young that season. She wore cheetah pants in purple, a cheetah hat and mittens, her hat pulled down over her eyes.

They stayed up late eating popcorn and they slept in their clothes in the mother's bed where the girl had been, far from the hospital, almost suddenly born. She asked her father to tell her the story.

"One thing. Tell about your sock I wore for a hat when that stuff was all over, right, that waxy stuff that was bloody was smeared all over my head? And, Papa, you drove," she said, "and Mama was just quiet. And Henry wasn't there, right? Henry wasn't born."

She stuffed her mouth with popcorn. She said, "I was in the accident, too, you know."

Popcorn shot out of her mouth as she talked. The father held up his hands in front of his face as though to shield it.

"Don't," said the daughter, and hit him, and she hit him again and again.

THE DAUGHTER SAID, "One thing."

She said, "Let's never go back to that hospital where they use all those whistly carts and stuff and Mama is just sort of *wah dee ga* and she just never listens? Remember she forgets? Remember that time she said that to me? She said she would fix my hair."

She said, "I want to stay home with my pictures."

The girl was cutting pictures of flowers out and of women in bikinis from catalogs. She couldn't wear any bikinis. That was not nice for girls. She pasted the pictures on a page together and X'd out all the girls.

Her mother hadn't picked her. That was what the daughter told her dolls. Her mother had longer to love her. She had been alive a longer time than Henry and also she was a girl. She was a little mother.

The daughter had a cut lip that was healing and both of her knees were not bony or loose the way they had used to be. They were puffy and hurt if she walked much but that was not going to make her—they weren't dashing *her* down to that hospital to fix her up again.

She carried her dolls in her underpants—two dolls tucked in at a time in turn so they would not be lonesome and they were all girls. If her babies were ready to plop out, *then* she would go to the hospital, but they were in her growing still and they were all girls. All God's little children.

She said, "Maybe you will die. Maybe God will want you."

She could not help it. All God's little children. She would say so long, good-bye.

THE DAUGHTER TOLD her teacher, "Henry's on vacation."

It was what she had said of her father, too: "He is taking a vacation from living with us still."

Still they had their days together—the ninth, the tenth, a few of the days that came after. The father closed up his house on the windswept farm on the curve of the road his children passed with their mother on the way from school.

It came again to be the father's job to ferry his daughter to school. He watched his daughter's face in the mirror as he drove. She looked sleepy, and puddled in the seat, blinking.

She said, "You should watch the road."

She brought her dolls with her in a clump by the hair, lassoed at the waist with a bolo tie.

"There you go," she said, and buckled them in.

And: "Amn't I a so good mother to you? I am buckling you right right in."

HE TOOK HIS daughter to school and back again and drank in the sun in the afternoon in the house he had been let to live in with them. He sat in the window with the sun on his face and listened for the coughing and spitting of the spigot that would mean the pipes had thawed.

There had been a day of rain and thaw. Now everything had frozen. The birches had laid down their heads in the snow and now the snow had seized them—the snow had them. The birches jerked in the wind. He found it funny, and called his wife. She was his wife still. The trees looked frantic.

He said, "They look like a bunch of old women out there frozen in by their hair."

He said, "I went ahead and built that bunkbed for them with the boards I measured and saved. I took the Christmas tree down. The pipes are frozen. Everything is frozen. I rolled the tree into the creek bed. Lucy bled all into the snow. She got a nosebleed—she was sledding—she bled all into the snow. God, the snow. It's been blowing. It's scoured. It's blazing out there. I can't see."

The house grew darker. The windowpanes rattled in their tracks in the wind and the wind drove the snow in between the panes into miniature drifts on the sill. The drifts darkened the house. The sun burned on the snow. The snow had a glaze poured across it that even the ox the neighbors kept did not, as it walked, break through.

The mother said, "He doesn't know me. He hasn't the faintest idea I am here."

THE MOTHER SLEPT in a chair beside the boy's bed and waked when anyone came in. She talked very quietly to him, not knowing if he could hear.

"When I was little," she said, "by accident, my mother set fire to my hair."

"A bird snatched a sandwich from me."

"My mother weaved a crown of flowers for me and I ran through the garden naked, painted up, making soups of sand and leaves."

She said, "Wake up. Wake up, Henny. Mama's right here."

The boy had a hose down his throat to breathe and he held it, the way a baby will, the way a boy holds the branch of a tree he has climbed and is swinging through the shadows from.

THE GIRL FELL on her back from the monkey bars from swinging in her mittens.

Her father came early to fetch her. He came at Thank You Time. She was thanking each one of her dolls. She thanked the nurse for her Band-Aid. She was wearing a Band-Aid stuck to her head where her brother's head was broken. She thanked her papa. He was a good papa. She said, "I always buckle my dolls."

"He makes me popcorn," she said. "I would like to thank him. Papa, thank you, Papa, for giving me this—what's it called again? This bolo."

She was swinging her dolls by the hair.

They had a Thank You Rock they passed, each to each. The teacher held out her hand for the rock.

"I amn't finished," the girl said. "He made a ladder for me. I like his brown spots on his hands. He smells like bread to me.

Thank you, Papa. Thank you for making me popcorn. Thank you for ice in my water. Okay next now."

She passed the rock. "Say you're welcome."

He could not say much: he had lost her. He would lose her again and again.

To her mother, she said, on the telephone, "You could have gone into the snow, couldn't you? It would not have killed you. You could have buckled us all all in."

The police, too, had questions they called with. The woman from the insurance company called to say, "Lady, your son can sue."

The mother said, "My son is two. His favorite color is blue, or it was. He liked to play blocks. He made a good sound like a siren. He's just small and he is sleeping and he will wake to himself and say *blanket mama me*. And you? You can't be—are you serious? You can't be serious. You are calling me and telling me, Lady, he can sue?"

"When he's older, ma'am."

"So sue me. Put me in jail and sue me. I was in my lane and here the guy came and there was nowhere for me to go. It was morning. We were driving up the hill in the snow. It went shadow and sun and shadow, and do you know what I was thinking? I was thinking, eight or nine? I was going to buy skates for my daughter and I couldn't think eight or nine, what the size was, I knew the color. Sun. And shadow and here he was. I thought I was seeing something. I waited for him to correct himself. I saw nowhere to go. The guy was driving a car like their father's and I thought if he was their father but it was not him. He was a guy from around. I patched him up once. I cut a rusty hook from his eyebrow once."

THE TWELFTH DAY passed and another. Nothing felt right—not going, not staying away. He hated to call but he called her. Did she need the clothes he had laundered for her or the potpie he had made or the bread?

"You made bread?"

"Well, I tried," said the father. Which he hadn't.

It amazed her—that anyone still made bread. That anyone tended lightly, easily, to the household, the press of tiny cycles, children's simple needs. *Blanket. Mama. Hungry. Pee.*

How many times had she wanted to run out screaming from him?

Dirty, ornery, noisy boy.

And now what would she—just to dress him, for a kick in the shin, to wipe his backside—what would she not give?

She rubbed his belly—hot, distended. He used to say, days ago, used to, "I want to feel your hot skin."

He was a boy who once lay so quiet in the grass a honeybee stood on his nose. The neighbor dog pissed on his bottom. She thought of him standing in a backyard pool hoisting an enormous zucchini. Of the ocean, she thought, the first time he saw it. A wave came over her head.

"I tried to run from it," his mother told him. "The wave was breaking. I was holding you over my head."

THE DAUGHTER CALLED to speak to her, to sing to her, something made up, come suppertime, a song of ice and trees. But her mother wasn't answering. Her mother had stopped answering the phone.

The girl spoke into the dead receiver. She bumped her nose against the counter to get it bleeding as she spoke.

"Papa's cooking," she reported. "He's a yogurt." (It was her brother's word for ogre.) "Now he's not. He's being that cooker that's fancy—right?—with the clogged-up nose. I got a nosebleed," she said. She tried to hide it. "And a fox came and ate up the melty stuff where I bled all down in the snow where the snow—"

"Papa, don't," she said. "I'm talking. Please don't turn that on."

The snow looked like a cherry slushy. In the morning it looked like a hole in the snow that a fox had come to see.

She said, "Mama, my tooth is looser."

And: "My papa fixed my hair."

She said, "I love everything you are cooking."

She liked him cooking. She liked the spots on the backs of his hands. She liked how if ever he took off his boots, he stood them back up again. They smelled of sawdust. There was sawdust packed into the treads.

She cleaned his boots for him, and shook talcum into the toes. She had an accident—and scorched his shirt with an iron.

They were like other days, these days, how they passed—her mother at the ER, her papa steady, home.

But they would be finished come morning.

In the morning, she would pour out cereal for her father and pick the caught bits from his beard. She'd find his calculator—his *cowcutator*—and take that. She'd take a rock to pass, a ball and jacks, a quiet pull-back train. Only quiet toys. Her father told her. You had to keep very so quiet there. You keep quiet when your brain is bleeding. You keep yourself so so still.

She bent her nose some, and drummed at it with her knuckles.

She found her brother's best sit-and-ride toy and rolled it out into the cold. The trees creaked and popped. She liked the sound of them.

She shoved the toy down the stairs to take. The ox fell down in the field. The girl mooed to him. Her papa mooed back.

They would see Henry Bear in the morning, unless the ice came, unless the snow.

THE MOTHER SETTLED into her chair as if to sleep.

He had brought fresh panties for her, and the line emblazoned on them kept repeating in her head. *More whiskey.* (A joke from the old days, a busty, puckish cowgirl, a lariat overhead.) *More whiskey and fresh horses for my men.*

The news was the same and the same and worse.

She drew her knees in, shut her eyes. Again the phone started up. They were after her: she was somebody else's mother. She was still somebody's wife.

The doctors appeared, went off, clammed up. Stingy bastards—pretending to hurry. Getting out, out the door, down the hall, man—quick, before she cries.

She should lock the door, yank the phone out. Doctor him herself.

She worked the ER. She had seen plenty. Things they never had seen, she had seen—manglings, flayings, freakish stuff, the slop and stink that didn't make the cut for prime time TV.

She had the head for it: the body gone at. The fat man disemboweled.

She had her face along the highway on a billboard.

SHE PUT CLEAN scrubs on. Her boy whimpered. He shut his hand, opened it again. When he opened his hand, the phone rang again.

"Officer Sweet here." You bet. "One question."

She dropped the receiver back onto the cradle again. Seconds passed, a minute, and up it started.

Her boy's hand opened when the phone rang, opened again, as though the ringing were a sound his body made and emitted through his fingertips. It sounded howly, living. The room was darkly purpled. She watched his hand move—a howling, pulsing flower, she thought, a bud caught in time-lapse footage, passing through the seasons, through the years.

He was two. He had not even learned to run quite. He still threw sticks backward.

She tried not to hear the phone. It seemed louder then. She tried to quiet it by listening.

Her boy thrashed in his sleep. She shook him lightly. He hissed at her when she shook him. Blood bubbled out of his ears.

THE FATHER SAID, "Up, up. Time to scoot."

The girl brought sticks for her brother she had dug from the snow. She brought dolls and the dresses she had made for her dolls. She made a long gown of raw bacon she poked twigs through the fat of to hold.

She told them, "Sometimes when your nose bleeds. Sometimes when your brain bleeds, you have to just swallow it down."

She rode in the back behind her father with her family of dolls. Her father rolled up the window on an out-folded map so the daughter's eyes wouldn't and her doll's eyes wouldn't sting in the so-bright sun. When he got the map right, he kissed her. She said, "Kiss Mama, too," and held up the doll who was the mama who was wearing the bacon gown.

The daughter's cheeks were shiny with grease and she was wearing a lacy pajama top and her hair had not been combed. He bent to kiss her again, her head tipped back, her narrow face turned up to him, a miniature of her mother's, and the daughter thrust her doll at him, saying, "Mama's right here."

"Cousin?" she said, addressing her doll. "Listen to me, cousin. I can show you. There's a thing with just marbles and springs we can see, and ditches with pops and whistles. This ladder thing carries this ball up. Okay? That is not for sick kids. That is for luckies like us."

IT WAS EASY for her to walk but he carried her and, as he carried her into the hospital, she sang.

This pretty planet, she sang,
spinning through space.

My garden, my harbor,
my holy place.

And then:

Bis bitty banet
binning boo bace.
By barben, by barbor
by boly blace.

The halls smelled of macaroni. She said, "I'm hungry, Papa. I want to eat, Papa."

He kept walking. She picked something out of his beard, tossed it into her mouth. "Better now?"

"No," she said. "No way, I'm not. No."

She felt like eggs, or candy. She felt like having a snowball fight.

"You're so stupid," she said. "She won't like it."

She said, "You should have fixed my hair."

The father found the room, the door pulled to. He swung it open and stood without walking in.

The bed was tucked and smoothed. The boy was laid out naked in his mother's arms—living, he didn't know, or dead. The father held on to the girl.

She said, "You're hurting me, Papa. Papa, stop."

Still he held her, awaiting the news of the day, the life ahead, unstoppable. His daughter slid down his chest and off and he felt he might float up. He tried to steady himself, make bone of the sand his bones became, put a stop to it. He was pouring into himself. Sinew and gristle, the renewable heart, the hard little beans of his kidneys—everything in him was mixing, slop, a caustic, grainy wash. He stiffened his skin to keep standing.

His wife waved at him. It rose up in her: the swarmy, passing happiness of seeing him again. She could smell him, it made her giddy: a man come in from the cold. *More whiskey,* she thought, and wished he would kiss her. Cross the room and kiss her. Fall on his knees and forgive her. For an instant, all at once, how hard could it be? She could ask him to forgive her.

He stood away from her, his hands folded over his zipper.

The daughter's doll began a dance, dancing gently, wildly, the bacon smacking against her legs. When she had finished, the doll fell on her back and glistened in the sun. In a whisper, the girl asked, in her doll's voice asked, "Do you think that dance was so pretty?"

"Oh, yes," her mother said.

"Not you," the girl scolded. "I asked Henry."

The sister reached in among the loops and straws and patted her brother gingerly, leaving little slicks of bacon grease. She pulled toys out to give him from the sack she had brought, saying, "Brother, I brought you this one, Brother, and that and that and that."

"The ox fell down in the field," she said. "I was swinging in my mittens."

She poked him gently. "You're not listening to me, Brother. He can't hear."

She blew into his ear and the hair lifted up.

He wasn't Henry yet. She wasn't any Henry's sister. She was a mother-girl with a bacon-doll with no little man to love.

"Hen, Hen, Hen," she said.

She kissed his head where he was hurt and stood up. She found the pull-back train in the sack she had brought and pulled it back across the floor to release it, to catch it up again. She would take it back home, she decided. The rest of the toys, he could have when he waked, finding that she had been near.

The daughter tugged at her father's knuckle to make him kneel for her, and spoke in a whisper to him.

"We can go now," she said. "He's just quiet. Little Henny's just lying quiet in the dream of his life again."

NOT SO THE DONKEYS

THE DONKEYS ARE EATING THE BARN. THEY'RE BORED, poor things. They are eating out the shape of a donkey, of a dull, sulking herd of donkeys, until at last, come spring, when the thaw comes again they wander out into the sun.

There they stand there. Flatulent. Yawning takes a full minute and you can jam a hand past their teeth. A bee zips in, plenty of time, and wets its wing on the painted dome. Spring at last.

Soon dark comes late and the donkeys, exhausted, lie down in the mud. They pass a night like this. Another, the bums. Beetles. Look, a bunny. A tender, inquisitive mouse, twitching her sealed vagina. In a week she'll reach lordosis.

Not so the donkeys. The donkeys go on warming the shapes of themselves in the commodious mud. Never mind the month's splendid exertions—a mole nosing darkly toward a parsnip, a raccoon sipping pearls of dew.

Here a wren sets down on the ridge beam. The barn shudders, slumps, collapses at last. The donkeys let down their sloppy members and kick up their heels in glee.

DUENDE

CAME UPON THE PINK PLASTIC LEG OF A DOLL IN A country where next to no pink people live, and soon upon the broken arm of the doll with its fanned-out supplicant hand. I thought about the girl whose doll it had been, whose doll it was maybe still. Like a brother from a war, his limbs missing. She had a father who crumpled his shirt at his chest and stroked his belly in the sun. She sang songs she made up to her mother and her mother, in her way, sang along.

I poured the sand out, salt, a scrap of shell, and carried the arm in my pocket.

I came upon the teeth of a man dead and buried in a grave the sea dug out. The teeth were the color of honey, lodged in an eaten bone. Ants in the bone, in the tunnels. How did I know these were a man's? I didn't. *Ser humano.* Ant farm. It doesn't matter but it did to him.

I came upon the cap my boy left on the shore between pangas with his shorts he'd had on. He'd had a girl out there where the pangas are and a thief swiped most of their clothes. Missed the cap.

You could have called me, I said.

He said, *Mother.*

His cap was blue, sir. She wore polka dots green and yellow. A flower in her hair. I found the print where they lay, I found their footprints—dents in the polished sand.

I came upon one of her flip-flops, her feet as small as a child's.

Upon a child washed to shore—but I didn't. But a child had washed to shore with his eyeballs burst on a tide from the neighboring town. A rag in his mouth. A body curdling. Brother, *cholo*, son.

A melon, an eel. The ragged fin of a whale. Each day for many days: yellow onions. Peeled clean by the sea and spit out.

I came upon a bead 400 years old that meant: ten chickens. One cow. Who really knew what it meant, what it counted? One bucket of milk. Two virgins. The bosque from there to here.

Repollo. Bizcocho. Huecito. Chorro.

Cabbage. Cake. Little Hole. Curly.

Did they know what had happened? They didn't.

In the cup of Chorro's hand was a parakeet blown off course from the jungle.

Macaco. Payaso. Carlita. Juan.

I asked anyone I found.

I found Adidas from Fukushima. Alligator handbags. Bowls that fit in bowls that fit in bowls, all bright. Flyswatters in little-kid colors.

I found a booby, dead, its feet like a duck's, a webbed and miraculous blue. Hawksbill. Olive ridley. A hammerhead as small as a hammer. A swallowtail, a bee. A wing bone weightless as a drinking straw, walking, I found these walking, until I couldn't walk or see anymore or think at all or breathe.

I was the mother—monstrous. A joke.

I was the mother shrieking at the bottom of a poisoned sea.

His father would say, What of it? So you drop to your knees. What comes?

At last I went home. I followed the sloppy, sandy track that climbed through the house to my bed. They were lying on my bed. Laughing. I was almost sure it was him.

You could have found me, I said.

He said, *Mother*.

The pangas are all named after women, he said, sisters, mostly, and wives.

My boy swam the mile home naked, the moon making glass of the waves. To be safe, he said. He was serious. He left a track of salt and sand through our house to the bureau where I keep my clothes. My son, my son. Did the girl know they were my clothes? My shawl. My skirt the yellow of honey. She was lying in my clothes and laughing with sand on her feet in my bed.

I wished the worst for her—a wicked uncle. A job scrubbing booths at a peep show.

She was silken, sixteen, untrammeled, at rest. She lived on nothing—on the fruit that drops from a tree. She hooked her leg around his leg to keep or climb him. Two beauties. Saved, a bullet dodged. They seemed to float there. Godly, jeweled. Salt on their skin the sun ignited.

My son was her life, her *rubio* now. Her movie, her catch, her prize.

She was flawless. No. She looked wolfish and her tooth was broken.

I had the arm of the doll in my pocket and if I lay it on the sheet beside her, the girl would think *duende* and flee. Duendes steal your socks if you sleep in them. They steal your teeth, your keys.

I pressed the fat of my thumb into the doll's hand and the hand took hold and squeezed. It was a duende's hand—beguiling. But the mother of the girl whose doll it had been hadn't known the hand was a duende's hand and by now the little girl was missing, spinning down in her sun hat through the darkening sea.

If I went to my knees?

If I called out?

Would the men I once loved beseech me? Throttle me again with their sweetness, their sudden, thrashing need?

I reached for my shawl. It was morning, but the brightness of the day had gone.

It was a yellow hat, sir. Sun in her hair.

A tasseled dress, sturdy and blue.

TALLY

KNEW A SOBER MAN WHOSE BROTHER HAD DIED DRIVING drunk on the high windy plains. The living brother, the sober brother, took to drink straightaway. He was belligerent and incompetent, drunk, and a gentle, almost girlish man, sober. He drank schnapps of every flavor and hue.

It was my job to pour and to tally, to feed a coin now and then into the jukebox when the quiet was too much to bear. Merle Haggard, Garth Brooks, Emmy Lou. "I got friends in low places—" every variation of that town and time is for me ferried by this one dumb song.

The man, the men—the sober man, the dead man—had a sister, inscrutable as a turtle. She appeared each night and drove her living brother home, for months in the same floral blouse. And then she didn't. She had given up, or gone elsewhere. And so the sober brother drove home wildly, drunk, the long way around, making turns that were not in the road.

One night after several months of this I let myself accompany him home. I drove us out to the turn his brother had missed and we lay in the grass for the stars. I felt pity, yes, and alluring. Enchanted by a grief that wasn't mine. We heard a bird in the dark we couldn't see. *Meteor, meteoroid, meteorite,* we remembered. *Sedimentary, igneous, metamorphic.*

After a time we stood up and he kissed me. In his hair the pods of a seed caught—feathery, silver, like something spit from a galaxy, space junk—luck—that sought and found him.

HIS PLACE WAS tiny, the bathtub dragged into the kitchen—the longest claw foot I had ever seen. You could lie in that tub without bending, sink beneath the glistening meringue of foam and entirely disappear. He went under. You cannot believe for how long. I couldn't see his face but his eyes showed—drastic, dark, sprung open. One eye disappeared, appeared again. He was winking at me slowly, the minutes slow in passing.

In bed, he moved as if blind. He was precise, and maddeningly patient. Once he whistled—one note—as to a dog.

The body opens, can be opened, a marvel, and still we live.

When he had finished, he filled the bath again. Carried me to it—not a word. Again the soap foamed up, great billowing mounds. It smelled of berries. In my cunt, a burning balloon.

The window glass shook. Water sloshed in the tub. We thought we'd caused it. We had lain in his dead brother's ashes, in grass where he had gone on ahead. It had not been my grief but I had claimed it. The mountains shuddered. The horizon bucked, it buckled—the boulders strewn and the grasses, erratic, the path of the glacier plain. This isn't metaphor. This was an earthquake, a moving ripple—ground I had thought of as solid warped, and returning to liquid again.

RINGNECK

HE SHOT PHEASANT WITH HIS COMRADE FROM KINDER-garten, flushed from the grassy swale. The men carried the birds out on their backs. They crossed the stream, the water cold, and pain flared in his toe. The gout years. Years of good bourbon beside a fire. Like a beacon, such pain, a knuckle pulsing in the night. They cut the trip short.

Took the toe, the doctors, when at last he was home, a bright nub on the heap to be burned. Brother at last to the black man. Foreskin of an infant; polyp; liver; lung—the array of what people live missing.

First the small knuckle, next the big. Next the foot—half the foot, next the whole foot, as in the song of a boa constrictor.

It hurt him, all, even missing.

Next the leg. To bear the pain in the leg he was missing, he rubbed the leg he had left in the mirror. Which helped. Some. Still he bellowed. Raged. Threw shoes at his wife.

He arranged to have lilies delivered to his wife on their anniversary for the next twenty years.

His wife was Pretty Shield—his pet name for her. Puddy Tat. At last: Doll.

The man's name was Wing.

Wing what? Wing what?

I have loved you for years, Wing Pepper, your hands like a girl's, your mouth.

BITTY CESSNA

BLUEBIRD DAY, A FINE DAY TO FLY. THEY TAXI OUT, NO radio, roiling dust, the airport bleak and uncontrolled. A vulture stands on the head of a cactus and displays its wings to dry. "What's *he* waiting for?" the instructor jokes. Of course he's flirting. Horny, disappointed man, too tall to fly the fighters and color-blind besides. He calls her Sunshine. A face like sunshine. First the climb, full on, the big blue he can't see. She's to stall, spin, recover. Pretty, a lay, college girl. She lives behind the hangars in a school bus. She turns the plane upside down. Everything in the cockpit is a missile now, launched, flying at their heads. Wallowing, sloppy, sickening plunge—the altimeter sweep, the stick clutched in her hands. "IT'S MY PLANE," he shouts, meaning, *let go, fool.* That we may live. May we seem to have lived. He sees again the spines of the cactus, the brainy face of the vulture, ravenous, a dream. Bitty Cessna, yellow as the dress his mother wore. Mother war. Mary. Gone to God. *Mine.*

KING FOR A DAY

ANTS STEAL OTHER ANTS' BABIES AND MAKE THEM INTO slaves. A fact. She cannot remember much more about it. She remembers Morocco, a man whose hand was hacked off at the wrist. He had been a stupendous musician. He was drawn into a trance at a drumming ceremony and lay down, coming home, in a heap of ants. Hours later, his brother found him. He had been eaten raw. Like meat, the brother told her. He lived another three days. A killer, the brother, the other a thief. The girl was nothing. His heart kept missing. His missing hand shook. But he was king for a day on the day he died and the ants in their perfect armor bore him in glory away. Singing. Song of feasting. Song of love.

LAST OF THE SWEET

THE WEATHER HAD KEPT THE HAULERS OFF AND BY morning with the snow coming down as it was the mare would be gone from sight. Already she was going, her rump to the wind, her tail where she had sunk to her knees in the field clamped to the fallen snow. First snow. Fields shorn, and stubble like teeth in dark rows. The almanac was right: winter had set in early. Spring would be brief and late coming, a year for ticks and mold. Early onset, an off year, an apple year, this last year, limbs breaking from the weight of it—bushels and bathtubs of fruit. Now wind plastered snow in the gashes the torn limbs had left in the trees, and in the grooved bark of the maple, the whitening windward face.

It was hard to feel warm, looking. But it was warm in the bright in the kitchen where the mother watched out through the snow. She counted the hours, a guess. Her daughter would be home by morning, late—grounded at some shabby airport. Buffalo, Erie. Icing and gusts and lake-effect snow and something about a boyfriend, she had said—ridiculous, unreliable, something about an old car.

What had she said, really—how hard? How hard to come home to your mother?

The last apples hung on the nearest tree and on the apples, too, the windward side, clinging: crescent of the first wet snow. The fruit was mangled but red and so pretty, the mother thought, the mother beyond hunger but thinking simply this: *if only.*

It was a game she could not stop playing. *If only an apple falls while I'm watching,* she thought. (Her daughter would reach home safely and soon. *If.*)

She had begun the game years—decades—ago, the baby due any day, any minute. And like something out of a fairy tale, high in a corner of the kitchen: a spider spinning her silver web. *If only she has her babies before I do,* the mother thought, *everything will be fine.*

But she hadn't thought much about it, not then she hadn't, not the way she was thinking now. Same game. Same unruly kitchen. Dusk coming down, a violet light the snow was slanting through. She could see her face in the window: surprise. *Next of the last of the last,* she thought. *Last of the next if onlys. But one. But one.*

Three apples. And in the corner of the kitchen a spider now in a different linty web. She had a wasp up there, its torn wings pinned; it would be shrouded and hollowed out. Food. Drawn through the straw of the mouth.

Was this so? Was this how it really happened in the world of wasps and spiders? A year for wasps and spiders. Mold.

I know, the mother thought, *next to nothing.*

Margaret would know, she would ask her. As a girl she picked anything up. Turned it in her hand. She kept bees now and sent a gift of honey for Christmas. The tall jars gleamed in the cellar, row on row, like a painting. A jar for every year at Christmas since Margaret had left home—not Christmas quite, Christmasish, the jar arriving weeks late in the mail.

Don't be petty.

She remembered her daughter asleep beneath the tree, in the light from the tree, the angel treetop, with a tape player on to catch Santa. Mind of a scientist, a court recorder. She would know. Whatever it was, her daughter would know it, and if she didn't she could make it up.

Soon—safely and soon, sun on the path, Margaret stumbling up through the snow. It would be a way to begin. A few questions. A few small things to know.

Which came first: The egg sac? The eggs?

And did the spider actually carry the sac?

And was she ever going to marry and have babies?

A papa's girl, this girl, out in the fields with a hoe. She would burst in flushed and breathless, carrying some creature in her hat. Mud on her boots and her hair clumped up, happy, happy, a girl in her papa's coat. It was her father who had thought to give her the mare to learn to care for and ride.

Where was he now?

End of the house. Second barn down. Elsewhere.

Once in the kitchen, tears in her eyes, Margaret spun round and asked him, "Kids don't have to get married, right?"

Plus she would never, ever have babies, no. Not in a million years.

Tomboy, hoyden, burrs in her hair, straw.

Margaret could tolerate ten, twenty minutes—years her braids hung to her pockets. Her hair a rat's nest, a thicket, snarls her mother worked out hurriedly with mayonnaise and a comb. *Sit still, sit still*—a chance to touch her. She couldn't sit. She could sit a horse, yes, that, sit a fence post, ride the tractor on her papa's lap.

Where had he gone, really?

The mother couldn't recall.

The house was quiet but for the hum of a light bulb, snow tapping dimly at the glass. Snow in the sills and gashes and the mare in the field on the slope of the hill the trees seemed to bend down to. Fields frozen hard as stone. Next, snow. First snow, and the white mare going down. And now the ground had gone soft beneath her, a shallow thaw as though spring had come while the last of her life passed through. The wind bent and fluttered her coat and her legs were as straight as fence posts though she had gone to her knees like—what had he said? Gone to her knees like jelly.

Why the knees? Why did fear so plainly lodge in the knees, and was this human, only, or mammal? The joints went soft and trembled, the body's stash blasting into itself and, if so, could you exhaust it, the mother wondered, and never be frightened again? Was this love—to be exhausted, finally? Exalted at last, unbound?

She remembered Margaret, years ago, slipping through the fence to sleep near the mare. Unafraid. *Unafraid*—imagine! And when September came and school again—clocks and bells and gossip in the halls, the mess of other people—Margaret braided the mare's hair into her braid. She had her mother's hair—dark and fine and the mare's hair—white—maundered through it like the vein of something molten.

Molten, ashen, ice.

How long since she had seen her? Months, was it, a year?

The planet tipped on its axis: leaves: weeks of windfall plums. The mother lay in the dim among strangers, bed rest, nothing to do, daybreak and falling night. She saw tapers of light and the color changed and these were the seasons passing. She heard wind in the trees, the patter of rain.

Once a deer stamped its feet in the grass.

Once the phoebes sang in the dark of her room their lovely, stubborn song. The rest had gone on without her, seed to stalk to threshing time and the skunk with her next batch of babies—cotillion day, on parade, tidy stripes and tails fluffed up, spring at last, she had missed it. Miniature identical skunklets—marching into the sunshine in a military row.

A baby skunk was called what? She had known this once. A skunklet, a margaret. Flown, the word, the sight of them, the infant mice, the rooster, the muskrat luxuriant in the velvety green of the pond.

Soon the apples grew round and red again and leaves tumbled over the barn. *So long. Until then.* She had to see it all without seeing—else hate everything, everyone who appeared, little pink swabs and cartoon smocks, and grayly, at last, for a moment, there: her father—no. Her husband, hesitating at the door. The sameness of it enraged her. And the smell! That was her, awful.

Good morning, good morning, and how are we this morning?

The same people appeared with new faces and whispered around the room. And the room was a boat and a room and a nest perched on a glassy building. Cloud. And the cloud hissed and warbled, and it banked and plunged like a bird.

And now at last, delicious—alone, the nurses snowed out, too.

The kitchen brightened and the pain came back. *Let it*, she thought.

Let me wake awhile. Let me see.

She saw a raven spook through the leafless trees, a shadow slipping softly through the falling snow. Snow cupped in the generous boughs of the spruce, the regal blue the mother loved, sap on her hands, and the smell she loved, minty and bright and blue. Blue the shade of the bower beneath the snow would sift down through; dry still, and soft and blue, a bed of fallen needles. As in a fairy tale, the mother thought, and thought if she could find her mukluks, her musty, quilted coat—but had they given these away?

Had they gone through her things already and kept only what she might miss?

She missed her ruby. Silly woman, there it was on her hand. This is your hand, Mother. Thin, thin, your ridiculous breasts, your poochy, sutured belly. Better never to see it, better to keep away. Buffalo. Erie. Exhausted, and Margaret would sleep in the flickering glare, her hat across her face, her mouth open, using her arm as a pillow. Delayed. Departing flights, arriving.

Oh, this. Long ago feeling. A marvel, to be flown, lifted away, buoyant in the dark and stars.

She had crossed the ocean on a boat, long ago; she had run off a cliff with a wing. The air was bright and singing and she was not afraid, the mother, not a mother yet—that was years away. *A girl.* Falling out of an airplane. She was making none of this up. She was plunging through the coppery blaze of the day with her downy arms thrust out. Alien, the thrill, illicit—and the wind passed through her stinging, cold, as if she were hollow, or heat. Nothing more. Nothing, sinking, achy, trying to hold her mouth shut. Tears blew from her eyes. Her face was changing places. Air rushed in and her cheeks billowed out and now the chute, abrupt, roared open. She seemed to surge upward and hang there and everything was still. She had held her breath and now she let the breath go and when she did, as through water, she sank again, in the rapture of cold and quiet. And the quiet was cold and something to feel and the chute blotted out the sun. She was cradled, buoyant, rocking—a flake of snow on a tether. Unafraid. She was drifting above the birds; they were marks on a page, hastily drawn, rising in spirals to meet her. She fell past them and went on falling; she would go on falling. She would fall through the earth as through beaten cream, alive, and live forever.

A rapture: a marvel the dream the mind invents to put an end to the body, and to carry it on and on. Her mind made softness of rock and tree and, of the cage of her room, a cloud. And yet there were rocks, there were trees, and the rocks and trees sped upward, familiar again, and the spider shook her web.

Now. Fix on something. Prepare.

Burn your letters, settle your debts. Change your nightgown, clip your toenails; paint your lips red, brush your hair.

Now pick out a smooth place to fix on and some tall thing to navigate by—the twisted oak a bolt of lightning struck, your father at the door. Stay loose. Be glad. Be soft and glad and loose in the knees and touch down running and roll. As if your bones are fished out. Hold to nothing. Becalmed, be afloat on the brassy Sargasso, sunshiny windless days. And if from beneath a raft of weeds the sound of a child comes to you, mad with thirst, depraved—cry out.

Out of the dark and mutinous. But one, but one.

Three apples.

SHE SAW HER face in the window, not hers—her Margaret. Her raven-haired girl ever flown.

And now the moon. If now the moon and the boughs of spruce and snow in the bluing light. Now the moon. She couldn't think what more she was thinking. And thought how lovely, how lovely and how unlikely it was: Margaret would let her mother brush her hair.

This was the sum now of what she wanted—the gift of repetition, row on row like a painting and the white hair woven through. She cared nothing any longer for the new; the mother wanted what she had, had had, had had and lost and wanted again, her musty coat, her ruby, her mukluks red as embers in the shaded blue.

The kitchen light dimmed and brightened.

And how are we now? And what do we want?

She wanted to brush Margaret's hair. Touch the snow. She wanted to crouch in the bower with Margaret and eat a cookie, eat an apple, mangled and sweet and cold.

Now the pain came and she went elsewhere as she had been told to do. She went with Margaret. The two, and it was summer, it was June, and she was holding a polished bowl of mash and the shadows moved on her arms. Margaret would marry. She was eleven, or nine, and rode in on her horse in a taffeta gown, to marry, she would marry, the altar was a swing lashed to a limb in the shade of the mothering elm.

Still the pain rose up. She felt it thicken, subside, and she tried to fall away beyond it, beyond Margaret remembered, anyone loved, past rock and field and bending tree, and as she fell she counted: yellow yellow blue, and yellow, and blue at last and white came and white was the blank of exhaustion. White was the drift, the beaten cream. The beauty, the supple joy.

How blue the band between earth and sky and how prettily it curved. A lark. And how spooky the mind, really, the softening it could do. So the room was a cloud and it dipped and swerved and the earth was beaten cream. Time was a stone held on the tongue and Margaret was coming home. *Soon.*

And years ago, and now again, the spider shook her web. She walked about on oiled feet and wound the cloth around her food while her babies grew and multiplied, tried their legs and prepared to live. They would live. They would burst from the ripened walls of the sac and swarm the web she had spun for them—eruptive, no sound, though there were hundreds, a thousand hungry baubles of skin on legs the light passed through.

All without a whimper.

The sun came up, the moon sank down: not a whimper, not a sound. So much else in the world muttered and screeched and rubbed its knees together. So little lived in quiet, patient, thinking ahead.

So maybe she was mistaken. Maybe Margaret would correct her, Margaret with her fine encyclopedic mind like her father's. Scientists; court recorders. *The spider emits a chuffing sound*— thank you, Margaret. Category, fact. They had no patience whatsoever for the approximate, the likeness, the whim.

The spider went on tidying—*like a woman hanging clothes to dry. Like a woman buffing her toenails* while in plain sight above her, the mountaintop spits fire and boulders melt and flow. The sac wobbled on her back—*a chute cinched shut.*

Could she take it off and go on?

Sleep on the floor like a gypsy, using her arm as a pillow?

It was true the mother knew next to nothing, but what did she need to know? That she waited. She was snowed in alone with a spider, an old woman in a nubby robe.

She had her questions, a way to begin. She had her husband, but where had he gone?

Buffalo? Erie?

Uniparous—was that a word?

Was a bough a branch, just a prettier word, or something different, really?

The sac was the color of the leaves of the beech that turned on the branch until spring. A branch; a bough. Snow cupped in the leaves furled to leeward, their crumbling backs to the wind.

Snow in the barbs of the fences.

She had fallen like a leaf through the sky. Beautiful. And from the barbs of the fence.

What was it? From the barbs of the fence her Margaret's hair and that was a name for weather. No.

From the barbs of the fence.

And the mare's tail: that. The mare's tail fluttered and twisted in the wind and that was a name for clouds. Mares' tails—wisped and scattered in the blue and blue the day come morning. And white the beaten cream. And the sac was the color of the leaves of the beech and veined like a hand and dry.

They would fall soon, they would never fall.

She would not live to see them.

Not leaves, not foals, the grasses green, spring again, and phoebes calling themselves by name. Not again the nodding fern, one among many—*shhh. See the fairy?* Margaret turned in the wind and whispered. *A fairy is waving hello.*

Hello, hello.

She couldn't bear it. Not another day, another minute.

To be seen, to go on, another day, and now the snow, and what did she look like, really? And wouldn't this be what Margaret saw, kept seeing, helpless, her mother, like a terrible dream, through the hoard of her life ahead? Would this be what she carried? This what waked and dogged her? Not love? Not the song for years her mother sang to her, not the polished bowl not the fern? Not the bent grasses they lay in, not the kite in the wandering blue?

Not love? Not love but a dream: you wake choking.

IT WENT ON, she lived on. And why?

And in the cupped leaves the snow caught.

And in the grooved bark of the trees.

And across the lake where Margaret lay—there snow driven like shattered glass sank from the face of the buildings. The airplanes were grounded and lacquered with ice and their wingtips quivered in the wind. The lake was ice, a great bellowing slab the wind ran snarling above. Snow stood in hard, scoured peaks and what was loose was driven on—and driven on, the sound of a bone being snapped, a rock split, and with it a hollow, moaning song as though a whale were caught beneath and smashed its head.

The ice was fractured, fissured, veined like a hand. Clouded, and in it were paper sailboats and little toy shovels and leaves. In it were naked babies with their bellies up and their hands—if that?

Would she have a baby then, her Margaret? If she could walk across and choose one and hack through the ice and go home?

They were cased in ice, the babies, but they melted if you held them, they moved.

They called you by name. They whistled.

As a spider whistles, the mother decided; it sings. The mother sings and tidies and boulders flow *bright as fire and spit like a stew and cool.*

For an instant she watched the babies emerge, grandly as from a vestibule in a military row—slavishly, submissive, born the size they would live to be. Like ants or bees, good colonials—and a queen—they would come home daily to.

Not so. But it didn't hurt to think it.

Sometimes it even helped—to believe a little, briefly, in tidiness, the comfort of the common denominator, the whip of the common good.

It wasn't so, but you could think it. Let your mind go. Let the sac burst. Her father at the door—her husband.

No. Nobody there at all.

And when the sac bursts?

When the sac bursts, the babies howl, a simple vowel, the *o* of the mouth—jubilant—and fall to feasting. But only spiders can hear it, and old women in nubby robes.

The mother heard the wasp in its winding cloth stop trying to shake free and live.

She heard an engine—no. Wind in the trees. Now quiet. Not even a wasp. The flakes tapped at the glass. Her hooves were freezing in. A snowflake swam in the dark of her eye and rode the raft its melting made until it shrank and was gone. Gone out. Sluggish, the mare's blood; it slowed; it stilled. And the ground grew soft and hard again and the grasses were flat and broken, the dirt of the field pressed smooth.

She slipped through—home from school, her Margaret, her hair flying loose, her book bag flung down. Her hair snagged on a barb when she slipped through the fence—no matter. Margaret was home, running barefoot over the field. She skimmed the seed heads, the nodding stalks. The mare lifted her head and nickered. Joy beyond measure or word.

Christmas already, was it Christmas, a jar of honey in her bag?

There were colored lights strung in the boughs of the spruce blinking faintly through the snow. Snow at the glass, a sound like a clock, like spiders flung at the sea. The mother had to lean in to listen. You heard the lights blink if you listened, the charge in the strand if you lay beneath the tree among the gifts that would soon be yours.

And all through the house—how did that go? *And all through the house not even a mouse.*

A fly rubbing its hands together—well. Maybe nobody really heard that.

But a roach makes a sound, scurrying, and you can hear the click of the jaw.

The mother knew one car from another by sound and the sound of the hooves of the deer. The sound of a moth catching fire. She knew the sound of a map being folded, being flattened; her husband spread it across his lap. Truckee. Cheyenne. Reno. Places he was yet to go.

She never went to Rome as she meant to. She meant to stand in a castle and listen to rain coming down on the stones. And wear pretty shoes, and her hair hanging loose, and a skirt that made a sound when she moved.

Her gown brushed across her legs—stringy, cheap—and the static, pinpricks—stars going out—you could hear that, too. Phosphorescence in the sea. Oh, the sea again. Glassy, and fish in the green of the lifting wave, faint—now foam, now flaring—loud, the broken white.

Surprising what you heard when you had nothing to do but wait for your next clump of pills. What you saw when you could see next to nothing.

Faintly again the lights blinked in the spruce—yellow, yellow, blue. Not even a wasp, a mouse in a drawer, but her breath she let out—that was something. The rapture of cold and quiet. She felt her gown catch on the skin of her knees—her mother gown, her winding cloth.

Hadn't he given her satin once, where was it now, was it Christmas?

Christmas. Mind of a court recorder. The jars gleaming row on row.

Christmas the year they gave her the mare and Margaret slept beneath the tree in her flower gown. Snow banked against the house. Glistening drifts. Her father led the mare down the path in the sun—a father's idea, a papa's girl, Margaret's favorite. He was giddy with the surprise. Her father tapped at the glass. Margaret flinched in her sleep. *Margaret. There's something you want to see.*

The mare smelled of hay, musty, of spring. Her breath came in clouds the flakes of snow spun and tumbled through. Something sang in the trees. *Wake up, wake up*—like a dream, like something the heavens sent—a white horse, hers to grow up with, yours, to speak a secret tongue. Tongue of the ecstatic, unencumbered love.

Something to care for, yes. Rain or shine—the long devotion the living teach us. Hers to doctor, hers to gentle. Ford the river. Clear the fence. *All yours*—the mare a steady and steadying love through the mess of everything else. A kind of practice.

Margaret lay in a stupor along the mare's back—Christmas day and days to come, in dress-up gowns, bikinis. Lanky, leggy, sullen child.

Years she pretended to marry. She would never marry.

But hadn't she, beneath the mothering elm—hadn't she pretended to marry, over and over again? One boy and another, any boy willing to play. Margaret arrived at a lope wearing taffeta, wearing sequins, her grandmother's kid gloves and tulle. Like sequins, the light, how it moved beneath the trees, gilded in the late breath of summer.

Next, snow. And the snow stayed on for years, it seemed, though of course this could not be true. Snow caught in the peeling crosses the mullions of the windows made and in the gray barbs of the fences, the wire strung round the field. A dog loped across the field. A bird called out: *Here, I am here.*

The old repeaters. Too soon for the phoebes but maybe she was wrong.

Maybe she was hungry: that was a new idea.

Nothing to eat but honey. Nothing to eat but apples, the white mare sinking in the snow.

She drew a hair from a slab of butter and flicked it into the sink. The sink was dripping. She considered toast: no. Pudding. Food she could not see through.

She found a grape in a bowl and held it gingerly in the dry ditch of her tongue. A stone—strange in her mouth and heavy. She pushed into it and felt the skin break and her teeth met in the cold. Surprising, the cold. So much of it. She drew the pulp with her tongue across the skin of her mouth, the veins she could feel and the ripples of her palate like something the tides had formed. The pulp was warm now and felt like tissue as if she were eating her mouth.

Last of the sweet.

She couldn't swallow. She walked to the door and spit out the pulp in a shower in the falling snow. Now the snow was pocked and she was sorry, the flawless blank concealing face—no matter.

It didn't matter. But it did. Every little thing.

She bent to touch the snow and felt nothing and wondered had she dreamed it up. She thought the mare could not have died but lay resting and would come to the fence to Margaret again until at last she felt the cold.

All so.

And the nurses would come back and she was dying.

All so.

And so how could this surprise her, over and over again?

She pushed her hand into the snow, deeper now, until snow came over the top to her wrist until her mind could play the trick that it was gone.

And if it were?

If her hand were gone and her husband, her ruby would be gone, too.

She turned her ruby on her finger beneath the snow, her ring finger, her marrying hand, while the cold sank faintly through—into

the joints, jelly and spur, a birdish fan of bone. She found a lump
of fruit still warm from her mouth, and tatters of grass, living still,
though the sweetness was gone and the green.

She had left the door ajar and now she closed it. Unmistakable,
this sound—a latch snapped into place. Daily, nightly. Nurses.
Her door opened onto the hallway, dark for months, and seasons
passed, and in a given day the mother heard—*that*—little snap—
how many times?

A given day. Was this a phrase? *Given night?*

And did a person give or take it?

Were these the same or different—*caregiver, caretaker?* They
must be.

Always the same pair of shoes. Different faces—why so different? Shouldn't they be the same? Givers, takers? Finders, thieves?
Wasn't *she* the caretaker, really?

She was out. She was out in her Christmas slippers. A gift from
Margaret. A china teapot. A flat rock lumped with Play-Doh for
her to prop her pencils in. Once, a broom.

Oh, a broom. The mother wanted a good broom to sweep with,
to sweep. A shovel for the snow, she was cold. No—thank you.
Not cold, not. She was Margaret.

Margaret—like a name in a poem but she had hacked at it and
asked to be called—Meg, was it? Maggie? No matter. She would
call her daughter Margaret as she always had.

She thought to shake the tree—but this was cheating. You
could do it but it did not count. *If an apple falls.*

If only. But: *only if*—this, also?

Her daughter would wander up the path, her hair cropped short, fuzz like a duck's. It wouldn't matter.

She would crawl. Pland through the snow—*pland* was a word. *Broom*, a word, Margaret's second.

Broom?

That seemed unlikely.

Twine—the broom that Margaret made—and loose straw lashed to a stick.

So was *broom* the word for it, really?

Was a bad broom a broom, really?

She had hung it in her closet with her pearls, the mother. Pearls. The mother.

Was it a word if it were your word only?

Pland through the snow the violet light. Last of the sweet.

She would crawl.

The snow was coming down like ash, the mother thought. Like snow, it was snow. Like feathers. Now cold fluttered in underneath her gown and now her skin was stiff and prickled. She was out. She was looking back at the kitchen. Miraculous. Appalling. She watched the sink drip—twice, the flickering light. Her hand on the latch.

Better try it. Better not.

Now the sink dripped.

Now the tree. Blue, the spruce, and one blue dew, and red like Snow White's apple. Little gray bird in the shadows. Two? Was there a third she could not see?

She needed mukluks. A touch of lipstick. Ratty, staticky, terrible gown—she knew exactly the one she wanted. Knew exactly where they were—her pearls. Her clump of pills. *Good on you.* Who was it said that?

Who: *What the Sam Hill?*

And now the pain came back. And her husband. *Husband* was a verb, yes, also? *To husband. Husbandry.* Steward of the land. Was it *stewart?*

Cheyenne?

Had he left her and she couldn't recall?

Now the pain. And the mare at the fence. A white horse—blue.

And a little white pill and a yellow. Smaller than the blue than the yellow. Days she could get them down.

She lay her cheek against the door and the sink dripped. Snow in the shadow at the corner of the house and a cloud in the ice dam melting. A face. Deer. They touched their muzzles to the glass. Curlews.

There had been a key beneath the mat beneath the snow. Now even the mat was missing. The trees leaned in, gauzy, like something about to dissolve. The mother was afraid to fall and falling and so dropped to her knees to steady herself and bled numbly into the snow.

Margaret, the mother thought.

To be Margaret. The hoard of her life ahead.

The mother felt her pulse in the cut in her knee where she had opened it on a stone. No pain. Not pain but the steady push of her blood and the lights synchronized in the tree. Now red blinked on, blue. Blue was raspberry. Blue was arctic. The grape was still in her mouth—the last shred.

If an apple falls.

If a Margaret.

No hope now of burying anything bigger than a shrew.

She pictured Margaret on a ledge and cars below, a window small as a washcloth.

A sling hung in the tree beneath the branches—a net—so the apples wouldn't bruise when they fell. Wouldn't drop and rot in the snow underfoot for the deer when there was nothing but apples. These were cider apples, not eating, late—chalky and tart. Still she would eat one.

Then she would live another month, another year.

The sling sagged as though an infant were in it, asleep and gently leaking. The hay lay gray and wispy in the field and the barn door beat on its hinge. Too much. And still the mare. The blackened door of her eye. A secret language but no one spoke it.

She would crawl. Shake the tree.

So it was cheating, so what. Three apples, but the mother counted two. Snow clung to the fruit as to the curve of the eye, like paint that is light and melts there. Pie, the mother thought. She would make a nice pie for Margaret, nutmeg, zest of lemon.

Wind. And in the wind the ruffled leaves turned and dumped their little buckets of snow. Snow in the barbs of the fences. There the ashen strands of the mare's tail caught and Margaret's hair, not her mother's hair, but dark and sleek and fine.

She had meant to die without a fuss but here she was.

She was listing. She let her tongue drag. Hair—not hair. Fuzz like a duck's.

You had to work at snow. You had to win it. Snow could be friendly—tender, fluffed—not fickle like air, not careless. She said her name to herself. Nothing. Something in the wind. Her father. With a shovel. With a broom.

And from the barbs of the fence. What was it?

Yes. She was listening. She was cold. Someone would have to tell Margaret. Yes.

The ashen strands of the mare's tail twisted in the wind and Margaret's. Yes. Tinsel. It was Christmas. She heard the phoebes. She heard wrens—the next batch, the litter, the brood. And the babies streamed out, baubles of skin, ravenous under the snow. Not likely. Not likely. But—there—yes, something. Was under the mother in the snow. It molted. A seal? It was not going to fall to the mother, she thought. It would not fall to her to tell Margaret—no.

A spotted dog?

No. Not likely. Cold.

And white the mare. Also violet. And *pland* was a word and white the mare and blue was, blue was arctic. And snow was beaten cream. Her eye was a door the wind sailed through and after that? Something. A door. Eye a door; I adore you. To lie beside of, the mother thought. Was it *beside of*? Was it *only if*? An *apple falls*? That game she had played? Two apples. One. Won. *Now* was *won*—backward, she knew. Were there two? Little gray birds? And her hooves frozen in? White, the mare. Happy. But she had gone to her knees like—*jelly* was a word?

Was it *lie*, the mother thought, or *lay*? And last before sleep, the prayer they once said? She knew nothing, next to nothing. *Now I lay me. Now I lay me.* And the babies in the ice? The face turned to see?

To sea, the mother thought. So—*pretty*. Fish in the lifting wave and snow, and in the barbs of the fences—pretty—and *pland* was pretty and *violet* and in the veined cups of the leaves. And Margaret. Margaret was pretty, a name like a bird the mother would not again see. Not again. All so. Not the sea, not again. Not Margaret. Her face in the snow still falling. Her face in the cup of her hand.

ACKNOWLEDGEMENTS

I WANT TO THANK EVERY SINGLE READER WHO HAS EVER thought or said anything nice about my work. Every one. Also my agent, Georges Borchardt, and the open-armed visionaries at Counterpoint, particularly Jack Shoemaker, Kelly Winton, Megan Fishmann, Ryan Quinn, Megan Jones, and Joseph Goodale. Thanks to the MacDowell Colony, for time in the trees and a sturdy bicycle. I thank Brad Morrow, who published many of the stories gathered here, and whose editorial hand continues to be illuminating and sure.

I want to thank my feral students, former and current, who are my kin and teachers—I hope to read you for as long as I live. Thanks to Lisa Olstein, Jason Schwartz, Leni Zumas, Hilary Plum, and Lauren Goodman—beautiful mavericks, careful readers, beloved friends. Thank you, Parker. And Chris Dombrowski. Thanks to Jane Ogden and Richard Blanchard, who keep their doors open. Thank you, dear Lance and Melanie. Thank you, Gordon—for your immeasurable gift, your terrible jokes, and the lesson of obsessiveness. And from the steamy mountaintop, for as long as I can shout it and as loudly, thank you, Sam.

Author photograph by Tiffany B. San Clemente

About the Author

NOY HOLLAND is the author of the novel *Bird* as well as three story collections, *Swim for the Little One First*, *What Begins with Bird*, and *The Spectacle of the Body*. A recipient of fellowships from the NEA, the MacDowell Colony, and the Massachusetts Cultural Council, Holland teaches writing in the graduate program at the University of Massachusetts, Amherst.

Printed in the United States
by Baker & Taylor Publisher Services